Gabri... the de... barely g... Rae's. At another time, with another man, the contact might have been innocent. But there was nothing innocent about this man.

No, Gabriel MacLaren was nothing but trouble. Rugged, stubborn, sexy, blue-eyed trouble. He made no effort to disguise the desire in those gorgeous blue eyes, and the sight of all that aggressive male need sent heat spiraling through her body.

She let her lashes drift downward, hiding her eyes. Oh, boy, she'd better watch herself.

Get out while you can, the rational part of her mind urged.

Logic dictated caution. But caution had never been her strong suit. What would it be like, she wondered, to be loved by such a man? Anticipation ran like wildfire through her veins.

This was a new experience for her. Compelling. Irresistible. *Dangerous…*

Dear Reader,

I'm not going to waste any time before I give you the good news: This month begins with a book I know you've all been waiting for. *Nighthawk* is the latest in Rachel Lee's ultrapopular CONARD COUNTY miniseries. Craig Nighthawk has never quite overcome the stigma of the false accusations that have dogged his steps, and now he might not live to get the chance. Because in setting himself up as reclusive Esther Jackson's protector— and lover—he's putting himself right in harm's way.

Amnesia is the theme of Linda Randall Wisdom's *In Memory's Shadow*. Sometimes you *can* go home again—if you're willing to face the danger. Luckily for Keely Harper, Sam Barkley comes as part of the package. Two more favorite authors are back—Doreen Roberts with the suspenseful *Every Waking Moment*, and Kay David with *And Daddy Makes Three*, a book to touch your heart. And welcome a couple of new names, too. Though each has written elsewhere, Maggie Simpson and Wendy Haley make their Intimate Moments debuts with *McCain's Memories* (oh, those cowboys!) and *Gabriel Is No Angel* (expect to laugh), respectively.

So that's it for this time around, but be sure to come back next month for more of the best romance reading around, right here in Silhouette Intimate Moments.

Yours,

Leslie Wainger
Senior Editor and Editorial Coordinator

Please address questions and book requests to:
Silhouette Reader Service
U.S.: 3010 Walden Ave., P.O. Box 1325, Buffalo, NY 14269
Canadian: P.O. Box 609, Fort Erie, Ont. L2A 5X3

GABRIEL IS NO ANGEL

WENDY HALEY

Published by Silhouette Books

America's Publisher of Contemporary Romance

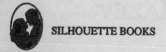

SILHOUETTE BOOKS

ISBN 0-373-07786-6

GABRIEL IS NO ANGEL

Copyright © 1997 by Chrysalis Enterprises, Inc.

WENDY HALEY

led a gypsy sort of life as a child, moving every three years or so. She continued this process as an adult before settling on the East Coast. A full-time writer, Wendy publishes romance, suspense, horror, young adult horror and mainstream fiction. She's written historical romances as Wendy Garrett.

To Jonathan—and the wave!

Chapter 1

Rae stood in front of the full-length mirror in the dressing room. Tiny brass bells tinkled as she adjusted the top of her costume.

"You've really, truly gone over the edge with this one," she told her reflection.

She'd gotten herself hired as entertainment at the biggest private gambling house in Baltimore. Rae Ann Boudreau, belly dancer and process server extraordinaire. Her old college roommate, Yasmin, had spent most of a year teaching her this skill. As a lark, of course. Who would have expected it to come in handy?

Rae Ann tossed her shoulder-length chestnut hair back and frowned at herself. Really, she should have turned this case down. Six years of experience had told her it would be a problem from the get-go. But she hadn't been able to refuse Barbara Smithfield, who was trying to collect two years' child support from the husband who'd deserted her. She'd come to Boudreau Professional Process Service in desperation, having been refused by every other process server in town.

"A twenty-nine-year-old soft touch, that's what you are," Rae muttered.

If only the woman hadn't brought her kids with her. Ah, those kids, Rae thought. Even if she'd had a heart of stone, those three children would have melted it. They were eight, seven and four. Big blue eyes. The youngest sucked her thumb and clutched a raggedy, loved-to-death teddy bear.

"It's the blue eyes," Rae groaned. "Ever since Jimmy Donovan in second grade, I've had this weakness for blue eyes."

Then she laughed. She'd spent at least sixty hours working for the thirty-dollar fee she'd charged Barbara Smithfield, and might as well enjoy the finale, belly dancing and all. Rae Ann Boudreau always got her man.

She wiggled her hips. The embroidery of her girdle caught the light in a rich, multicolored gleam, which was echoed by the large fake sapphire she'd pasted into her navel. Actually, she thought the skimpy costume flattered her. Belly dancers were supposed to have curves, of which she had more than her share. No one could ever call Rae Ann Boudreau skinny. In fact, it wouldn't have hurt her feelings one bit if there'd been a smidgen more room in the skimpy bra top.

Someone knocked on the door. "They're ready for you, honey," a man called.

"Well, I'm ready for them, too, sugar," she cooed.

After checking one last time to make sure the subpoena was securely tucked away, she sashayed out to the main room.

Automatically, she scanned the area, tallying possible escape routes. There were too many doors for comfort; she'd have to be sharp to keep Smithfield from getting away from her.

The decor tended toward paneling and mirrors—some two-way—and the muted gold of the carpet and walls made a nice, rich contrast against the gleaming wood. Nice, Rae thought. Gaming tables were scattered throughout the large room, piloted by clean-cut employees whose friendly smiles didn't once flicker as they raked the house's winnings in. Rae would have given a lot to know who owned this place. Whoever it was, he had a mighty slick operation going.

The buzz of conversation became hushed as the men realized she'd come in. Rae spotted a familiar face or two, but doubted they'd connect the rouged, mascaraed and thoroughly veiled belly dancer with the all-business process server who'd thrust subpoenas into their unwilling hands.

She also spotted her quarry. Peter Smithfield had a weak, almost pretty face. Dissipation made him look years older than the picture she'd seen, and his mouth held a downward-turned curve of dissatisfaction.

Evidently, it hadn't been a good night for poker. Well, his evening wasn't about to get any better.

"Gotcha," she murmured.

Then she caught sight of another face in the crowd, a rough-hewn, intensely masculine face. And oh, God, eyes to die for.

They were ice blue, as clear as cracked glass, and startlingly pale compared to his black lashes and flaring dark brows.

Secrets lurked in those eyes, things that sparked both her interest and her caution. Her gaze drifted involuntarily to his wide, sensual mouth. Lines bracketed those hard, well-cut lips, giving him a look of world-weary cynicism. He didn't belong here. For he was not the kind of man who played games, even one as dangerous as gambling. Her interest sharpened even more. She'd always been good at pegging people, but he eluded her.

Well, whatever he might be, he was male with a capital *M*, and reaction spurred along her nerves and sank deep into her body. This had never happened to her. Rae had always thought of herself as immune from the usual feminine weaknesses; she was self-made, self-contained, self-reliant.

So then why did his gaze feel like a caress on her skin? Why did her blood run through her veins in a sweet, hot tide, and why did her pulse race faster than it had any right to do?

She reined herself in sternly, reminding herself that she'd come here to do a job. If Rae Ann Boudreau took on an assignment to serve a subpoena, it got served. She wasn't about to let libido jeopardize that perfect record.

Slowly, sensuously, she raised her arms and clanged her finger cymbals. She could feel the crowd's attention sharpen and focus. Against her will, her gaze drifted back to the man with the dangerous crystalline eyes. Heat sparked those pale depths as she began to sway.

She didn't know what came over her—she really didn't. But somehow, everything changed. No longer did she move dispassionately, her process server's mind clicking away behind the ritualized patterns.

No. She danced for him. Only for him. The ancient, graceful movements became the medium of communication between them, and the message was hot.

Some small, sane corner of her mind was glad they weren't alone. For this was magic. Powerful and dangerous, infinitely seductive.

She couldn't stop. Her gaze locked with his, trapped by the pure male desire in those blue, blue eyes. He wanted her. She wanted him to want her. She told him so with every glance, every movement of her body. Arousal coiled along her limbs, making her movements even more sensual.

He watched. He knew. She could see that awareness jolting through his eyes, in the tightening of his mouth. If he'd touched her now, this moment, she'd probably go up in flames.

Then she spotted Peter Smithfield oozing along the wall toward the interior doorway, and she snapped back to reality. She had no business getting star struck and losing track of things. Barbara Smithfield and those three kids needed help, and Rae was the only one who cared enough to try.

Slowly, unobtrusively, she danced her way closer to her quarry. An absurd nursery rhyme began running through her head: "Bells on her fingers, and rings on her toes..." And a subpoena in her girdle.

Darn. She hadn't gotten to the end of her dance yet, and Smithfield was almost to the door. She hated to lose her cover by racing after him, but she'd prefer that to letting him get away. As she spun, she caught a glimpse of her blue-eyed devil. Something in his expression startled her, but she didn't have time to think about it.

Getting out of the room was going to be harder than she thought. Evidently, the audience had *really* liked her dance; hands reached out for her as she made her way toward the door. She twirled out of reach of a man who wanted to put a twenty-dollar bill into her girdle. And twirled again, setting her gauzy veils spinning around her in a multicolored whirl as she avoided another man's grasp.

Finally, she was clear. She stopped, her head bowed, her arms stilled in a graceful arc. The veils drifted back into place.

Applause exploded in the room. Instead of bowing, Rae went for an inscrutable lift of her head, a flashing glance that speared straight to a pair of sensuous ice blue eyes. Then she ran lightly from the room.

She heaved a sigh of relief as she spotted Smithfield standing just outside the rest room. Thank you, thank you, she thought. She started toward him. The bells on her anklet jingled exotically, and a smarmy smile spread over his face.

"Hell-o, beautiful," he said.

Still opting for mysterious, she smiled. Another doorway led to the rear of the house, she noted. Casually, she moved to stand between him and it. Draping herself against the wall, she studied him from beneath her lashes. He liked her, obviously. But his eyes held wariness, as well as admiration, and she knew this was going to be tricky. He'd proved himself to be very good at spotting possible legal complications, and light on his feet, as well. If she played it wrong, he'd run from her, and it would be a cold day in Hades before he'd let her get near him again.

Then his gaze dropped to her chest, and she knew she had him. He wasn't going to walk away—at least until it was too late.

A loud crash of shattering wood rang through the room she'd just left. She whirled to see men in bulletproof vests burst in through the doors, guns drawn.

"Police!" one shouted. "Everybody on the floor!"

A bust, Rae thought. Darn, darn, *darn!* "Not now," she muttered, reaching toward her girdle.

Peter Smithfield bolted for the door. Rae grabbed him as he raced past her, and they fell to the floor. Unfortunately, he landed on top. She held him by the front of his shirt while she tried to reach the papers tucked into her girdle. If only he'd stop squirming, she could...

A big, square hand seemed to come out of nowhere. It wound itself in Smithfield's collar, hauling him up with a jerk.

Rae focused on a rough-hewn face and a pair of furious ice-blue eyes. What was *he* doing here? Astonishment stilled her for a moment.

"Get out of here," the newcomer growled, flinging Smithfield toward the door.

Rae scrambled to her feet. "Hey!"

Smithfield didn't stop moving. Rae sprang after him, only to be caught in midleap by a hard arm around her waist.

"Not so fast," the man said.

"Let go!" She squirmed frantically, but his grip didn't ease at all. "Let go, damn it! I've got unfinished business with that guy!"

"I bet you do."

His voice was deep, with a brandy-and-smoke huskiness that made her nerve endings quiver. It was also angry enough to freeze the air around them.

Rae twisted in his iron grip. A cop, she thought. She should have known. He wasn't the kind of man who'd play games. Well, she wasn't playing, either.

"Get your hands off me," she snapped.

One side of his mouth went up, but he didn't let her go. His gaze made a sweep of her body, then made another, slower one. A tingle raced through her, heat and temper and anticipation all rolled together.

Desire flared into his pale eyes, turning them hot. Rae found herself staring at his mouth. It was hard and male, yet there was a sensuous curve to his bottom lip that made her want to taste it.

This is bad, she thought. Or maybe very, very good.

Then she realized that his smile had turned cold and cynical, and that he was still holding her. And yet his hands felt hot against her skin, and his grasp had a possessiveness to it that made her pulse stutter and leap.

He felt it, too, and it was obvious he didn't like it. His eyes turned smoky and narrow, and the line of his jaw hardened.

"You ought to get a real job, darlin'," he growled.

"A real..." Rae's temper flared. "You've got your nerve!"

"Nothing to match yours," he drawled. "Ever heard of the notion of privacy? Or maybe he paid you enough not to care?"

Astonishment silenced her for a moment. He'd thought that she and Smithfield were... Oh, Lord. Anger washed through her, as hot and primitive as her desire. She jammed her hands on her hips and glared at him. "I should have known. You're a cop."

"You got it, sweetheart."

She let her breath out with a hiss. "You know, you guys are all the same. You think the worst of everyone."

"That's a laugh, coming from a—"

"Oh, excuse me," she said. "I was unfair in my assessment. You're a vice cop. You *know* everyone's bad."

"You've got it pegged, darlin'," he said. "Now, just for curiosity's sake, how much did he pay you?"

"Enough," she retorted, too furious for caution. "Why? Thinking of making an offer?"

His eyes chilled. Rae stood for a moment to let her disdain sink in, then turned and started to walk away. She didn't get far; his hand closed around her upper arm, pulling her to a halt.

She jabbed backward with her elbow, only to find both her wrists imprisoned in his inexorable grip.

Then she felt the cold metal touch of handcuffs.

"Hey," she raged, glaring at him over her shoulder. "What do you think you're doing?"

He spun her around to face him. Even in her fury, Rae felt something warm and heavy slam into her chest as she met his gaze. He pulled her closer. Then he slid his hands up her arms to her shoulders slowly, almost as though he didn't want to—and couldn't help it.

Her breath grew shallow as his long fingers curved over her flesh. It wasn't an ungentle touch, but it held a darkly veiled aura of possessiveness that made her heart beat much too fast.

Then she lifted her chin, a defiant gesture. Rae Ann Boudreau had never been unnerved by a man in her life, and she wasn't about to start now.

"What the devil are you doing?" she demanded.

"I'm Detective Gabriel MacLaren, vice squad," he said. "And you're under arrest."

"Arrest!" she yelped. "What for?"

He grinned at her. "Prostitution, honey-child."

Chapter 2

Feeling weary down to his bones, Gabriel propped his feet up on his desk. God, he hated late shift. He glanced up briefly as two beat cops hauled a very intoxicated, very large and loud man past him.

"Not another one," he muttered.

He wished he could stop thinking about the belly dancer. But oh, boy, she'd settled into his mind and wouldn't leave him alone. He'd felt an actual physical jolt when their gazes had met that first time. It bothered him.

She bothered him. A mane of red-brown hair, skin like creamy silk, tip-tilted eyes the color of warm sherry, a body as lush and curved as sin itself... His blood ran hot just thinking about her.

She'd looked straight at him as she danced. For one brief, astonishing moment, something magical had sparked between them. She'd been his own private fantasy made flesh.

Then he'd found her rolling around on the floor with Peter Smithfield.

And his fantasy had turned to ash.

It shouldn't have made him angry. But it had. He didn't

even know her name. She'd clammed up on him the moment
he'd put the handcuffs on her, and he'd booked her as a very
defiant Jane Doe.

"You don't want to know her name, MacLaren," he muttered.

Sure. Right. He should have known better. As a vice cop,
he saw the worst of human nature. Every night, every place
he went. Men, women, kids doing things the average citizen
couldn't even imagine. He'd gotten used to it.

The belly dancer had turned out to be only what he should
have expected. The only surprise was his own disappointment.

The sound of bells cut sharply through the everyday noise
of the station. If he'd had one foot in his grave, he would
have recognized that sound. His body tensed in a reaction as
powerful as it was unwelcome. Scowling, he glanced over his
shoulder.

She looked as exotic as an orchid in this place. Curves
everywhere, that mane of chestnut hair gleaming beneath the
unrelenting fluorescent lights. Every man in the station
watched her. Wanted her. Married, single, young or old, cops
or lawbreakers, they wanted her.

Gabriel scowled, possessed by a sudden, hot sweep of irritation. Crazy as it seemed, he had the irrational urge to grab
her and lock her up where no other man could look at her.

He studied her as she strode toward him. She was all
woman, and his pulse stuttered and cranked into high gear.

"It ought to be illegal for a woman to look that good,"
one of the other detectives said. Loud enough for everyone
to hear, of course.

"It *must* be illegal," somebody else called. "MacLaren
arrested her."

Laughter rippled through the room as the belly dancer
stopped in front of his desk. Gabriel abruptly realized that
everyone else knew something he didn't.

Alarm bells went off in his head. He'd transferred to this
precinct six months ago, and his fellow detectives hadn't

missed an opportunity to capitalize on that fact. This might be bad.

"Hey, Boudreau!" a detective called. "How about a dance?"

"In your dreams," Rae retorted, without taking her gaze off Detective MacLaren.

Gabriel's alarm bells shrilled louder. Boudreau. He'd heard that name. Ray Boudreau was a private process server with the rep of being very smart and very effective. But a woman?

His gaze dropped to her breasts, which were barely contained in the tiny costume top. Yup, he thought. Definitely a woman.

An angry woman. Whom he'd just arrested for prostitution.

She planted herself in front of his desk and stared down at him as though he were some particularly unsavory type of pond scum.

Unfazed, he met her gaze levelly. She was even more beautiful close up, with her pale, creamy skin and those eyes that fairly sizzled with resentment and challenge. He liked a challenge. A faint, exotic scent teased his nostrils, distracting him. Some kind of flower, he thought.

"Detective MacLaren," she said.

"Ma'am?"

Rae studied him from beneath her lashes. He looked like a great cat lounging there in front of her. Impressive. Insolent. She felt at a distinct disadvantage. How could she deal with him when the very sight of him sent her nerves jangling with reaction?

She opted to echo his attitude of cool detachment. She was not about to let him get to her. Uh-uh. He'd called her honeychild, for God's sake.

"So you're Ray Boudreau," he said.

"Rae," she replied. *"R-A-E."*

He ran his thumb along the angle of his jaw. "You told me your name was Jane Doe."

"Better that Jane Doe gets busted than Rae Ann Boudreau."

His brows rose. "Did it occur to you to maybe mention what you were doing there?"

"I tried," she said. "But you were more interested in flexing your handcuffs."

She crossed her arms over her chest. Gabriel's gaze dropped involuntarily. If he'd been a weaker man, his jaw would have dropped right onto his desk. Man, oh, man, but she was one fabulously sexy woman! Lush curves swelled almost to overflowing, and his hands itched with a sudden, powerful desire to touch her.

They stared at each other silently for a moment. Rae felt as though he'd looked straight through to her soul. It was a very disturbing feeling.

She needed boundaries, and his eyes didn't allow any. With a sharp inhalation of breath, she started to turn away.

"Hey," he said.

His voice was deep and dark, smoky with desire. It held her when she would much rather have moved away. A thrill ran up her spine, alarm or anticipation or perhaps both.

"Hey?" she repeated, raising her brows. "Boy, you really have a way with women, Detective."

"Don't know anything about 'em," he replied too cheerfully. "Like every other guy on the planet. It's a common failing."

Rae was not in the mood for clever repartee. "Did you have something else to say?"

"Yeah," he said. "Why *were* you following Peter Smithfield?"

With elaborate casualness, Rae propped one hip on the corner of his desk. "Why don't you want me following him?"

"Because," he said.

Rae's nostrils flared. "You want a lot without giving anything in return."

"It's a man thing," he countered.

"Not at all," she replied. "I expect that's a personal trait of yours. Comes from being a cop too long."

"I'm perfectly willing to go down to the courthouse and look it up," he said.

She pushed a stray curl away from her face. Much as she'd like to continue baiting him, good sense dictated a truce.

"All right," she said. "We might as well get this thing straight."

Gabriel licked suddenly dry lips. With her scarves and veils disarranged the way they were now, a whole lot of skin was showing. She had more curves than the law ought to allow. Of course, he held a purely male admiration for a beautiful, sexy woman. Strangely, however, her eyes held more interest for him than her admittedly luscious body. They were good eyes, straightforward and honest. Intelligence and humor sparked those warm brown depths, and something more. He didn't know what that something might be, but it appealed to him powerfully, drawing him to seek more of the woman within.

He almost came out of his shoes when she started fooling with the girdle thing that rode low on her hips. She wasn't going to take it off, was she? But she merely extracted a folded paper from beneath the coin-encrusted band.

"Take a look," she said, dropping the paper into his lap.

Gabriel unfolded it and began to read. His brows went up at the familiar sight of a subpoena. Clipped to the top was a business card. It said Boudreau Professional Process Service.

He pulled the card free and dropped it onto his desk. "Not many people would learn belly dancing just to serve a subpoena."

"I already knew how to dance," she said, gazing at him along her straight, slim nose. "I just applied it to the situation at hand. Special circumstances require special solutions."

He stared at her for a moment. Then he began to laugh.

"Special solutions...belly dancing process service. Oh, God, that's rich!"

Rae repressed the urge to shove him out of his chair. "Are you making fun of me?"

"Making fun?" Still grinning, he shook his head. "Not at all. I'm impressed with your dedication. Not many people would have thought of that ploy, let alone have the guts to use it."

He grinned at her. Rae found herself caught in the crystal-line depths of his eyes, surrounded by heat born of desire and admiration. Drawn by something more powerful than herself, she leaned toward him.

He slid his hand across the desk, until his fingertips barely grazed hers. At another time, with another man, the contact might have been innocent. But there was nothing innocent about Gabriel MacLaren. He made no effort to disguise the desire in those gorgeous blue eyes, and the sight of all that aggressive male need sent heat spiraling through Rae's body.

The line of his mouth softened, and she knew he wanted to kiss her. It was no surprise to Rae; she wanted him to kiss her. If they'd been alone, it would already have happened.

Rae felt oddly disconnected to anything but him, as though the rest of the world had gone spinning away. It was a pow-erfully intimate moment. All those barriers she normally kept between herself and the world had been stripped away, leav-ing her exposed and vulnerable.

She would have expected to see triumph in his eyes, but she saw only her own emotions mirrored in those ice blue depths. Rae was stunned by the realization that she'd expe-rienced something with him she'd never shared with another human being, even her ex-husband.

"I..." she began, then closed her mouth as she realized she didn't have the slightest idea what she was going to say.

Her voice broke whatever spell had been woven around them. His eyes changed as though a switch had been clicked off, shutting the emotions behind a featureless wall. Rae knew it for what it was: a cop's disengagement. It was a more effective shield than the hunk of metal he carried in his wallet.

She straightened. He leaned back in his chair, studying her from beneath thick, dark lashes.

"Why did you let Smithfield go?" she asked. She knew the answer already, or most of it, but she felt compelled to fill the awkward moment with something other than too-swift breathing.

Gabriel's alarms went off again. He knew she'd figured out the deal the moment he'd told her he was a cop. So why ask now? Games, he thought. Get the most play from his reaction to her admittedly gorgeous self, then sling a question at him he didn't want to answer.

He didn't like games. At least other people's. Hell, hers was working all too well. It was all he could do to keep from sliding her across the desk and into his lap.

Disappointment stabbed deep again. Why, he didn't know. He only knew that she affected him in a way no other woman ever had, and that from the moment he'd met her, he'd wanted her to be something special.

Damn.

"You cost me my service tonight," she said.

He held his hands up, denying the charge. "Hey, that wasn't my fault. You were lying on the floor with the guy on top of you. I only made the natural assumption, considering the circumstances."

Rae considered a number of responses, then discarded most of them as counterproductive. "The only reason you'd let a sleaze-ball like Smithfield slide out of a bust is that you want him for something else. Or need him."

"Um…"

"He's your snitch," she said.

Gabriel set his feet on the desk, trying to look a lot more casual than he felt. "I couldn't tell you that if I wanted to."

"Look," Rae said, "he owes two years in back child support, and his wife and kids are desperate. All I want to do is serve him that subpoena, and then I'll be out of your hair."

Gabriel winced inwardly, but his duty had required harder things than this. "Sorry."

"Sorry?" she demanded. "Is that all you have to say?"

"It's all I *can* say."

"I'm not buying, Detective. If you can give me a reason to assume your case is more urgent than a woman and three kids…"

"It is."

"Why?"

"Because I said so," he growled, testy because he didn't want to feel guilty, and he did. Big time.

"I want Peter Smithfield," Rae said, equally testy.

"You can't have him."

Rae studied Gabriel from beneath her lashes. Given the circumstances, she should have written him off. But she saw something in his eyes that looked an awful lot like regret. It was unexpected, and more welcome than she would have believed.

Until this moment, she hadn't realized how much she'd wanted him to be more than the cynical cop she'd expected. That flicker of emotion had given her that. He did care. Way, way inside, where he thought no one could possibly see, beat a real heart.

She let her gaze drift along his big, lean body. This was no indolent house cat. No, Gabriel MacLaren was a tiger, his power restrained but ready. Oh, Lord, she thought, not this man. He'd be nothing but trouble. Rugged, stubborn, sexy, blue-eyed trouble.

She let her lashes drift downward, hiding her eyes. Oh, boy, she'd better watch herself. For that heart was deeply buried, so deeply that he might have forgotten how to use it.

Get out while you can, the rational part of her mind urged.

Logic dictated caution. But the brief flashes of emotion in his eyes had stirred her unbearably, and caution had never been her strong suit. What would it be like, she wondered, to be loved by such a man? Anticipation ran like wildfire through her veins.

Simply, she was compelled. It was a new experience for her. Irresistible. Dangerous.

"Ms. Boudreau."

She blinked. "Huh?"

"Snappy comeback," he said, slashing a grin at her.

It was a decidedly cynical smile, and made her think she'd imagined those brief, stirring glimpses of emotion. He'd turned all cop, as hard and impenetrable as steel.

Her temper kicked in, goaded perhaps by disappointment as much as by anger. "Are you going to tell me where Peter Smithfield is?"

"Nope."

"Thanks for nothing, Detective," she snarled.

"My friends call me MacLaren."

"What do your enemies call you?"

"Lots of things."

"I bet." She studied him from beneath her lashes, awash with resentment for her own helpless attraction to him. "All right. Keep your smelly little bureaucratic secret. But don't blame me for messing up plans I don't know exist."

Gabriel pushed aside the irrational urge to apologize to her. This was business, nothing more, nothing less. And she was pushing too hard. Still, he couldn't keep his gaze from straying. It was worth it, he thought, noting every satiny curve, every luscious inch of skin.

Then he grinned. "You lost your jewel," he said.

Rae stared at him in astonishment. Then, in yet another sally at clever repartee, she replied, "Huh?"

Lightly, he slid his fingertip across her navel, where she'd worn the big sapphire stone earlier. "Your jewel. Must've gotten stuck on Smithfield while you were rolling on the floor."

It took an effort of will for Rae to keep from gasping. His tone might have been playful, but his touch was anything but. Neither was her reaction. A flooding wave of arousal started at that small point of contact and spread like heat lightning through her body.

She lifted her chin, denying it. "You've got your mind up and locked," she said. "But we'll talk again when I find Smithfield."

His eyes narrowed. "If you interfere in police business, I'll have to arrest you."

"So what's new, Detective?" she retorted.

She slid off the desk and walked away, moving with a fluid grace that drew every gaze in the station.

Gabriel sighed in pure male reaction. As she disappeared through the door with a shimmy of satin hips and a flutter of gauzy fabric, he had the strange feeling that she'd taken something of his with her.

Absently, he picked the business card up and held it to his

nose. It smelled like her. Wildflowers and woman. He inhaled deeply, savoring the scent.

"MacLaren!"

He glanced over his shoulder to see Captain Petrosky beckoning him from the door of his office. Gabriel swung his feet off his desk and strode across the room.

"Close the door," the captain said.

Flinging himself into his battered executive chair, Petrosky propped his feet up on the desk. His shaved head gleamed in the bright overhead light.

"So that was Ray Boudreau," he said.

"Rae," Gabriel said. "*R-a-e.* She wants to serve a summons on Peter Smithfield. Child support."

The captain snorted. "We've got somebody high up in the city government involved with an illegal gambling business. He's smart, and he's got power. This guy has used political office to set himself above the law. I'm going to be real unhappy if some overzealous process server screws this case up."

Gabriel smiled. "We don't want you unhappy, sir. But she's a pro, and very determined. If we explained the situation—"

"No. Any leaks, we can throw this case in the trash. You don't tell Boudreau. You don't tell anyone."

"She'll interfere."

Petrosky's grizzled brows swept downward. "So I'm making her your responsibility. Keep her out of it if you can, use her to find him if you can't. You've got the smarts to handle it."

A feeling of impending doom settled on Gabriel's shoulders. "Yes, sir."

Cursing silently under his breath, he left the office. It would have been hard enough to get her out of his mind; now he was probably going to drive himself crazy with wanting her. Wanting to know her. Wanting to find out if the promise in her eyes was as good as it seemed, and if the unfamiliar new feelings he had for her were as powerful as he thought.

He gave himself an inward shake. "She's nothing but trouble, MacLaren," he muttered. "Big trouble."

Still, an undercurrent of anticipation edged his annoyance. He'd see her again. The thought tugged at something inside him, something he hadn't been aware existed. But there it was, undoubtedly and exclusively hers.

It bothered him. It bothered him a lot. He was thirty-five years old, and had been convinced that he knew himself inside and out. But a few minutes in Rae's company, and his insides had somehow become turned inside out and upside down, and he had no idea how to get them back to normal again.

You're doomed, whispered his cynical policeman's mind.

And then another voice surfaced, a laughing rogue of a voice that spilled like quicksilver through his brain. But what a way to go, it said.

Oh, yeah.

Chapter 3

Rae slipped one fingernail between the slats of the miniblind and peered outside. Gabriel leaned against the fender of a dark blue Taurus parked a short way down the street. He held an open newspaper, but she knew he was watching her building in his side-view mirror.

"The Angel Gabriel himself," she muttered. "My very own guardian angel."

She let her breath out with a hiss of cynical laughter. If there were anything angelic about Gabriel MacLaren, she'd eat her desk. She'd checked him out, of course. Thirty-five years old, sixteen years on the force, a slew of commendations and an impressive arrest record.

He'd never been married.

"Probably hates women," she said, cataloging in minute detail the way his black T-shirt followed the ridged musculature of his back, not to mention the battered jeans that clung to his long, strong legs and outlined the nicest—

"Whoa, girl," she murmured, catching that thought before it quite began.

Sunlight glinted off glass as he adjusted his side-view mirror. Very diligent, Detective MacLaren. She'd spotted him the moment she'd stepped out of her apartment building this morning, of course. A rueful smile curved her lips. If she'd been blind, her personal radar would have homed in on him instantly.

Gabriel MacLaren had made an impression. Definitely. She'd hoped a good night's sleep would have rid her of him, but he'd taken over her dreams. Torrid dreams, dreams full of sensuality hotter than a summer storm. And yet, as wild as that passion had been, those dreams had been laced with something sweet and tender, something she wished were real.

"Might as well ask for the moon," she told herself. "Reality is that he walks and talks and breathes police work, and doesn't even notice the string of broken hearts he leaves in his wake."

She raised her voice, although there was no way he could possibly hear her. "And you've got nothing better to do than to follow Rae Ann Boudreau."

He laid the paper aside and stretched. Oh, boy. He looked as lazily masculine as a panther, and as dangerous. Rae wanted to drop one wing and run in circles.

"This isn't good," she said. "Not good at all. I don't like cops. I don't trust cops. I never, *ever* date cops."

Sure. That's why she stood here with her insides surging with pure female reaction to him. She let her breath out in a sigh of frustration. Life had been simple until last night.

She shot a glance at her computer monitor, which displayed her favorite screen saver, a boldly lettered logo that read I Am Lobo, I Hunt Alone.

"Alone" had felt good. She had her profession, which was challenging, fun and sometimes downright exciting. She had a few good friends with whom to spend her free time. Well, maybe there hadn't been all that much free time. But she'd been happy. Well, she amended again, she'd been content. Something had been missing.

Surely, though, that something couldn't—absolutely, positively couldn't—be Gabriel MacLaren.

"Go away," she said, glaring down at him.

Of course, he didn't. Rae let the blind slip back into place and turned away from the window. Her office was her home, more so than the apartment in which she spent so little time. She'd grown fond of the big, spacious room that held her desk, filing cabinets, a pair of big, comfy armchairs and a battered sofa on which she'd slept many a night. And, of course, the all-important computer. Plants had not survived her inattention, so out of kindness she'd decided to leave green things to those more suited to them.

Domestic, she was not. But she was a good process server, and had built a successful business. Rae Ann always got her man.

Corny, but true.

She dropped into one of the armchairs and propped both feet on her desk while she considered the situation. She could go about her business, letting Gabriel follow if he so desired. But she couldn't. Rae Ann Boudreau always did *something.*

"Now, Detective," she murmured, "what will I do with you today? What will you absolutely, completely loathe?"

She tapped her bottom lip with her finger. A smile curved her mouth as she got her best idea of the week.

"You are too cruel, Rae Ann," she said with a laugh.

A few minutes later, she stepped out into the sunlight. Shielding her eyes with her hand, she scanned up and down the street. The Taurus was still there, but Gabriel had disappeared. He was good; she'd have to give him that.

She strolled toward the business district, stopping to peer in every store window she passed. As she passed Mr. Fedderman's flower shop, she couldn't resist buying a great big bouquet of fresh flowers from the sidewalk stand.

"Hello, Rae Ann," the florist said, wrapping the blooms in slick green paper.

"Hi, Mr. Fedderman," she replied. "I bet you never expected to see me buy anything living again."

"After you killed the poor ivy, no. But the cut flowers will die anyway, so I am not committing a crime by selling them to you."

Rae laughed. "If you think I'm dangerous around plants, you ought to taste my cooking."

"So tough," he murmured. "Don't you get tired of buying your own flowers?"

She'd never been able to convince Mr. Fedderman that she didn't want another husband. "No," she said. "Have a good day, Mr. Fedderman."

She turned away, juggling flowers as she tried to put her wallet back in her purse. Then she caught sight of her reflection in the store window and stopped. She looked...prettier somehow, the lines of her face softened by the flowers beneath her chin.

Then she caught sight of Gabriel MacLaren's reflection over her shoulder. He stared at her with heavy-lidded eyes, and his expression held such hunger that her knees went weak for a moment.

It wasn't simply desire. No, this was much more. A strange, unexpected wistfulness tempered the desire in his eyes, gentled it and made it infinitely more compelling.

"Oh, Lord," she whispered, turning away so abruptly that the reflection of the flowers blurred to an indefinable jumble of color.

Sternly telling herself that this was no time to get flustered, she slowed down to a seemingly casual pace. Gabriel stuck right with her. On impulse, she turned and entered the gleaming brass-and-glass luxury of Gaylord's, the city's swankiest department store.

A glimpse in a nearby mirror showed Gabriel nearly getting himself run down in his haste to follow her. She didn't blame him; this would be the perfect place in which to lose a tail.

If she'd wanted to.

She moseyed along the perfume counter, pausing to test a scent that cost more per ounce than she made in a day. She glanced in the mirror to catch Gabriel's reflection.

Judging from his expression, he didn't like to shop. She smiled. "We're going to have lots and lots of fun, Detective," she murmured.

She went from department to department, browsing, stopping frequently to try something on. An hour passed, then another. By the time she hit the lingerie department, Gabriel looked as though he were ready to strangle someone. Probably her.

A cream-colored nightgown caught her attention. Rich, understated, sexy, it was more lace than otherwise. Rae had never been one for fancy lingerie. Her taste leaned toward nice, big T-shirts. But this gown was pure sin.

She couldn't afford the nightgown. She couldn't afford Gabriel MacLaren, either. Still, she couldn't help a bit of wistfulness over them both.

A long arm reached past her and plucked the nightgown from the rack. "Buy the damned thing," Gabriel growled in her ear. "Hell, I'll buy it for you if you'll just stop this nonsense."

Rae turned. And found herself almost nose to nose with one very annoyed vice cop. Her nostrils flared as she registered his impact down to her soul. He smelled of soap and mint and what was inimically MacLaren. If he'd walked up to her in pitch darkness, she would have known him.

This was bad.

She couldn't let him know how he affected her. "Why, Detective MacLaren, what a surprise—"

"Bull," he said. "You spotted me an hour ago."

She smiled. "Actually, I spotted you the moment I walked out of my apartment building."

His eyes narrowed. "I want to talk to you."

"Why?" she inquired, all innocence.

"Don't play that game with me," he snarled.

Gently, Rae took the nightgown from him. "You're crushing the merchandise."

"So buy it and let's get out of here."

She turned and hung it back on the rack. "It's three hundred dollars. I'll be too old to wear it by the time I can afford to pay for it."

"Now, that," he murmured, "would be a shame."

Astonished, she looked up at him. His eyes had turned crystalline and hot. Obviously, he was imagining her in that almost-transparent confection. Danger signals went up all through her mind, but her body didn't listen. Arousal pooled warm and heavy at her core.

"What do you want, Detective?" she asked.

The moment the words were out, she realized how they'd sound. She blushed. She hadn't blushed in at least ten years. Gabriel MacLaren was definitely getting to her.

To give him credit, he didn't take the opening. Instead, he grasped her by the arm and turned her toward the staircase.

"Call me MacLaren," he said. "Or Gabriel."

She made an unsuccessful attempt to pull her arm out of his grasp. "I don't know if I want to get that personal," she said.

Before she could reply, he swung her around to face him. They stood so close that their chests were almost touching. Rae had to make a conscious effort not to lean toward him.

"You don't know if you don't," he said.

"What?"

"Get personal."

Rae looked into his eyes. It felt as though she were falling off a cliff. No man had ever looked at her like that, ever. Oh, MacLaren was still plenty annoyed with her. But beneath the irritation lay a desire as hot and primitive as a desert storm.

It should have frightened her. After all, she knew cops. And this one had a streak of cynicism a mile wide. She'd been there, done that. And she had a failed marriage to prove it. She had no business being tempted by any cop, especially this one.

But she was. Despite caution. Despite experience. Despite everything, she was tempted. No, no and no. Definitely.

"I'm really busy today, Detective," she said, meeting his gaze levelly. "And I've already wasted most of it leading you around. So, if you don't mind—"

"I do mind," he replied with infuriating coolness. "I want to talk to you. Now."

She studied him from beneath her lashes. He *was* an arrogant so-and-so. He was playing with her. And enjoying it.

Somehow, she had to find a handle on this. On herself. She

had to learn not to react, or at least to make him react more. Definitely a challenge. Suddenly, she smiled, and a heady thrill of recklessness shot through her. She'd always enjoyed a challenge.

Tilting her head back, she looked straight into his eyes.

"Are you going to handcuff me?" she asked softly.

"No." After a moment, he smiled. "At least, not yet."

He steered her out of the store. Still riding that wave of recklessness, Rae let him.

"Where are we going?" she asked.

"Lunch."

She hadn't expected lunch. The rational part of her mind gave a hoot of cynical laughter. *What did you expect, twit? To be beaten with a rubber hose?*

His eyes were crystal clear and guileless in the sunlight as he walked along with his distinctive male-tiger stride. Her heart revved, and not from the effort of keeping up with those long legs.

He led her to a tiny, dark cubbyhole of a deli named simply Doukas. Behind the counter stood a vast hulk of a man, a man who was tall and wide and sprouted a mustache that looked as though it might flap right off his craggy face.

"Hey, Gabriel," he called, his pure, sweet tenor a startling contrast to his appearance. His gaze shifted to Rae. "Wow."

"Mike, Rae," Gabriel said. "Rae, Mike."

"Graceful introduction," Mike countered. "Pleased to meet you, Rae."

She reached over the counter to shake hands. His grip was firm, but gauged to accommodate her smaller hands. Rae liked him; so many guys tended toward limp hands, which she hated, or grips calculated deliberately to hurt, which she hated even more.

"Mike's known me since I was young and stupid," Gabriel said.

"Yeah?" Mike retorted. "You might not be so young any more, but you're just as stupid as ever."

"There's no time limit on stupid," Rae added, diving right in.

With a flourish, Mike took an enormous cleaver from a nearby rack and began to chop meat. "Yeah, but the majority of people at least learn to hide it."

Gabriel snorted. "Sure. And most people learn not to put chopped jalapeno peppers on smoked turkey—"

"Hey!" Mike yelped.

"Hot jalapenos," Gabriel said. "On that obnoxious city inspector's sandwich—"

"Hah!" Mike brandished the cleaver, sending wicked flashes of light skittering around the room. "Could I help it? I thought it was pickle relish."

They all exchanged glances. Rae was the first to laugh, but the men joined her a heartbeat later. A customer came in, took one look at the cleaver and quickly ducked out again.

Beneath the laughter, Gabriel found himself watching Rae. Most of the women he'd brought around had been intimidated by Mike's size and boisterousness, but Rae had joined their repartee as though she'd been doing it for years. Gabriel didn't think much intimidated Rae Ann Boudreau. He admired her for it.

"I've got to know," Rae gasped. "Did you pass inspection that day?"

"Heck, yeah. You don't think I gave him that sandwich *before* he passed me, do you?"

That set Rae off again. She reached blindly behind her for a chair. "Oh, boy," she gasped.

Retrieving some measure of control, she scrubbed the tears away with her sleeve. Only then did she register Gabriel's laugh. It was a great laugh, deep and rich and full of joy. She wouldn't have believed the tough, cynical vice cop had it in him. The sound raced through her like hot wine, setting up a matching resonance deep in her body.

She studied him from beneath her lashes. He was much man, she thought, her gaze drifting to his mouth, then lower to the clean, strong line of his neck. She wanted to press her open mouth there, right there where the pulse beat beneath the skin.

He stopped laughing suddenly, and she knew he'd noticed

her watching him. Look away, you fool! But she couldn't. Amusement drained from his eyes, leaving her gaze impaled on pure desire. Hot. Raw. Powerful. And yet it was tempered with that same tenderness she'd glimpsed before, making it more compelling than simple passion could ever be.

Heat rolled through her until she thought her very bones would melt. She was glad for the solid support of the chair beneath her; it wouldn't do for tough, independent Rae Ann Boudreau to sink to the floor like a jellyfish.

Then Mike cleared his throat, giving her a welcome respite. "So, tell me, beautiful lady," he said, jabbing his thumb in Gabriel's direction. "What are you doing with *him?*"

"He arrested me," she replied.

Mike snorted. "That's how he gets all his dates."

"Why am I not surprised?" Rae said.

"It's only fair to warn you," Mike began, winking at the detective. "He's got a lot of faults, even for a cop. I could tell you stories—"

"Hey," Gabriel protested. "You promised you wouldn't breathe a word to anyone."

"Awful stories?" Rae asked.

"Horrible," Mike said, grinning fiendishly. "You'd run screaming before I got to the really bad stuff."

Rae gave a mock shiver. "Ooh. Should I be afraid?"

"Terrified," both men said in unison.

"Mmm. Then you'd better feed me. I do terror best on a full stomach."

Mike swept the cleaver in an expansive arc. "Anything you want, beautiful lady."

"Roast beef on wheat," she said, adding after a pause, "No relish."

Both men snickered. With a jolt, Rae realized that she was having fun. With Detective Gabriel MacLaren. This shouldn't be happening, she thought, even as her heart began to pound. Anything but this. If she didn't watch herself, she'd start to like him.

That would be bad.

"What about you, Gabriel?" Mike asked. "You want the usual, or are you gonna try something new for a change?"

Gabriel raised his hand in a warning gesture. "Uh-uh. You've experimented on me enough. I'm sticking with the usual. And two cups of coffee, please."

Rae wanted coffee. But she didn't want coffee if Gabriel wanted her to have it. Absurd, yes. Still, she had the strongest feeling that she'd be giving something up by letting him make any decisions for her, even one so simple. Gabriel MacLaren was rather like a force of nature; if she didn't hold tightly to herself, he'd sweep her up and whirl her away.

"I'd rather have iced tea, if you've got it," she said.

She shot a glance at Gabriel. He met her gaze squarely, a cynical half smile curving his hard-cut mouth. He knew what she was thinking, and knew why she was thinking it.

With an effort, she pulled her gaze away. And found Mike watching them both with an I-know-what's-going-on-here expression on his broad face.

"You do not," she said.

He didn't even try to pretend to misunderstand. "Do, too."

"Do not."

"Do, too."

"What the hell?" Gabriel asked.

Mike smiled at Rae. "See? I told you he wasn't all that bright. But he'll figure things out eventually."

With swift, economical movements, Mike wrapped the sandwiches and thrust them into a large white bag with Brenda's Hairstyling blazoned in pink across the front.

Rae lifted one brow. "Brenda's Hairstyling?"

"Advertising," Mike explained. "She's my niece."

"You're a nice man," Rae said.

He lifted both hands in mock horror. "Please. Don't tell anyone, you'll ruin my reputation. Get her out of here, MacLaren. And try not to embarrass me, will you? She knows my name."

"And I'm holding you responsible," Rae countered.

"You can come back anytime," he said, chuckling. "And you don't have to bring him with you."

"Thanks." Smiling, Rae shook hands again.

"Come on," Gabriel said. "I've played straight man long enough."

He led her down a side street to a tiny, V-shaped park tucked between two office buildings. Flowers bobbed in waves as the breeze riffled through them, and two dogwood trees laid patterned islands of shade beneath their branches.

"I've worked in this city for six years, and I had no idea this was here," Rae said, settling onto the grass in one of those shady spots. "Nice. Very nice."

Gabriel turned to look at her. No restlessness shaded her warm-sherry eyes now. The breeze lifted her hair, turning it to a red-brown aureole around her face.

His heart lurched, an honest-to-God physical reaction to the sight of her. It astonished him. He'd known prettier women. He'd known women who were smart and independent, women who were sensual. But until now, he'd never known one who could reach him so powerfully, and in a way that went far beyond attraction.

"This *is* nice," he said, easing down beside her.

Rae registered his closeness with every cell in her body. And every cell reacted. The sunlight seemed abnormally bright all of a sudden, the breeze warmer on her skin than it had been a moment ago. Gabriel's unique, musk-and-mint male scent blended exotically with that of the flowers.

She had to do something, anything, to keep from leaning toward him. Reaching out, she took the bag from him and retrieved her sandwich. The moment she unwrapped it, the delicious aroma of fresh roast beef wafted to her nose. She held the sandwich up, admiring it. Thick slices of homemade wheat bread held a wealth of pink-tinged meat layered a luscious inch high. Lettuce and tomato made bright slashes of color against the beef.

Sheer greed washed through her. She took a bite, closing her eyes in ecstasy as the bevy of flavors burst into her mouth.

"Oh, boy," she breathed, a wave of hunger washing through her. "That man really knows how to make a sandwich."

Riveted by the look of pure pleasure Rae's face, Gabriel stopped chewing.

"Mike is a great guy," he said, pretending that his insides weren't jumping crazily. "He's had some hard times. Married his childhood sweetheart and spent twelve years in bliss, then lost her to cancer a couple of years ago. I thought for a while he'd just shrivel up and die. But he made it. As he says, it takes guts to live. And even more guts to live alone."

The story brought unexpected tears to sting Rae's eyes. To cover them, she hastily took a bite of sandwich. When she looked up again, Gabriel was gazing at the tree branches above them.

"It's ironic," he said. "So many people marry, divorce and end up hating each other for the next fifty years. Mike was one of the few who are lucky enough to find true love. And then he had to lose her."

Rae's brows soared. "Detective MacLaren, are you telling me that you believe in true love?"

His reaction was instinctive and instantaneous; give one inch here, and he'd get himself maneuvered into a corner. As the saying went, the best defense was a good offense. "Don't you?"

"I gave up childish fantasies a long time ago."

Gabriel lay on his side, propping himself up on his elbow. Her eyes had turned wary, emotion closed off as though it had never existed. And all because of the mention of love. Interesting. A prudent man would have left it alone, but he'd never been prudent.

"Who hurt you?" he asked.

Rae's stomach dropped hard. She felt naked, vulnerable, her past exposed to a man who'd use his knowledge any way he could. Handling this would be tricky. Retreat was dangerous here, and so was attack. She kept her gaze on his, trying to lay a veil of casualness on feelings that weren't casual at all.

"Why would you think that was your business?" she countered.

"I'm a cop," he said. "Curiosity is my stock in trade."

"Mine, too," she replied, surprised at the edge that had come into her voice. "So...why aren't *you* married?"

Gabriel started to say that he just hadn't found the right woman yet, but that statement would be too revealing. He'd never made himself that vulnerable to another person, and he wasn't about to start now.

"I guess I'm just not the marrying type," he said.

Rae stared at him for a moment. She'd noticed a tiny hesitation in his answer, and knew he'd done some editing before speaking. She wondered what he'd hidden.

"Why not?" she asked.

"Maybe I'm just restless," he replied, shrugging.

Her gaze remained speculative, and Gabriel knew she wasn't finished. He also realized that she'd deftly turned the tables on him. One moment, he'd been asking the questions; the next, he'd been answering—and on the defensive. She was good—he'd give her that. There weren't many people who could distract him.

His gaze strayed to her mouth. A tiny spot of mayonnaise glistened on her bottom lip. Intending to fluster her, he reached out and cupped her chin in his hand. "You've got something on your lip," he said. "Hold still."

"That's okay," she said. "I'll—"

"Hold still," he growled.

Slowly, with deliberate sensuality, he slid his thumb along her chin toward her mouth. A sudden impulse caught him. Instead of wiping away the fleck of white, he spread it over the sweet curve of her bottom lip. The heat of their bodies melted it, turned it into a film that slid slickly along their skin.

Her breathing quickened. He registered it with his mind, his heart and his body. Of its own accord, his breathing shifted pace to match hers.

Suddenly, everything changed. The game was no longer vice cop using his skill to tweak her reactions. It had become purely sensual, both more complex and more dangerous than the one he'd begun. He didn't care. His eyes slitted almost closed as he ran his thumb over her lip again.

A jet roared overhead, shattering the moment. She pulled away from him, and Gabriel felt regret down to his toes. He didn't regret touching her. Oh, no. He regretted stopping. His hands ached with the desire to touch her again, to keep touching her until he'd assuaged this powerful need.

Stunned by what had happened, Rae reached up to touch her mouth. Her skin seemed to retain the memory of his touch as though it had been burned into her. He hadn't even kissed her.

"So," she said, fighting to regain some semblance of normalcy, "tell me about Peter Smithfield."

"What?"

His gaze showed no understanding of words, but it was definitely communicating on another level. Rae tried to resist the heat in his blue-crystal eyes, but found herself drawn deep, deep, deep. Desire ran in white-hot rivulets through her body. He wanted her. He wanted her in a way no other man ever had, and she was drawn to him by everything that made her a woman.

"I..." She swallowed against a throat gone tight and dry. "I asked you about Peter Smithfield."

With an effort, Gabriel disconnected from her eyes. Damn, he thought, she packed one hell of a lot of voltage. It took him a moment to remember why he'd brought her here. Rae Ann Boudreau seemed to take over his being, focusing him so completely on her that he lost his hold on everything else.

He was in trouble. Deep trouble.

"Why do you want to talk about Smithfield?" he hedged.

"Because you have him and I don't, and I have a subpoena to give him."

"This is one service you're not going to make," Gabriel said.

"Wrong," she snapped.

"Are you always this big of a pain in the neck?" he asked in exasperation.

"You bet," she said. "And I always get what I want."

"Let me give you a bit of friendly advice," he said. "Want something other than Peter Smithfield."

"Gee, Detective, I'd really like to accommodate you, nice guy that you are. But unfortunately, I've taken somebody's money to deliver a subpoena to him."

Gabriel would have liked to wring her neck. No, he amended silently. He'd like to do a number of things to her, all of them pleasurable.

"You'd do better to work with us than against us," he said.

"Why?"

A typical Boudreau response, he thought, gritting his teeth. "Look, Rae. We need Peter Smithfield right now. Badly. Once the case is finished, he's all yours."

"Is the case almost complete?" she asked.

"Ah..."

"No," she finished for him. "And do you know *when* it might be expected to be complete?"

She waited for him to lie to her. The intent lay plain in his eyes.

"No," he said, "I don't know when it will be complete."

Relief flooded through her. She didn't know why an honest answer mattered so much, but it had.

"That's fair enough," she said. "But you have to realize that Barbara Smithfield and her children can't wait. They need that child support, and they need it now."

"Damn," he muttered. There were times when his job required him to do things he didn't like, and this was surely one of them. "You know where I stand on this, Rae."

"And you know where I stand."

"If that's the way you want it," he growled.

"It is."

Locked in resentment and desire, they glared at each other a heartbeat longer. Then Rae snatched her trash up and scrambled to her feet.

"Thanks for lunch, Detective," she snarled. "I'll see you around."

His eyes had turned cold and cynical, and his smile with

it. He looked her up and down, and Rae felt as though he'd peeled flesh and bone away to look straight into her soul.

"Count on it, honey-child," he said.

Chapter 4

Rae stalked away. If she hadn't been so annoyed, she would have remembered to stick her nose in the air.

"Hey!" Gabriel called from behind her.

Casting a glance over her shoulder, she saw him coming after her with long, efficient strides. She dived into the lunchtime crowd, then abruptly made a one-eighty turn and mingled with a group of women.

It gave her a lot of satisfaction to see Gabriel turn the wrong way. Hah! she thought. Even arrogant, know-everything vice cops could learn a thing or two—with the right teacher.

"Boudreau, you are an idiot," she muttered. "Letting yourself getting snookered into lunch... Putting your brain on hold, hormones raging all over the place... Having *fun* with the man, for God's sake... You ought to be taken out and shot!"

She'd spoken the last sentence a bit louder than she'd intended, and a briefcase-toting businessman shied away from her. Rae hardly noticed him.

Stepping off the curb, she flung up her arm to summon a

passing taxicab. The vehicle screeched to a halt beside her. She pulled the door open and got in, nodding to the driver as he turned to look at her.

"Where to, ma'am?" the driver asked.

"Twelve twenty-one Harcourt Street," she said, reaching to close the door.

It was pulled out of her hand. Gabriel appeared in the opening, his mouth smiling but his eyes blazing hot with annoyance. He slid in beside her.

"Hello, sweetheart," he said. "Mind if I ride with you?"

"Yes," she said.

The driver laid his arm on the back of the seat. "Look, buddy, if the lady doesn't..."

Gabriel showed his badge. With a grunt, the driver turned forward again. Rae scooted across the slick vinyl seat, intending to make a quick escape out the street-side door. Gabriel scooted with her, however, securing the door handle before she could get a grip.

"Not so fast," he growled.

As the vehicle swung back into traffic, Rae crossed her legs and stared straight ahead, wishing she were anywhere else. No, she amended. This was her cab. She wished *MacLaren* were anywhere else. But there he sat, big and gorgeous and arrogant, his shoulder and thigh pressed so tightly to hers that she could feel the hard-muscled heat of him through her clothes.

This was bad. Very bad. She needed some boundaries, and fast. Anger was always useful. She clutched hers, using it to protect herself.

"That was lousy," she snarled.

"What was lousy?"

"Using your badge to get what you wanted."

He raised his brows. "But this *is* police business, Ms. Boudreau." Enough, his cop's mind told him. But the man in him wanted more. Wanted to jog her into an admission that he'd gotten to her, too. "Or did you think there was something personal?"

That really made her mad. She'd been struggling all along

to keep her emotions out of her dealings with Gabriel, and
had lost the fight every time he looked at her...like that.
Damn him, he was doing it again. Looking at her as though
he'd like to have her for dessert.

"Trust me, there's nothing personal," she said.

Gabriel smiled. "So what's the problem?"

"The problem is that I didn't want to share my cab with
you." Rae drew a deep breath, trying to still her churning
emotions.

Gabriel ricocheted between the urge to shake her until her
teeth rattled and the urge to kiss her senseless. Actually, he
amended, the urge to kiss her was very much stronger. But
since he had the feeling *he'd* be the one rendered senseless,
he resisted that urge.

Rae turned to glare at him. He was staring at her, his gaze
almost frighteningly intense. It seemed as though he'd peeled
her layer by layer, until her soul lay exposed. It frightened
her. She didn't want her soul exposed to any man, and particularly not to this one.

"Don't you have anything better to do?" she demanded.

One corner of his mouth went up. "Nope."

"Wouldn't it be more of a public service to go bust some
drug dealers?"

"Why don't you like cops?" he asked.

The question took Rae by surprise. She drew her breath in
sharply, shocked that she'd been so transparent. And that her
resentment against her ex-husband had so thoroughly soured
her feelings toward all cops. It had. And it wasn't fair. She'd
always prided herself on her fairness, so this didn't sit well.

"I was married to a cop," she said, fixing her gaze on the
back of the driver's head.

"Ah." Gabriel knew that the emotionless tone came from
tightly held control. Whatever had happened to her marriage,
it had hurt her badly.

A wave of tenderness rolled through him, both unexpected
and powerful. He shouldn't care, damn it. He didn't want to
care, and she obviously didn't want him to care. But he did.

He wanted to know what made her tick, what made her happy or sad, all the things that made her inimically Rae.

"It ended badly, I take it," he said.

Rae didn't look at him. Couldn't. She had no intention of telling him the sad, sordid tale of her marriage's demise, her ex-husband's constant harassment and the callousness of his fellow officers when they'd refused to go against one of their own. It had taken her a year to amass the evidence that had finally convinced her ex's captain to take action. She'd handled it quietly, and that, too, had backfired. Even now, the other detectives in that department thought she'd hounded Danny right off the force. Truth was, he'd ruined his career all by himself. Unfortunately, no one else believed it.

Gabriel wouldn't, either. He was a cop, and cops stuck together. Always.

"What happened?" he asked.

"With what?" she asked, being deliberately obtuse.

"Your marriage."

"Can't we talk about something else?" she demanded.

"No," he growled.

"We were married, it didn't work out and we split," Rae snapped. "End of story."

Gabriel leaned back against the seat and studied her with narrowed eyes. She'd lied to him.

So, why not? that little voice whispered. After all, they were on opposing teams here. But this had nothing to do with Peter Smithfield. This was personal.

Impossible. No, it was nuts. He had no business even *thinking* about anything personal where Rae was concerned. But even as that thought crossed his rational mind, his voice was saying something entirely different. Something personal.

"Do you ever see him?" he asked.

"None of your business," she retorted.

He scowled at her.

Seeing that scowl, Rae smiled. "What's the matter, Detective? Don't you like my answers?"

"Damned straight."

She batted her lashes at him. "It will do you good not to get your way for a change."

"I don't—"

He broke off as the taxi drew to a stop in front of her office building. The driver hooked one elbow over the back of the seat and looked back expectantly. Gabriel ignored him. He studied Rae closely, watching the emotions flitter through her eyes. She wanted to escape—badly. He'd dug too far down this time, and he'd dredged up things she'd rather keep hidden.

Good, he thought. He wanted to shake her up. Hell, he wanted to do a lot of things—things that would send her screaming from the cab if she knew.

"Hey," the driver said, "if you're gonna have a lovers' spat, take it outside. I got a living to make."

Lovers' spat? Rae recoiled from that. She *really* had to get out of this taxi. "What do I owe you?"

"I've got it," Gabriel said.

"It was my cab," Rae protested.

Stung by a sudden, powerful wave of annoyance, Gabriel snarled, "I'm paying."

"Ooh, how *masterful,*" she cooed. "I wouldn't dream of arguing."

Before he could react, she flung the door open and stalked out. By the time he'd paid for the taxi, she'd disappeared inside. He cursed under his breath.

"Take my advice, pal," the driver said. "You've really got her cranked. Let her cool off."

"What makes you the expert?" Gabriel demanded.

"Hey, I been married four times. If anybody knows when to lay low, I do."

With a grunt, Gabriel added five dollars to the fare and got out of the car. The taxi zoomed away.

"Four marriages," Gabriel muttered. "Sheesh!"

He glanced down at his watch. Three hours until his shift was over. There was no point in spending the time sitting in his car when he could spend it aggravating Rae. She'd certainly gotten more than her fair share of aggravating *him.*

Whistling under his breath, he took the stairs two at a time up to her third-floor office. The door was locked. Okay, he'd expected that. He knocked softly.

"Go away," she said, her voice muffled by the door.

"Come on, Rae," he called.

"I've got work to do."

He took a deep breath, controlling his temper with an effort. Oh, she was *very* good at this aggravation thing. "Open the door."

"Do you have a warrant?"

"Damn it, Rae—"

"If you don't have a warrant, you can go straight to—"

"I took the express there the moment I met you!"

Her response was a silence so cold he could feel the chill all the way out here. He resisted the impulse to knock the door right off its hinges. Damn, but she'd gotten to him. Every primitive instinct he'd known about—and a few he hadn't—was rampaging through him right now.

He stared at the door a moment longer, then forced himself to walk away. Not because he wanted to, but because he didn't trust himself. Maybe distance would give him some perspective.

Rae opened the blinds and watched him walk out to his car. Lordy, Lordy, but that man could move. He sauntered along with long, catlike strides, looking more male than ought to be legal. And boy, did the females respond! One woman nearly split her power suit trying to keep him in sight.

What was that nasty little feeling poking into her stomach? It felt cold and clammy and decidedly green. "I am not jealous," she said aloud. "I've never been jealous in my life."

She returned to her computer, plopping into the chair with perhaps more force than was necessary. But it didn't take long for her to become enmeshed in the puzzle of tracking down Peter Smithfield.

Her mouth curved in a mocking smile. She didn't need to pound the pavement to find Peter Smithfield. With her computer, the Internet and a little creative thought, she could find almost anything, anywhere.

MacLaren-based annoyance nagged at her while she logged on, while she connected with the database containing all the vacation rentals in the area. Her mind conjured up the memory of that business-suited woman turning to ogle MacLaren. That green, queasy feeling settled in Rae's belly again.

"Probably the pickles," she muttered.

The sun eased down toward the west, painting a glorious banner of red and orange across the sky. This was Rae's favorite time of day. Whenever the weather allowed, she'd jog home. Today was perfect, and she slipped into the sweats she'd brought with her.

Of course, Gabriel would be waiting.

But like mosquitoes, potholes and rattlesnakes, he could be ignored. She hoped.

Pulling her hair back into a ponytail, she jogged downstairs and out into the street. Gabriel's Taurus sat in the same spot it had been in all day. He leaned back in the seat, one tanned, sinewy arm hung out the window. As her gaze moved to his face, he pulled his sunglasses off and smiled at her.

It wasn't fair, she thought. She'd always considered herself a strong woman, but one glimpse of those eyes turned her insides molten. It didn't matter that he was an arrogant so-and-so, or that his smile was feral enough to belong to Shere Khan.

"Get thee behind me, temptation," she muttered.

She moved off down the sidewalk. Out of the corner of her eye, she watched Gabriel reach to adjust the mirror to keep her in sight as she approached.

He eased into gear, keeping pace with her as she ran. She glanced up and down the street, wishing she'd had the foresight to take a taxi. Unfortunately, there wasn't one anywhere in sight.

"Want a ride?" he called, steering with one hand.

"Go away," she retorted.

"Hey, you could hurt my feelings."

"If you had any," she countered.

He chuckled. "That's what I like about you, Rae. No wishy-washy cooperation, no coddling of my fragile male ego."

"I don't think your ego needs a whole lot of help," she said. "Hey, what if I cross-my-heart-and-hope-to-die promise not to leave my apartment until morning?"

"Ahh…no," he said. "You might as well get used to me, honey-child. Because until this case is over, we're going to be spending a lot of time together. A *lot* of time."

She resisted—barely—the urge to stick her tongue out at him. Instead, she put her nose in the air and kept moving. He idled along beside her, grinning like the Devil himself.

A van pulled up to the curb, blocking Gabriel's lane.

"Hah," she muttered.

Gabriel, however, was not so easily vanquished. He merely slapped his portable blue light onto the roof of his car and turned it on. The van moved.

"Smart aleck," Rae muttered.

She, like a complete idiot, was jogging along in her oldest sweats with an attention-grabbing police escort flashing alongside. She'd be lucky if this didn't make the eleven-o'clock news.

Gabriel tried to keep his attention on the road, but he had to admit that Rae was definitely distracting. None of those prissy parachute-silk or Spandex running clothes for Rae. No, she wore a pair of battered running shoes and well-worn sweats that clung to every luscious curve of her body.

And oh, man, could she move. He'd never thought of running as sexy before. But he was captivated by the unconscious efficiency of her pace, the fascinating flex of her smooth female muscles and the eye-popping sway of her ample breasts with every step she took.

He wasn't the only guy who noticed, either. Rae didn't seem to see the men who turned to watch her once she'd passed. But Gabriel did, and it set up a clamor of emotion in him. Primitive emotion. Unfamiliar emotion. To say it simply, he didn't want any other men looking at her.

"Are you sure you don't want a ride?" he asked.

"Positive."

He became fascinated with the thick, curly ponytail that bounced with every step she took. It was obvious that she didn't realize how beautiful she was. She'd cultivated being tough and independent, and had forgotten about being a woman.

And that, he thought, was the most fascinating of all.

"This is the strangest kind of surveillance I've ever heard of," Rae said, although she knew silence would have been safer.

"True," he agreed. "But we aim to please. Whatever the situation requires, that's what we do."

"You've got to sleep sometime."

"True again," he said. "But then somebody else will watch you until I come on duty again."

Rae shot him a glance. Cops, she thought. She'd intruded in their precious bureaucratic bailiwick, and they were determined to make her life miserable because of it.

"The only thing I insist on," he continued with a grin, "is that I'm the only one who gets to arrest you."

"What's the matter, Detective? Have they passed a law against jogging, and you want to lock me up again?"

Hell, yes, he thought, he'd like to lock her up. He'd like to lock her up and keep her all to himself until he figured out finally and completely why she affected him the way she did. Why did he feel that strange tenderness for her? Sure, he wanted her in the most elemental of ways. Desire. Passion. Those, of course, he'd been familiar with since he turned thirteen. But this blind, driving urge to know her down to her soul was new to him.

Things ought to be simpler, he thought. Then he laughed. He'd been a cop too long to think that things could ever be simple. Rae Ann Boudreau wasn't going to be just a beautiful woman he wanted to experience; of course, she had to be involved up to her eyeballs in a case that could be the destruction of his career.

And she wasn't going to get in his car simply because he wanted her to.

"Come on, Rae," he called. "I'll take you to dinner."

Rae's breathing changed, grew swifter and more shallow. She told herself it was the exertion of running. She told herself it was anything but the prospect of spending more time with Gabriel MacLaren.

"Are you trying to bribe me, Detective?" she asked.

"Absolutely."

"Well, I'm incorruptible."

She turned her face toward him, and her ponytail fanned out behind her. Gabriel was possessed by a vision of her lying on a bed—no, *his* bed—that glorious chestnut mane spread across the pillow, her eyes heavy lidded with passion. Incorruptible? He hoped not.

"Rae—"

"The answer is no," she panted. "Whatever it is you have in mind, no."

After that, Rae maintained a determined silence. He drove along beside her, tenacious as a pit bull, flashing that dratted blue light whenever anyone threatened to get in front of him.

Rae's apartment building loomed ahead, its white-frame walls turned orange by the setting sun. She sped up slightly, anxious to reach the haven it offered.

But Gabriel wasn't about to make it so easy. He zoomed past her as she turned onto the sidewalk leading to the entrance. She knew he was going to park. If she could just get in ahead of him...

"Forget it, Rae," he said, jogging past her with a fresh, bouncy stride she couldn't hope to match after the mile run she'd just completed.

She wasn't even shocked that he'd all but read her mind. They'd been on the same wavelength from the beginning.

He held the door open for her, his gaze clear as crystal and as guileless as a baby's. The snake. Rae held her head high as she went past him. He sped past her again to ever so solicitously press the elevator button for her.

"What a gentleman," she snarled.

"I was taught manners, honey-child," he replied.

Rae opened her mouth to say something scathing, but the elevator doors slid aside and she found herself standing in front of Marlene Britton, the worst gossip in the county. Maybe the whole continent. If there wasn't any gossip to be had, Marlene invented it. Rae, being single—and worse, uncooperative—had been the focus of her attention for years.

Mrs. Britton swiveled her head to look from Rae to Gabriel and back again. Not a single hair stirred with the movement. "Rae, dear!" she exclaimed. "And with a man! I see that you've finally decided to end your self-imposed celibacy!"

How typically Marlene, Rae thought with an inward grimace. The amazing thing was that she prided herself on her manners, and was quick to point out anyone else's lapse.

"Actually," Rae drawled, pinning the bleached-blond busybody with a look that should have freeze-dried her instantly, "he's not a man. He's a cop. He arrested me, and is now delivering me to home-bound probation."

Marlene's mouth opened and closed soundlessly for a moment.

"What…what did he arrest you for?" she finally managed to ask.

"Prostitution," Rae said.

"So much for celibacy," Gabriel muttered, fighting to keep from laughing. It was obvious that Rae didn't like this woman, and equally obvious why. He should let her handle it.

Then he stepped forward. Rae might not care about her reputation, but he did. *What am I saying?* that oh-so-rational cop's voice whispered. *Chivalry? From a vice cop? A week ago, he would have said that chivalry was as outdated as the nickel phone call.*

"She's teasing you, ma'am," he said, ignoring the hoots of laughter that cynical voice left in his mind.

"Oh, really?" Marlene asked, arching well-plucked brows.

"Really," he said.

"*Are* you a police officer?"

"Yes, ma'am."

Her steel gray eyes homed in like tracking devices. "And did you arrest her?"

"The only woman I've arrested recently was a Jane Doe," he replied without cracking a smile. "We get lots of those."

"Ah." She swung around to glare at Rae. "Darling, you really ought to stop playing these silly games. You know we only want to see you hooked up with a nice man."

Rae let her breath out with a hiss. "Who said he's a nice man?" she retorted, stalking into the elevator.

Gabriel thrust out a long arm to keep the doors from closing.

Slipping into the elevator with Rae, he slapped his hand over the Door Open button. "You must forgive her, Ms...."

"Marlene to you," she said, batting her lashes at him.

"Ma'am. Don't hold it against Rae that she doesn't tell you anything about her personal experiences. She's had a real hard life, and she'll be the first to admit that she has difficulties with opening up to people."

"Some people," Rae snarled.

"But I plan to change all that," Gabriel continued.

Malice creased the Britton woman's face, and he knew this encounter would provide gossip fodder for weeks. Suddenly gripped with an irresistible wash of pure devilment, he let go of the button and swept Rae against him in one swift motion.

Rae drew a breath, ready to protest. As she did, he claimed her mouth in a kiss that shocked her so badly she forgot to close her eyes. The last thing she registered as the doors snicked closed was Marlene's astounded, openmouthed stare.

"Hey," she gasped, pushing him to arm's length. "What—?"

"Shut up," he said. "I'm protecting your reputation."

"What?"

Gabriel didn't give a damn whether he made sense or not. This had begun as a joke, but he was damned serious now. All the powerful, confusing emotions she roused in him had come to a head, and he only cared that she was finally in his arms.

"Look, MacLaren—" she began.

"You talk too much," he said.

He leaned closer, fascinated with a tiny dimple at the corner of her mouth. Her eyes registered his nearness, echoing the sizzle of arousal that he felt toward her. He watched as her mouth softened, her lips parting as though to invite his kiss. No man in his right mind, he thought, would pass up an opportunity like this.

He'd always had good reflexes.

Wrapping his hand around her ponytail, he fitted his mouth to hers. She tasted like heaven. He tilted his head, seeking greater contact as he slipped his tongue deep.

Rae sighed as he slid his free hand up her back, spreading his fingers wide in a gesture both tender and possessive. No one had ever touched her like this. No one had ever made her *feel* like this, hot and cold and shaky all at the same time.

She sighed again as he ran his tongue along the tender insides of her lips, then traced the edges of her teeth. Desire ran wild through her body.

This isn't me, she thought dazedly. I don't react this way, I don't, I don't. But she did. Everything inside her had turned to fire, and every leaping flame, every rushing tingle of arousal, had Gabriel MacLaren's name on it.

Reality went spinning off. For this moment, caution didn't exist, nor did restraint. There was only Gabriel. Rae met his tongue boldly with hers, inciting him, inciting herself. His sigh was as helpless as hers had been, as fraught with passion.

She slid her hands upward along the hard male muscles of his chest and shoulders. Winding her fingers into his thick dark hair, she held on while he took her on a magic-carpet ride of sensation.

"Wow," he murmured, coming up for air.

Rae sank her fingers deeper into his hair. "You talk too much."

Gabriel wasn't about to waste time disputing that. She was lush and curved and as passionate as he could have imagined, and all he wanted to do was kiss her again. Slipping his arm around her waist, he lifted her more closely against him.

The elevator chimed to announce their floor. Still holding

her against him, Gabriel jammed his thumb on the Door Close button.

"Now, where were we?" he muttered.

But Rae's bubble had popped. She sprang away from him, frantically smoothing her hair. There was no smoothing her emotions, however. Shock and dismay mingled with the sweeping tide of desire still coursing within her.

"Open the door," she said.

Gabriel studied her with narrowed eyes, damning the limitations of the situation. He wanted privacy, and Rae. If they'd been anywhere else...

"Rae—"

"Don't say anything," she said. "This is embarrassing enough."

"What's embarrassing about a kiss?" he asked.

She crossed her arms over her chest. "Haven't you heard the term 'conflict of interest'?"

"Yeah, but this—"

"Is."

"Damn it, Rae."

"Open the door."

Gabriel's gaze drifted down to the Emergency button. It ought to take a couple of hours to get them out of here.... But a couple of hours alone in an elevator with an amorous Rae Ann was a completely different prospect from being trapped with Rae Ann in her present mood.

With a muttered curse, he lifted his thumb from the button. The doors snicked open. Rae strode out into the corridor, then turned to look at him. Resentment darkened her eyes, but he couldn't miss the flicker of desire heating the shadows.

Something important had happened here. He knew it. She knew it. But Rae was nothing if not stubborn, and she wouldn't have admitted it if it had been printed on her forehead.

"You can't make it go away by pretending it isn't there," he said.

"I don't know what you're talking about," she retorted.

He smiled. "Your lips are swollen."

His words brought memories crashing back through her mind, too-vivid tastes and feelings and sensations she didn't want to remember. She turned and walked away from him.

Gabriel felt as though something important had been ripped out of him, and she'd taken it with her. He ought to go pound on her door, break it down if he had to…anything but to let her walk away like this. Everything that made him a man cried out for him to claim her—and take back whatever it was she'd stolen.

But he wasn't just a man. He was a cop with a job to do.

So, instead of following his instincts, he pushed the Lobby button.

Downstairs, Gabriel found another detective ensconced in one of the comfortable armchairs scattered throughout the lobby.

"Hey, MacLaren," he called softly.

Gabriel joined him. He didn't know Brett Wilson well; the tall, sandy-haired detective had transferred in from another precinct a few weeks ago. He seemed capable enough, however.

"Are you my relief?" he asked.

"Yeah." Wilson rubbed his thumb across his jaw. "So Rae Ann is up to old tricks, eh?"

Gabriel's attention focused, sharpened. "What do you mean?"

"Rae Ann was married to my cousin Danny. He was a cop, too, stationed with me over in Balfour Hills. When they broke up, man, did she mess him up. Kept complaining to his captain, and once even went to the commissioner with her lies. Eventually got him run off the force."

Shock numbed Gabriel's mind. "How did she do that without evidence?"

"Hey, this is the nineties. You don't need evidence—all you've got to have is politics. Don't ever get involved with Rae Boudreau, that's all I can say." Shooting a speculative gaze at Gabriel, he added, "Oh, man, tell me you haven't—"

"I haven't," Gabriel growled. "And if I had, I'm a big enough boy to take care of myself."

"That's what Danny said. He's selling insurance now."

Gabriel found himself not liking Brett Wilson very much. Strange, he should have been grateful for the warning. Hey, he would have been the first to say that Rae was trouble. But not like this. He would have bet his life that her kind of trouble was straightforward and honest, like her warm-sherry eyes.

"Damn," he said. But not because of Danny whoever-he-was. Because of Rae, because she wasn't the person he'd thought her to be.

And because of his own bitter disappointment.

"Hell of a thing, ain't it?" Wilson asked.

"You've got that right," Gabriel agreed.

Chapter 5

Rae twisted and turned, aware of her restless movement even in sleep. Gabriel MacLaren had invaded her world, her peace of mind and now even her dreams.

She could feel him, actually feel him. His hands were as hard and gentle as they'd been in reality, his mouth as hot as when he'd kissed her.

In her dreams, she had no defenses against him. Didn't need any. They came together in passion, in love, in trust. Nothing between them but skin and heat. She became lost in his eyes, and it seemed as though she floated in a blue crystal sea, held safe in the hard strength of his arms.

Desire thrummed through her veins like a swift, powerful drumbeat. Her heart took up the rhythm. It was a dance as old as time: man and woman, woman and man. Passion as deep as the ocean, as uncontrollable as a thunderstorm. Primitive. Compelling. And oh, so very beautiful.

Her dream lover rose above her. She arched her back, welcoming him. No. Inciting him. His crystalline eyes blazed with passion, and she knew he'd given himself up to her completely. She curved her hand around his neck, ready, oh, so ready—

The telephone shrilled, and the lovely mood shattered like so much glass. Rae sat straight up, her hair all but standing on end. She felt as though every nerve in her body had been twanged like badly played guitar strings.

The phone rang again. She fumbled to answer it, only to find the cradle empty. "Darned cordless phones," she muttered, groping along the top of the nightstand. "Where the devil did I leave it?"

Finally, she found the fugitive handset buried in the clutter that always seemed to accumulate beneath her bed.

"Hello?" she panted.

"Miss Boudreau, this is Barbara Smithfield. I hope I didn't wake you."

Rae glanced at the clock—5:10 a.m., she thought. Barbara Smithfield wasn't the sort to be calling about something frivolous. "Don't worry about that, Barbara. What's the matter?"

"We're being evicted this morning and... I hate to bother you, but if you think you might be getting close to finding Peter, I might be able to convince the landlord to wait a few weeks—"

"I wish I could tell you yes," Rae said. "I almost caught up with him Saturday night, but he got away from me."

"Oh." Barbara Smithfield's voice blurred, as though all her hope and will had drained out. "I'm sorry to have bothered you—"

"Barbara, where do you plan to go?" Rae asked.

The other woman hesitated a moment. "I heard of a place down on Washington Street—"

"That's a shelter," Rae said. "And only temporary."

"Yes," Barbara replied with quiet dignity, "I know. But right now that's better than the alternative."

Rae was possessed by a wave of outrage so sudden and powerful that she actually began to shake. "I won't have it!" she snapped.

"What?" Barbara gasped.

"Get those kids in a taxi and come over here," Rae ordered.

"But—"

"If you don't have the money, tell the driver to come up here with you and I'll pay him. We'll figure the rest out later."

"We couldn't impose—" the other woman began.

"Enough," Rae said, completely exasperated. What was she supposed to do, let them get thrown out onto the streets? "Just do what I tell you. For your kids' sake if not your own."

"Yes, Rae." A lighter note had come into Barbara's voice.

Rae had the feeling she was being teased, but Barbara hung up before she could find out for sure. She sat for a moment, scowling at the phone and wondering how Gabriel would have felt had he taken that call. Would he just shrug, accepting the situation with that infuriating cop's cynicism?

Probably, she thought. The only surprise was how much it hurt.

One thing was certain: if he still thought that his stupid little bureaucratic secret was more important than people, then he had no heart at all.

Rae stood in the doorway of the spare bedroom. Barbara Smithfield and the three children lay snuggled in the bed. The kids looked completely relaxed, as though a great weight had been lifted from their shoulders.

With a sigh, Rae turned away. Mike, the eight-year-old, had informed her that he was "the man of the family." His little brother, Joey, hadn't said much, but he'd quietly slipped his hand into Rae's when she'd offered him a cookie. And the youngest, Sarah, had clutched her ragged teddy bear and watched Rae with an expression that looked an awful lot like hero worship.

"You're lost, Boudreau," Rae muttered.

She slung her briefcase over her shoulder and let herself out of the apartment. Her temper might not be running so high if she hadn't known that Gabriel would be waiting for her. If he said one thing to her, one little thing… Scowling, she stabbed the elevator button with her forefinger.

The first thing she saw in the lobby was Detective Mac-Laren. He sat sprawled like a tiger in one of the armchairs, a newspaper open in his lap. Of course, he'd been watching for her.

Her heart gave a strange little leap as that crystalline gaze traveled her from head to toe and back again. Warmth raced through her in a molten tide. She saw a matching heat flicker to life in his eyes, and she nearly groaned in frustration.

This was terrible. Awful. She had it bad. Whatever *it* might be. She'd used the saying a thousand times without wondering what it really meant.

She'd already been annoyed before coming down here. Now, with her very body betraying her, she passed straight into anger.

Gabriel smiled at her. She was sailing high and hard this morning, he thought. Probably that kiss last night. He'd hardly slept at all last night, tormented as he'd been by thoughts of her heat, her passion, her lushness. And now, seeing her in the flesh, he wanted her more than ever.

Rae, however, had been more accommodating in his dreams. He watched her walk toward him, her jaw set stubbornly, her eyes resentful. Still, she was so beautiful this morning that his heart felt as though it were turning flips in his chest. Her skin gleamed like rich cream in the bright sunlight, and red highlights burned in the depths of her hair.

She wore a green, long-sleeved tunic over gray leggings, and looked absolutely delicious. He had the feeling she thought the loose top hid her body, but she was much too curvy for that. But her unconscious sexiness was more stirring than any deliberate sensuality could possibly be.

No-nonsense Rae, striding toward him like pure temptation. He smiled appreciatively as she neared. But she stuck that slim, delightful nose in the air and sailed past without speaking, and he had to jump up to follow her before she got too far.

"Morning, Rae," he said, falling into step beside her.

"Men are toads."

Gabriel studied her for a moment while he pondered a response to that one. Had the toad remark come simply from temper, or was it a ploy to make him angry enough to walk away— leaving her alone to pursue Peter Smithfield?

"Ribbet," he said.

Rae surveyed him with a look that should have burned him instantly. "I don't have time to play with you today, Detective. I've got work to do."

"I'll be very quiet. You won't even notice I'm around."

Fat chance, Rae thought.

Her beeper went off, startling them both. Rae slapped her hand over the device to keep Gabriel from seeing the number display. It was her answering service, doubtless with a rush job.

"Excuse me," she said, turning away. "I've got to find a phone."

Without cracking a smile, he handed her his cellular. Rae made the call. It was a typical one for her: some lawyer needed papers served ASAP on a man who was flying in from Omaha this morning.

She studied Gabriel, calculating her chances of ditching him. It could be done. But not easily—she needed to choose the moment carefully, for maximum usefulness.

"Look," she said, pinning him with a level stare, "it's obvious that I'm not going to get rid of you—"

"You've got that right."

"So, I might as well accept the situation."

"Absolutely."

She fell silent for a moment. Gabriel repressed a smile while he waited for the other shoe to drop.

"Then you won't mind driving," she said.

"Not at all."

He grinned at her, a bad-boy smile the Devil himself would have envied, and took her by the arm. Her breathing suddenly became shallow. Tingles ran in all directions from the spot where he held her, and she felt as though she'd been dipped in fire.

"Why do I suddenly feel like the proverbial lamb being led to slaughter?" he inquired.

"Why, Detective," Rae drawled in her best Scarlett imitation, "whyevah would you think that?"

He laughed, and that deep, husky sound brought her gaze down to his mouth. A tight, restless ache bloomed deep in her body, a woman's affirmation of desire.

Once in the car, she studied him out of the corner of her eye. His face looked as though it had been carved from granite— rugged, handsome, unyielding. He was sure, so blindly sure, that his decisions were the best for everyone. But he was wrong. After looking into the eyes of Peter Smithfield's children, Rae knew what was most important.

He slipped the Taurus through a break in traffic that would have intimidated another driver. Startled, Rae stomped a non-existent brake pedal.

"What's the matter, Rae?" he asked, shooting her a glance.

"I've grown accustomed to living," she retorted. "When something threatens that, I react."

"You wound me. I'm a very competent driver, you know."

"Sure. But have you ever checked your rearview mirror to see the mayhem you leave in your wake?"

The creases bracketing his mouth deepened, although he didn't actually smile. Very sexy, in Rae's opinion. In profile, his face looked sharp hewn, with an aggressive jawline and an alarmingly rapacious look to his mouth. It was the face of a man who knew what he wanted, and who took it.

"Why haven't you ever tried to get your driver's license back?" he asked.

She stared at him, her mind knocked off balance by the unexpected question. "How did you know—? Never mind," she said. "You're a cop. You regularly pry into other people's business."

"Having your license suspended can hardly be considered private," he said, "Besides, you're the subject of a police surveillance. As of now, your life is an open book."

"I doubt that, Detective," she retorted.

He shot her a look from the corner of his eye. "Six years

ago you had a rash of tickets, from parking too close to a fire hydrant to reckless driving. You ended up with a year-long suspension.''

"That's the story," she said.

"It's nothing to be ashamed of. You were going through a divorce at the time. Stressed out and emotional."

Her tone turned arid. "Yup, that's me."

She lapsed into silence, not even tempted to tell him the truth of that story. It stung, even to this day. Not because her feelings were hurt, or even because she'd lost her license. But her sense of fair play had taken a bruising on that one.

Simply, the system had failed her—because it was being abused by the very people who were supposed to protect it. Her ex and several of his cop buddies had harassed her for months. They stopped her at least once a week. She'd complained, of course. But her word was nothing against that of the police officers.

It didn't matter that she'd eventually won, gathering enough evidence to go to both her ex's captain and the commissioner. Her idealism was gone, shattered, and she'd never get it back again.

"A penny for your thoughts," Gabriel said.

She blinked, returning to the present in a rush. "My thoughts are *much* more valuable than that," she retorted.

"Hmm. It might just be worth the investment to know what scheme is going through that tricky little brain of yours."

"Detective," she said in mock indignation, "surely you aren't suggesting that I would try something nefarious, when you're only doing your duly appointed job?"

"In a New York minute."

She smiled at him, a secretive, intensely female smile that had all Gabriel's instincts humming. She was a real player, this one. As her ex-husband could no doubt testify.

"There's the lawyer's office," she said.

He ducked his head to look up at the building's expensive brick facade. "I know this guy," he said. "I arrest a lot of his clients."

"Your cynicism is showing," she said.

His eyes narrowed. "Maybe I should have smiled."

Rae wished for a moment he was anything but a cop. He'd had more to do with the Peter Smithfields of the world than with decent people, and his perceptions were shadowed accordingly.

"I..." she began. Then she sighed. "Oh, never mind."

She turned away. But he grasped her by the hand, bringing her back again. The moment his long, warm fingers closed around hers, the world gave a spin. Then it settled down into a new configuration, one centered on Gabriel MacLaren.

Rae found herself staring into his eyes, unable to break away from the passion flaring in their depths. His thumb strayed to the back of her hand and began to stroke. Back and forth, back and forth. Heat swept through her in a wild rush. She felt light-headed, as though up and down had suddenly switched places.

"What is it?" he asked.

His voice ran through her like a physical touch. One word, one touch, and nothing else seemed to matter. It wasn't just desire, although there was more of *that* than she'd like to admit. Whenever he touched her, her spirit seemed to go rushing toward him, pulling the rest of her along whether she wanted to go or not.

Did she want him? Yes. Did she want to want him? Oh, no.

With an effort of will, she pulled her hand from his. "I've got to get to work."

"I'm not stopping you," he countered.

One corner of his mouth went up in a smile that was as sexy as it was cynical. Rae got out of the car to escape it, although she would have died before admitting her own weakness.

It only took her a few minutes to collect the papers, but that respite gave her a chance to get her wayward emotions under control. By the time she returned to the car, she'd regained all the barriers he'd torn down before.

She hoped she could keep them. If she could keep from getting lost in those blue crystal eyes...

"Hey," he said. "Where to, boss lady?"

"The airport." She checked her watch. "I'm in a hurry—"

Her head snapped back as he screeched away from the curb. She shot him a glare and found him grinning at her like a wayward kid.

"Wanna work the siren?" he asked, waggling his brows.

"Yes!" she said in a sudden rush of delight.

He got her to the airport in record time. Exhilarated by the wild ride, Rae laughed as he pulled up in front of the entrance.

"I'm going to have to get one of those things," she said, pointing to the blue police light.

Gabriel turned to look at her, and his stomach did a headlong plunge into his knees. Rae actually seemed to glow, as though lit from within. And why? Not for baubles or even for love, but simply the pure, unadulterated delight of a fast car ride.

No woman had ever had his effect on him. Ever. If she knocked him for a loop with a laugh, he thought a bit hazily, then what would she do if she came to him in passion?

He reached for her before his conscious mind had caught up. Fortunately for both of them, she'd already started to leave the car. By the time she bent to look in the window, he'd retrieved his wayward hand and put it back on the steering wheel.

"Wait here," she said. "I'll be out in a couple of minutes."

He nodded. The moment she entered the terminal, he followed her. He had no trouble keeping her in sight; everything that made him a man had tuned in to her. If he'd been blind, some sort of male sonar would have enabled him to pick her out of a crowd.

She cast a glance over her shoulder, and he knew she'd spotted him. That look had Keep Off signs all over it. He smiled when she swung around and came toward him.

She stopped in front of him and put her hands on her hips, an action that pulled her top tightly against her breasts. Gabriel couldn't keep his gaze on her face. He couldn't. Hell, the woman had more curves than the law ought to allow.

He took a leisurely visual journey down her body, his gaze skimming those full breasts, the sleek curve of her waist and hips, the long, shapely legs....

"MacLaren, if you mess this up for me, I'll—"

"What?" he inquired.

"I haven't decided yet." She gazed at him from beneath her lashes. "But it will be bad."

He grinned at her. "I can hardly wait."

"Listen, MacLaren. You look like a cop," she said. "This guy's the suspicious sort. Stay away from me."

"Yes, ma'am," he said, ripping off a salute.

With a final glare, Rae turned away. She stopped briefly to buy a bouquet of flowers from a nearby kiosk. Then she blended in with the people waiting just outside the security checkpoint.

She spotted her quarry right away, recognizing him from the photo the lawyer had shown her. Then she whistled under her breath. The attorney had shown good judgment in not telling her more about the guy—like the fact that he must have been six foot six. And proportionately broad.

"You knew I'd charge more, you snake," she muttered.

The man strode along as though he owned the world. Rae waved her bouquet at an elderly woman behind him, as though greeting her long-lost aunt.

With one smooth motion, she pulled the summons from her pocket and stepped in front of the man. He had good reflexes; she'd give him that. Before she could say anything, he knocked the papers from her hands and ran back toward the gate.

Rae had good reflexes, too. Before he'd gone three paces, she scooped the papers up off the floor and ran after him. Uniforms materialized in front of her as airport security reacted.

"Police!" Gabriel called from behind her. "Out of the way!"

The uniforms vanished. Rae hustled after her quarry, but he'd disappeared. Then she noticed the door to the men's room easing closed.

"Hah," she said under her breath.

She went in after him. Only one other man was in the rest room, and he left in a hurry. Rae walked along the line of stalls. Spotting a pair of what had to be size-fourteen shoes, she extended the summons over the metal door.

"These legal papers are for you, Mr. Shackleford," she said. "You might as well take them."

"Oh, hell," he said, and did so.

A moment later, he came out of the stall. "You're not shy, are you?" he asked, indicating their surroundings with a wave of his hand.

"This would definitely be the wrong job if I were," she agreed.

Shackleford unfolded the summons and began to read, then peered at her over the edge of the paper. "I don't suppose I could offer you something to tell the attorney that you didn't see me—say, a couple of thousand?"

"No," she said. She didn't even get angry; she'd been offered bribes before, and by better men than this.

She also knew what was coming next. First the what's-a-nice-girl-like-you-doing-in-a-place-like-this routine, then admiration for her honesty and, finally, a pass. Men really were toads.

"I've got to admire your integrity," he said.

"Thanks."

"Buy you a drink?"

"No, thanks."

She turned away. As she neared the exit, she spotted Gabriel tucked into the alcove behind the door. He fell into step beside her as she left.

"I heard the guy offer you a bribe," he said.

"That stuff happens all the time," she retorted.

"Do you usually get asked out on dates, too?"

"Sometimes."

"Do you ever accept?"

Her nostrils flared. "Bribes?"

"Dates," he growled.

"I don't see where that can be considered police business," she said.

Gabriel wasn't sure what he'd wanted from her, but a snotty answer definitely wasn't it. Actually, he didn't even know why he was so annoyed. Yes, he did, damn it.

He was jealous. Green-eyed, teenage-irrational jealous, and just because another man had asked her for a date. He had no right to his jealousy, as Rae had so graciously pointed out. Their relationship was strictly business.

Yeah, right. So why was he standing here, seething with annoyance at the thought of her going out with another man?

He wanted her for himself. He didn't know why he wanted her, or exactly *how* he wanted her, but want her he did.

"You owe me dinner," he said, deliberately slinging one from left field.

Rae blinked. "Huh?"

"You owe me, Rae. You'd still be explaining things to Airport security if I hadn't come along."

She studied him from beneath her lashes, wondering what game he was playing now. Wondering if it were a game at all, or something much deeper and more dangerous. Tension fairly radiated from his body, and something hard and hot had come into his eyes. It was almost as though his facade of civilization had cracked, revealing a glimpse of the predator below.

Another woman might have been intimidated. But Rae was not any woman. He roused something reckless and untamed within her, wildness calling to wildness. It burst through her like flame, burning everything else aside.

Gabriel's eyes demanded her answer. But there was no choice for her, not really. Maybe there never had been. From the moment she'd met this man, she had been tied to him somehow. Danger didn't seem to matter. Nor did caution, nor common sense.

Her answer had been made for her long before now. In this one, rushing moment, however, she realized it.

"Yes," she said, perhaps agreeing to more than dinner.

Chapter 6

Gabriel gazed across the table at Rae. She was worth looking at. Definitely. She'd pulled her hair up in a prim knot, obviously hoping to project an air of propriety.

Trouble was, propriety didn't work on a woman with such reckless eyes. She wore a dark green sundress that would have been merely flattering on another woman. On her, it looked like pure sin. The square neckline delineated the full swell of her breasts, and although it was cut modestly high, it revealed a wedge of skin so smooth and creamy it made his mouth water.

"You look—" he hastily edited the phrase *good enough to eat* "—gorgeous."

"You were going to say something else," Rae said.

He leaned back in his chair. "Don't you know how to have a normal conversation?"

"What's a normal conversation?"

"A normal conversation is when two people sit down and talk about things that interest them, hoping to find one or more subjects of *mutual* interest."

"Oh," she said. Propping her elbows on the table, she

leaned her chin on one palm. "We're both interested in Peter Smithfield. Let's talk about him."

"Let's not." Gabriel raised one finger, summoning the waiter. "We'd like another bottle of the chardonnay, please."

"Are you trying to stupefy me with alcohol?" Rae asked.

"Ms. Boudreau, I can't imagine any situation in which I could successfully stupefy you."

I could, Rae thought, remembering that kiss. The moment his lips had met hers, her brain had gone into suspended animation. Her body had swept into the breach, and everything it had said meant trouble.

It wouldn't be so bad if Gabriel weren't so incredibly sexy, a condition intensified by the dim lighting of the restaurant. Sepia shadows lurked in every angle of his rugged face, making him look even more the predatory male animal.

There were so many contradictions in his eyes—passion and tenderness, cynicism and a smoky sensuality hot enough to make steam. He'd go after what he wanted. And he wouldn't stop until he got it. If that happened to be a woman, specifically Rae Ann Boudreau... Oh, boy. It would be like getting swept up in a hurricane, or maybe burned alive.

Her pulse stuttered into high gear. She'd better think about something else, fast.

"Why did you go into law enforcement?" she asked.

He lifted one broad shoulder. "Why do you want to know?"

"Call it a stab at normal conversation," she countered.

"I wanted to have a part in making the world a better place," he said.

Rae hadn't expected idealism from him. It stirred her, and disturbed her, too. She let her gaze drift away across the restaurant. It was a very stark room, white linen tablecloths and napkins, white-on-white china. And it had nothing to keep her attention from drifting back to Gabriel's fathomless ice blue gaze.

"Did you?" she asked.

"Did I what?"

"Make the world a better place?"

Ordinarily, Gabriel would have said something flippant, something designed to hide his real feelings. But he wanted Rae to understand. More, he needed to know she *could* understand.

"I used to think so," he said. "But sometimes I don't know anymore."

She didn't answer, just kept looking at him with expectant, sherry-colored eyes. He'd given her a provocative answer; now he knew he had to explain it.

"I get frustrated when I arrest the same girls night after night," he said. "I've tried talking to them, telling them the risks. 'You're going to die,' I tell them. 'AIDS, drugs, some john who goes too far.' They don't listen. I bust kids who are selling drugs to other kids. They've got no conscience, no future. I take them in, the courts let them out."

She nodded. "Do you ever get used to it?"

He hadn't. He'd tried to, because a thick skin was the only way to survive the job without getting flayed. But every time he saw a new girl walking the street, still looking fresh and healthy, he hurt. And a cop couldn't let himself hurt.

"Sure," he said. "I'm used to it."

It seemed as though a shutter had snapped down over his eyes. He'd closed up, tight and smooth as a glass wall. It had happened so often with her ex-husband. After a while, she hadn't been able to reach Danny at all.

Rae knew there was no chance of getting through that barrier, and she'd had too much experience even to try. Her only protection was to retreat behind barriers of her own.

"Now," she said, "about Peter Smithfield."

"Can't tell you a thing," he said.

"Won't."

He smiled. "That's right. Won't."

Rae leaned back in her chair. Lifting her wineglass, she ran one fingertip around the rim. "I've spent a lot of time getting to know people," she said. "People who like to keep their finger on the pulse, so to speak."

"So who hasn't?" Gabriel carefully kept his voice neutral,

but his stomach had begun to churn. He had a feeling he wasn't going to like what came next.

"Some of these people know the same things the cops know," she continued.

He was right; he didn't like it.

"And?"

"You don't know where Peter Smithfield is, MacLaren. Might as well admit it."

He smiled at her. "Rule number one, Rae, learned firsthand from every felon on the street. Never admit anything."

"I'm going to find him first," she said.

Something sharp and uncomfortable poked at Gabriel's conscience. Because no matter how good she was, if she found Smithfield first or not, she wouldn't be allowed to serve that summons. And he'd be the one to take her victory from her.

He pushed that thought away. Twinges of conscience were something he wasn't allowed to have. He had a job to do.

Rae saw the detachment in his eyes. Then everything changed. His smile turned from cynical to sensual, and the desire in his eyes warmed to megawatt voltage.

Her blood sang through her, turning her body molten and her brain to mush. Stupid, yes. Controllable, no.

"Would you like dessert?" he asked, his voice as soft as a caress.

Her gaze went to his mouth. "Are you having any?"

"I thought I'd try that chocolate-passion thing the waiter suggested."

"Chocolate passion," she repeated. An unfortunate title, she thought. It evoked thoughts that weren't at all sweet.

"If you dare," he said.

She didn't think he was talking about the dessert. But a challenge was a challenge, and Rae wasn't about to let him back her down. In fact, she decided to up the ante. "After that steak, I don't think I can eat a whole one," she said.

His eyes warmed further. "Then we'll share."

Call and raise, Rae thought. Oh, boy.

The waiter appeared. Rae studied Gabriel as he ordered

coffee and chocolate passion, and tried to quell her churning emotions.

Chocolate passion was the biggest, highest, richest-looking cake Rae had ever seen. The icing looked like pure fudge, and the top fairly bristled with slivered almonds. It was all she could do not to snatch up her fork and pounce.

"Enjoy," the waiter said, setting his burden on the table with a flourish. "Everyone says it's sinful."

"Hooray for sin," Gabriel said, watching Rae's eyes.

He'd never been jealous before. Even as he registered that revelation, his cynical cop's mind began to hoot with laughter. Gabriel MacLaren, jealous of a piece of chocolate cake!

Ah, but this wasn't just any cake, he thought. *This* cake was being regarded by Rae in pure, unadulterated lust, and that was something he wanted for himself. Only for him. Compelled by an impulse he could neither understand nor resist, he pulled the cake closer to him.

"I hope you're joking," Rae said.

"What if I weren't?"

"Then I'd have to do something."

"Like before?" he inquired. "Something…bad?"

"Real bad," she agreed.

"Mmm." Deliberately, he took a bite.

Rae watched him, shocked by the open sensuality in his eyes.

Shocked, too, by her reaction to it. She had a powerful urge to kiss him and see if he tasted like chocolate. He would. He had to. Her lashes drifted down of their own accord, and it was all she could do to keep from climbing into his lap like a great big house cat.

"Ready?" he asked, his voice low and slightly hoarse.

She had the feeling he was talking about something besides dessert. Holding her gaze with his, he slid a bite of cake onto his fork and lifted it to her mouth.

The taste of dark chocolate and almonds captured her senses. Ah, they'd named the cake well. It was as rich as desire, treacherous as sin and yet sweet as the rush of passion through her body. She licked icing from her bottom lip, and saw something raw and powerful leap into Gabriel's eyes.

"You missed some," he said, reaching to run his thumb across her upper lip.

Rae felt that touch down to her toes, a wild rush of sensation that had every nerve quivering with expectation. He stilled for a moment, and she saw something raw and primitive surge into his eyes. Then, with deliberate intent, he moved his thumb along the sensitive corner of her mouth, then downward to her bottom lip. He rested there a moment, his gaze burning into hers, then slid his thumb along the warm curve of her bottom lip. Her breath went out in a sigh she hadn't intended to make.

The soft sound broke the web of sensuality that had claimed her. Dread settled like a cold hand on her heart. She'd let herself get carried away, and she'd let Gabriel see it. Bad. Oh, very bad. She sat back, out of his reach.

Gabriel set his fork down because he couldn't trust his hand not to shake. His body ached, actually ached, for her. And his heart was doing strange things, too. Hell, he'd lost it. Rae had him so wound up he didn't know up from down.

"Lady, you pack a wallop," he said.

"Don't—"

"Don't talk about it?" His brows contracted. "Pretend it didn't happen?"

"That works for me," she retorted.

He studied her, assessing the stubborn set of her jaw against the smoldering sensuality in her eyes. He wanted to touch her again. "You were moving right along with me, Rae."

"I don't know what you're talking about," she said.

"Liar."

"So sue me," she snapped.

Gabriel's interest sharpened, focused. Despite her sassy reply, there was real retreat in her eyes. It was almost as if she'd been frightened by the powerful emotions they'd both felt. Strange, he thought, coming as it did from a woman who had shamelessly hounded her ex-husband right off the force.

It was a contradiction, something that didn't add up, and it interested him. He'd always liked solving puzzles.

"Want another bite of cake?" he asked, smiling.

Rae didn't like that smile. It was too knowing, and much, much too cynical. He was trying to make her back down. She smiled back at him, holding his gaze for a long moment, then picked her fork up from the table.

"Neutral ground, mister," she said, pointing at the plate.

He pushed the cake toward her, positioning it in the exact center of the table. "How's that?"

"Perfect."

She took a bite. His gaze fastened on her mouth, and she took great pains to lick every bit of chocolate icing from her lips.

"You're pushing it," he said, his voice hoarse.

"I'm eating cake," she replied loftily.

"Rae..."

Heedless of the warning in his voice, she took another bite. She took that bite as if it was the most sensual—and sensuous—thing she'd ever done. In a way, it was. She savored the chocolate even as she savored the flaring reaction in his eyes. Arousal washed goose bumps along her spine as she watched it happen to him.

She took another bite. Another. He didn't even attempt to pick up his fork; all his attention was focused on her mouth. She shouldn't do this, she knew. There would be consequences. But recklessness had her in its grasp, and she intended to ride it no matter where it took her.

Noticing a tiny dab of icing on the tip of her index finger, she licked it off. Slowly. While staring right into Gabriel's eyes.

And then she smiled.

"Okay," he said, standing up. "That's it. Check!"

The waiter appeared as if by magic. Gabriel dumped the contents of his pocket into the man's hands.

"Hey, thanks," the waiter said, eying the pile of bills. "I guess you liked the cake."

"Yeah," Gabriel growled, pinning Rae with a burning, ice blue glare. "Let's go."

"Am I under arrest?" she inquired.

He cursed fluently under his breath, barely resisting the urge to throw her over his shoulder and carry her off. He'd had it. Finally, truly had it. "Let's go."

"I don't know," she said, batting her eyelashes at him. "You're awfully big and scary right now."

"Get!"

Rae got. Or rather, she sashayed, swinging her hips with deliberate insolence.

She expected an argument once they'd gotten outside, but he didn't say a word as he walked with her to the restaurant's tiny parking lot. He even seemed relaxed as he strode along beside her. Triumph bubbled through her veins. He'd played his little game, and had his bluff called. Maybe next time he'd think before playing again.

"Thanks for dinner," Rae said as they reached the car.

"Although it was supposed to be my treat. Just—" Her voice trailed off into nothingness as she got a good look at his eyes.

They were as clear as blue ice water...and not even remotely civilized. Anger lit those crystalline depths, partner to a desire so hot Rae could feel the impact of it right down to her soul.

She'd miscalculated.

Gabriel MacLaren was not a man to be trifled with, and she'd stepped way over the line. He would not be manageable just now. He wouldn't even be reasonable.

"Now, MacLaren—" she began.

Words became a gasp as he swept her against him with one hard arm. Rae wasn't a weak woman, nor a docile one, but she found herself in the car before she could even consider reacting.

"Hey!" she yelped.

Gabriel came in beside her. She raised her hands to fend him off, but he grasped her by both wrists and tugged her off balance. She found herself sprawled across his lap, imprisoned against the hard wall of his chest.

He slid one hand into her hair, loosening it from the knot. Her skin felt hot, oversensitive, and she shivered as the hair came tumbling down upon her almost-bare shoulders. His breath went out in a hiss, and he gently combed his fingers through the mass of curls. Desire flared hotter in his eyes, burning everything else away.

He claimed her lips in a kiss so hot it seared her to her toes. Her conscious mind suggested resistance. She even managed to bring her hands up between them to push him away. Instead, however, she laid them flat on his chest. He was hot to the touch, and his heart hammered hard against her palms. Against her will, against all caution, she spread her fingers out across the hard shelf of his pectorals.

He tilted his head to deepen the kiss. Rae sighed. Or maybe he did. *Somebody* did. Then she stopped wondering, because he felt so good. His tongue slid across hers in a caress that sent arousal coursing through her in a sweet, hot tide.

She shivered as he cupped the back of her head with one big hand. The gesture was both erotic and tender, and stirred the fires of her passion still higher. Mindlessly, she slid one hand into his hair and hung on tight.

The world seemed to begin and end here in his arms. She forgot the cramped seat, the streetlight outside, everything. For this moment, only Gabriel MacLaren existed.

She met his roving tongue with her own, eager to taste his passion, his heat. And he gave it. All of it. Everything. It felt as though she'd stepped in flame. There was no thought of restraint, no thought of anything but pleasure gained, pleasure given.

He broke the kiss slowly, slowly, drawing her bottom lip into his mouth on the way out. Rae gasped, a soft, urgent sound of arousal. He ran his tongue over her lip, then traced a wet, hot path across her cheek to her ear. She shivered as he traced the delicate shell shape, then delved inside to evoke responses she didn't know she had.

"Oh," she whispered, sighing into his mouth.

Gabriel nearly lost it then. He'd begun this to teach her a lesson, but it had become something else entirely. The moment he'd touched her, his annoyance had been burned away in a wild torrent of desire. He only wanted to touch her, kiss her, possess her.

He ran his hands down her back and was gratified when she arched in response. Like a cat, he thought dazedly. A beautiful, sexy tigress—complete with claws. It excited him. Her back fascinated him, the smooth, strong sweep of her spine, the taut female muscles, the fascinating curve where her waist met her hips. He thought about stopping there. But he'd fallen into the clutches of a passion much too strong to resist, and he had to have more.

Slowly, giving her ample time to stop him, he slid his hands up her sides. She didn't stop him. Breath suspended, he moved higher, cupping the sweet weight of her breasts in his hands. He groaned softly as he felt the hard points of her nipples against his palms. Damn, but he wished they were somewhere private!

Gently, he rubbed those erect nubs with his thumbs, his heart revving into high gear when she gasped in sheer, voluptuous pleasure. He bit softly at her mouth, inciting her further. She arched against his hands. Almost beyond control, he kissed his way over her chin and down her throat, pausing to press his open mouth on the frantically beating pulse point there. He moved downward, savoring the smooth skin of her chest, then ran his tongue across the beginning swell of her breasts.

Rae clenched her hands in his hair, holding him against her. He gave her what she demanded, laving her skin with his tongue, making teasing little forays beneath the edge of her dress. She could feel him hot and hard beneath her. The awareness of his arousal stirred her so powerfully that she couldn't keep herself from rubbing against him.

His breath went out sharply, a hoarse, urgent sound. He looked up at her. His eyes were passion glazed, his face taut with passion. The sight stirred her unbearably. She traced the hard line of his lips with her fingertip, then delved for a moment into the wet heat of his mouth. She saw it impact in his eyes, felt it in the surge of his erection beneath her.

Anxious to get to his skin, she fumbled open the top three buttons of his shirt. She slid her hand beneath the fabric, skimming muscle and hair and heat. He groaned against her chest as she skimmed her fingertips across his small, tight nipple.

"You like that," she whispered.

"I like that," he agreed.

Slipping two fingers beneath the bodice of her dress, he explored the lush curves of her breasts, her heat, the differing textures of her skin.

"Oh," she gasped, nearly undone by the sensation.

Gabriel stilled, awash in need. A moment more, and he wouldn't care where they were or who was watching. And Rae deserved better than that. He wanted to make love to her without worry, without reservation, without restraint.

"Rae," he groaned. "This isn't the place for this."

She stiffened as the world intruded, bringing all its conflicts and complications with it. She had no business being here, hung like gift wrap around Gabriel MacLaren. Bolting from his lap, she slid into the other seat.

"Take me home," she said.

"We need to talk about this."

"No, we don't."

"Rae—"

"Don't." She smoothed her hair with shaking hands. "We can't be doing this. You know why."

Gabriel studied her with narrowed eyes. Sure, he knew why. Conflict of interest. He'd had no business kissing her, now or ever. But she'd tweaked him to the point that his testosterone had done his thinking for him, and he'd fallen right into the trap. And now she had the gall to sit there looking aroused and outraged and too damned gorgeous for words.

Clever girl. If he wasn't careful, he'd end up selling insurance like her ex-husband.

"You were right along with me," he growled, annoyed because he couldn't keep from saying it.

Rae glanced away. "I know. Look, MacLaren. I'm no tease. You caught me at a…weak moment, I guess, and things got a little out of hand. I'm sorry."

A little out of hand? he thought incredulously. Hell, they'd both been ready to make love right now, right here. He didn't think things would be different tomorrow. She had sparked his very soul, and things weren't going to cool down until he'd found a way to get her out of his system.

He studied her a moment longer. Then he reached out, pulling her back into his lap. Instantly, his body reacted, and he wanted nothing more than to start touching her all over again.

She felt it, too. Dropping his gaze to her breasts, he saw her nipples beneath the bodice of her dress. Triumph shot through him. Maybe, just maybe, this game was even. She couldn't touch him without being touched in return, and her body seemed to be determined to betray her.

"What are you doing?" she asked, her voice just a bit breathless.

He smiled. "Just taking you home, honey-child."

Slipping out from beneath her, he got out of the car and walked around to the driver's side.

Rae watched him surreptitiously as he drove. Now that she had some control over her emotions, she began analyzing the night's events. Unfortunately, two plus two kept coming up five. Still, there was a solution. Since Gabriel's touch seemed to send her brain into a tailspin, she'd just have to keep him from touching her. Good. Great. Ought to work.

As though reading her mind, he turned to look at her. The moment their gazes met, her stomach fell straight to her knees.

Oh, brother! She could control the touching thing—she hoped—but how was she going to keep from looking at him? She felt as though she stood at the very edge of a cliff, one foot sliding, the other on a banana peel.

He pulled up in front of her apartment building. Putting the Taurus in Park, he swiveled to look at her.

"Your bedroom light is on," he said. "It wasn't on when we left."

"That's what I love about cops," she retorted. "They always notice what's none of their business."

She pushed her door open and got out. Before she'd gone five steps, Gabriel caught up with her. She stopped, swinging around to glare at him.

"What?" she demanded.

"You didn't answer the question," he said, his voice silky with menace.

She tilted her head back to meet his turbulent gaze levelly. She'd had enough of Detective Gabriel MacLaren for one night. Still, even now, irritated as she was, her body thrummed like a well-oiled machine simply because he stood beside her.

If he touched her, he'd know it. She couldn't risk it. Her body she might be able to ignore. But he seemed to be able to twist her emotions out of kilter, and that she couldn't trust.

"Back off, MacLaren," she snarled.

"No," he growled. "Answer."

She studied him with narrowed eyes. "You've become monosyllabic, Detective."

His fingers spread out over the curve of her shoulders. Rae's pulse rate skyrocketed, and she was appalled by the treachery of her own body.

"I'll come up with you," he said.

Rae would have extracted her teeth with a spoon first. "I've got company," she said.

"Who?"

"Company."

They stood toe-to-toe for a moment, locked in conflict. Then, with a muttered curse, Gabriel let her go. She wasn't going to give an inch without a major fight.

Besides, it wasn't his business who her company was, as long as it wasn't Peter Smithfield.

He watched her walk into the apartment building. Of

course, Rae never just *walked.* She moved with a graceful sensuality that aroused him powerfully.

He didn't want to feel like this. He didn't want her to have that kind of power over him. Naturally, his treacherous memory chose that moment to conjure up the remembrance of the first time he'd laid eyes on her. She'd looked like pure sin in that skimpy belly dancing costume, a vision of smooth, feminine curves, skin like cream-colored silk and moves that had dried his mouth and made the rest of his body burn.

She'd looked at him. Only him. And she'd danced for him. Only him. He'd felt matched to her in that strange, magical moment, soul to soul, and he'd wanted nothing more than to carry her off and claim her.

Just before she went inside, she turned to look at him. He swallowed hard. She was in half profile, giving him a clear view of the lovely curve of breast and hip. The light from the open door turned her hair into a bronze halo around her head, and there was such sensuality and insolence in her eyes that he took a step toward her.

Then she turned and went inside. He clenched his hands into fists, resisting the urge to follow her. Somehow, he managed. After a moment, he even managed to turn back to the car.

Who was up there?

It was none of his business, as Rae had so graciously pointed out. Theirs wasn't a romantic relationship. Hell, theirs wasn't a relationship at all. Just because they struck fire whenever they touched, just because she tweaked emotions in him he hadn't even known he had... Involuntarily, he glanced up at that lighted window again.

Who was up there?

"Stop being a boob," he growled under his breath.

He was a cop. Cops were objective.

Without his permission, his gaze drifted back to that lighted window. Yeah, right. Objective.

It was going to be a very long night.

Chapter 7

Sleep fogged, heavy with the MacLaren dreams that had haunted her all night, Rae staggered into the kitchen the next morning. Little Sarah sat at the table, eating a bowl of Froot Loops.

Rae perked up. "Hey, I love Froot Loops."

"Mama bought them yesterday," Sarah said. Morning sunlight turned her hair to spun gold and gilded the long lashes rimming her blue eyes. "We got Frosted Flakes, too."

"Frosted Flakes!" Rae groaned, wallowing in a wash of memories of early mornings spent at the kitchen table at home, a table so familiar that every speck in the Formica top was like an old friend. "I've got to have Frosted Flakes."

"What, no bran?" Barbara asked from the doorway.

Rae smiled over her shoulder. "I'd rather die. Hey, I noticed you cleaned the place up. Thanks."

"It was the least I could do after you took us in."

"I'm not much of a housekeeper, I'm afraid," Rae said.

Barbara came into the room, a shy smile on her face. "Well, we all have our talents. But look, we can't impose on you like this forever. It's time we started looking for a place."

"Now?" Rae was surprised that she was so reluctant to have her solitude back. "How much money do you have, Barbara?"

"Well—"

"Twenty-five dollars and sixty-one cents," Sarah announced.

Barbara blushed. "I—"

"I don't mind you being here," Rae said. "Not that I want you to think this is charity or anything, I mean, uh…"

"I know what you mean," Barbara murmured.

Before Rae knew what was happening, the other woman gave her a quick, hard hug. Rae blushed, to her astonishment.

Barbara laughed. "What's the matter, Rae? Are you afraid someone might think you're a softie inside?"

"Oh, hell," Rae muttered. "I need a cup of coffee."

"I saw my daddy yesterday," Sarah announced.

Rae and Barbara turned in unison. "You did?"

The child nodded. "When we were at the store. I was looking out the big window in the front, and I saw Daddy getting on a bus."

"Why didn't you tell me, hon?" Barbara asked.

Sarah shrugged. "Sometimes you cry when we talk about Daddy."

"Ah." Barbara's chin took on a determined tilt. "That's all changed now, sweetheart. You can tell me anything, okay?"

"Okay."

"Which way was the bus going?" Rae asked.

The girl shrugged.

"We were at Morton's Grocery," Barbara offered.

Rae crouched beside the child. Taking two spoons, she laid them at a ninety-degree angle. "Okay, sweetie. Here are the streets where Morton's is. And here—" she placed the salt at the intersection "—is the store. Can you tell me which street the bus was on?"

Sarah pointed. "That one."

"Now, can you tell me which way the bus was going?"

"Uh-uh. Can I watch TV?"

"Sure." Rae patted the girl's shoulder. "You did good, sweetheart."

Once the girl was out of earshot, Rae turned to Barbara. "I need any name that might be associated with your husband. Previous wives, family names, names of friends, business associates... Better give me addresses, too."

"I'll make a list. Do you think you can find him again?"

"I'm going to do my best," Rae promised.

A short time later, armed with a list, Rae headed for work. She rode downstairs with several of her neighbors, including the new guy who'd just moved in down the hall. He was quite the hunk, Rae thought. Tall and tawny haired and with a twinkle in his eye that was mighty attractive. Nice, too— shook her hand as though he meant it when he said he enjoyed meeting her.

It was a shame she'd become fixated on a low-down, conniving, drop-dead-gorgeous cop.

The elevator doors opened, revealing said low-down, conniving, drop-dead-gorgeous cop. Dark circles shadowed his eyes, and his jaw was furred with a day's growth of beard.

"See ya," she said to her handsome new neighbor. As she walked past Gabriel, she added, "You look terrible."

He didn't so much as glance at her. His gaze was focused on the handsome neighbor, and there was enough hostility in those ice blue eyes to start World War III.

For a moment, Rae was surprised. Then she smiled. He thought...he thought the *neighbor* was her overnight guest. And if she wasn't mistaken, that hostility had a definite tinge of green to it. Oh, this was too good!

"Coming, Detective?" she cooed.

He made a growly noise deep in his throat as he followed her outside. The sky was full of scudding dark clouds that matched the surliness in his expression.

"You must be one of those people who aren't human until they get that first cup of coffee in the morning," she said.

Gabriel resisted the urge to shake her. Her eyes were full of laughter and secrets, and she stirred him to his soul. "Who was that?" he demanded.

"Who?" she asked, all innocence.

"You know who."

She put her hand on her hip. "You're a detective, aren't you? So detect."

With that, she turned and walked away. She wanted to glance over her shoulder, but that would spoil the effect. It gave her a great deal of pleasure—something her conscience might have to deal with later—to discomfit him as much as he'd discomfited her.

"Rae."

Gabriel's dark-velvet voice sent goose bumps racing along her arms. She kept walking.

"Rae."

Out of the corner of her eye, she saw him driving slowly alongside her. She turned her gaze forward and kept walking. If he started with the flashing lights again, she didn't want to know.

"Hello, Rae!"

She turned to see Mr. Fedderman, the florist, waving at her from behind a bank of multicolored blooms. "Morning, Mr. Fedderman," she said, joining him.

"Did the flowers last all right?" he asked.

Rae blinked. She didn't have the slightest recollection of what had happened to the bouquet. But Mr. Fedderman looked so earnest that she didn't have the heart to tell him. "Sure, they were great," she said.

"I've got something else for you," he said.

She put her hands up in a warning gesture. "I forget to water them, I forget to feed them, I forget to open the curtains—"

"This one will tell you when it needs to be fed."

"Huh?"

The old man bent, retrieving something from the basket at his feet. Something that squirmed and whimpered and wagged a tail....

"No," Rae said. "Mr. Fedderman—"

"Bertrice had pups," he said. "Full-blood Australian shepherd, this little man is."

"No."

He thrust the little beastie at her. Rae found herself holding a warm and wiggly puppy. He licked her hands and wrists—everything he could reach—then turned adoring eyes to her.

"Blue eyes!" she wailed.

"He likes you," Mr. Fedderman said.

Rae held the puppy against her chest. He immediately started chewing on her buttons, creating a wet, slimy spot on her skin. Something soft and very unwelcome bloomed in her heart, and she groaned, realizing that she was lost. "That was rotten," she said. "You knew he was cute, you knew he'd lick me—"

"Take him, Rae Ann," the florist said. "He's yours."

"Now, look—"

"Take him, Rae Ann," another, deeper voice said.

"Mind your own beeswax, MacLaren," she snarled.

"Feisty, isn't she?" Gabriel asked the florist. "And she seems to be mad at me. Do you think flowers would help?"

"Would I be in this business if I didn't?" the old man asked. "Now, you let Fedderman give you some advice, son. For the man in just a little trouble, a mixed bouquet. If you're in deep do-do, nothing but roses will do."

"I'm not angry at him," Rae said.

Mr. Fedderman shot her a bird-bright glance. "No?"

"In fact," she continued, "I hardly know him."

"Ah."

The old man was fairly beaming now. Accepting it as a lost cause, Rae tucked the puppy into the crook of her arm and started off down the sidewalk. She hadn't gone ten feet when Gabriel's big hand wrapped around her upper arm, pulling her to a halt.

"That wasn't funny, Rae," he growled.

"You just don't have a good sense of humor," she retorted.

"Get in the car."

"I'm on my way to work."

"I'll drive you there."

"That won't be necessary," she replied. Loftily.

"Get in the car."

She eyed him speculatively, weighing the price of defiance. Too high, she decided. He looked annoyed enough to toss her over his shoulder and carry her if he had to.

Not a good idea, she thought. Not with her nerves thrumming like wires and the blood surging through her veins in a molten tide. Oh, no.

"Oh, all right," she snapped.

Holding her arm as far from her body as she could, she waited for him to release her. After a moment, he did. He stepped past her to open the car door, handing her in with extreme courtesy.

"Remember," Mr. Fedderman called. "Roses!"

Gabriel waved to the old man, then swung out into traffic. He glanced at Rae out of the corner of his eye. He'd spent the night in utter torment. Damn her. Only the most stringent willpower had kept him from marching up to that apartment, kicking the door in and staking his claim to his woman.

His woman? *His* woman? His cynical cop's mind hooted with incredulous laughter. Rae Ann Boudreau was the subject of police surveillance on an important case.

He shot her a look. She held the puppy close, pretending not to notice that he was licking her neck. Gabriel didn't blame the dog; *he* had a definite urge to lick her neck, too.

"What are you going to name him?" he asked.

She shrugged. "I've never had a dog."

"He's got to have a name. Something that fits his personality."

Rae cocked her head to one side, studying the dog. "I dunno," she said slowly. "He's awful wriggly and slobbery. No dignity at all. If I name him something that fits him now, he'll never live it down."

"So give him a name he'll grow into."

"Okay." But Rae's mind remained blank. Finally, in desperation, she said, "Tom. I'll call him Tom."

Gabriel's brows went up, a gesture far more eloquent than words. Rae instantly went on the defensive.

"It was my grandpa's name," she said.

"Rae, this is a dog."

She shot him a glare. "Okay. I'll call him Tom the Dog."

"Let me see him," MacLaren said.

Rae handed the puppy to him. Cradling the little beast in one big hand, he held him up. "You look awfully pleased with yourself, fella," he said as the dog tried frantically to reach him with his tongue. "Found yourself a cushy deal, didn't you?"

"What's cushy about it?" Rae demanded.

He glanced at her, and there was such need in his eyes that her throat went dry. He handed Tom back to her, and for a moment she thought his hand shook.

"You're thinking about putting him to work?" he asked.

"Doing what," she retorted. "Herding deadbeats around?"

"Sure. Let him serve summonses. Then you could retire."

She laughed. "Right. He'll probably grow up to be a lazy slug and eat me out of house and home. And speaking of eating, there's a pet store a few blocks up on the right. Would you mind stopping? I want to pick up some things."

"Like puppy food, doggie treats?"

"Well, yeah."

"I told you, Tom the Lucky Dog," Gabriel said.

Tom barked, apparently agreeing with that assessment. Then, before Rae could react, the puppy launched himself at Gabriel. The little dog seized the detective's belt loop and savaged it happily.

Instead of pushing the puppy away, Gabriel laughed.

That deep, joyful sound impaled her, made her feel as though she'd been struck with lightning. Her heart gave a lurch, then stuttered into high gear.

Gabriel reached down with his free hand and wiggled his fingers. Tom, sensing live prey, pounced. Amusement sparkled in Gabriel's eyes, and his grin almost matched the puppy's in pure delight. For the first time, Rae saw him with all his barriers down. It was devastating. *He* was devastating.

"Hey, watch this," he said.

He rolled Tom over onto his back and began to gently scratch the little dog's rounded stomach. Tom's hind leg began to rotate. The harder Gabriel scratched, the faster the puppy's leg rotated. Finally, Tom's eyes glazed, and his jaws went slack.

"Look at him," she said. "He loves it."

"Works every time," Gabriel said.

He looked up at the very moment she lifted her gaze to his face. Everything in her focused to a single point: Gabriel MacLaren.

And then she knew what had happened to her.

Her stomach went into a steep dive. Everything seemed preternaturally clear, edges sharper, colors brighter than she'd ever seen before. This shouldn't be happening. She'd spent the three years since her marriage building a fortress against this very thing. And Gabriel had sneaked over the walls and into her treasure room while she was still trying to defend the drawbridge.

She'd fallen in love with him.

It had happened in that strange, powerful moment when their gazes had first met. Her heart had known, and her soul.

Oh, no. Not this, not with him. He'd tear her heart out for his job. She had to find some defenses, fast, or she'd regret ever being born.

She fled the car the moment Gabriel pulled to a stop in front of the store. But she soon found that the pet store held hazards of its own. There were too many choices, and she had too little knowledge. Finally, the clerk took pity on her.

"Do you need some help, miss?" he asked.

Rae nodded. "I need puppy stuff."

The clerk smiled, and Rae got a definite whiff of spider-to-the-fly pheromones. "No problem, miss."

Twenty minutes later, she headed back to the car. She carried a bulging shopping bag in each hand.

"What did they get you for?" Gabriel asked.

Rae tossed the bags into the back seat. "Fifty-seven eighty-one."

"Happens with every free dog," he said.

"If I'd known then what I know now..." she muttered darkly. Then she looked at Tom, who lay on his back in Gabriel's lap.

"Cute, ain't he?" Gabriel asked.

Rae's gaze dropped to his mouth, an involuntary response to the surge of her own desire. She loved this man. Hopelessly, helplessly, drawn to him like a moth to a flame. He would surely burn her.

Apparently unaware of the agitated state of her emotions, he put the car in gear and headed toward her office. A few minutes more, she told herself. She'd get away, back to the safe, solid reality of her life. Maybe then she could get her emotions back into some semblance of order.

The moment he pulled up in front of her office building, she reached for the puppy, intending to slide out and escape. But Gabriel captured her hand with his, trapping it against his thigh. Rae's breathing changed. His leg was iron hard beneath her hand, and warm.

"Don't run off yet," he said.

"I've got work to do, MacLaren."

Something hot and raw came into his eyes. "Who was that man?"

The wise thing to do would be to tell him about Barbara Smithfield and the kids. But Rae didn't want to do the wise thing. He'd entered her world like a tornado, sweeping all the comfortable, conventional barriers aside. She wanted to back him off, to keep some part of her life inviolate.

"Why should I tell you anything?" she asked.

"Don't push, Rae," he growled.

"Don't push?" she echoed incredulously. "Don't push? What's with you? You're acting like a...a..."

"What?" he prompted.

Goaded, she said it. "Like a lover!" Her chest hurt as she pulled a breath in. "You have no right, MacLaren. No right!"

Tucking the puppy beneath one arm, she snatched her bags out from the back seat and got out of the car. Without a backward look, she marched up to her office.

After setting out food and water in the shiny chrome bowls she'd just bought, she laid an old newspaper on the floor. Then, arms akimbo, she stood looking down at Tom the Dog.

"You know what that paper's for, right?" she asked.

He gazed adoringly into her eyes and wrung his stub of a tail.

"I'll take that as a yes," she said.

She booted her computer up. The screen saver seemed to mock her: I Am Lobo, I Hunt Alone.

"Yeah, right," she muttered.

Now, in retrospect, she couldn't believe she'd said what she'd said to Gabriel. Lover. It was a dangerous word, a provocative word, and she was sure she'd regret it.

"Back to work, Rae," she said. "You know better than to let the personal intrude in your business."

Determinedly, she put Gabriel MacLaren out of her mind. First, she called up a map of downtown Baltimore. This wasn't any old map; she'd been working on it for years, adding the names of buildings, stores, restaurants, hotels, anything that might conceivably help in locating someone. She found Morton's Grocery and traced the paths of the two intersecting streets.

The one running north and south didn't interest her. But Fells Point, the east-west road, did, because it ended at the city's waterfront area. Hotels abounded there, and the throngs of tourists would make it an ideal place for Smithfield to hide.

A whimper came from beside her. Distracted, she looked down to see Tom sitting beside her feet, looking plaintive.

"No," she said. "You can't come up. I'm working."

He whined. Those round blue eyes seemed to get bluer and rounder. His mouth opened, and a long, drawn-out wail emerged. It bespoke utter loneliness and need.

"I'm *working*," she complained.

Those eyes never wavered. After a moment, she scooped him up and set him in her lap. Happy now that he'd gotten his way, he curled up and went to sleep.

"Males," Rae grumbled. "They're all the same."

She returned her attention to the computer screen. She liked the waterfront angle. Plenty of short-term rentals, lots of tourists—the perfect place to disappear for a while. Now, if only she could track him down.

Pulling the telephone closer, she called an old friend who

just happened to own a travel agency. Amy had been of help before, and eagerly agreed to track down any reservations that might have been made in names on Barbara's list.

"Better call me on the cellular," Rae said. "Thanks a lot, girlfriend. I owe you."

"Don't worry about it," Amy replied. "I'm an old married lady who gets vicarious pleasure out of your exciting life."

Rae couldn't help but laugh at the irony of the whole thing. She'd been working like a donkey for three solid years, and hadn't had a date in all that time. And Amy thought her life was exciting? Sheesh!

But then, things had been looking up since she'd met Gabriel MacLaren. Unfortunately, she wasn't sure the upturn had been an improvement.

Cradling the sleeping puppy, she went to look out the window. MacLaren's Taurus was gone, but a brown Crown Victoria that fairly screamed *unmarked police car* occupied the same spot. Rae smiled. Apparently even arrogant vice cops needed to sleep sometime.

A half hour later, Amy called back. Propping the phone between her shoulder and jaw, Rae called up her computer map again.

"I've got something for you," Amy said. "First, a Peter Smithfield registered at the Days Inn from the twenty-third to the thirtieth of last month. Then a John H. Walsh—"

"That's his cousin's name," Rae said, consulting her list.

"Right. Walsh stayed at the Villa Bay from the thirty-first to the fifth. Then Peter Johnstone checked in to the Arabian from the eighth to the fourteenth."

"Peter Johnstone is an alias he's used before," Rae said.

With her forefinger, she touched the map. The three hotels were all within walking distance of Sweetbrier Road, and the bus.

"Now," Amy said, "the pièce de résistance. I've got a long-term condo rental by a Sylvia Applegate—"

"His girlfriend," Rae said with a glance at the list.

"More fool she. Anyway, on the fifteenth, she took a three-month lease on a two bedroom in the Garden Towers on West Terrelton Avenue—4B.''

Rae found the building on the map. "I see it. Hmm, the Tropical Breeze Hotel is right across the street. The time has come for me to take a little vacation down by the water. Thanks, Amy. You're a gem.''

"Yes, I am," Amy replied with a laugh.

Rae started to say goodbye, then stopped. "Hey, do you happen to know who owns the condo?''

"Give me a minute, it's probably on the listing…oh, here it is. Elliston Enterprises, Ltd.''

"A corporation?" Rae asked, surprised.

"Sure. Happens all the time.''

Rae bid her a hasty goodbye, knowing that she had to move on this, and fast. First, she had to ditch the cops. Gabriel had proved to be very hard to unload. But this other guy, now…she might be able to work with him.

"Why didn't you leave town?" she muttered, staring at the screen. "If I were in your shoes, I'd be in Alaska by now.''

Interesting. For a brief moment, she found herself wishing she could work with Gabriel on this. She had the feeling they'd make a very effective team. Hah! Rae Ann Boudreau helping the cops. That would be the day.

Beneath the cynicism, however, lurked a cold little kernel of regret. She saw it, turned away from it. After all, one couldn't regret something that had never existed.

She and Gabriel were on opposite sides of the fence. They always would be. She'd have to change the man himself, and she'd learned the hard way the impossibility of that task.

No, she'd have to find Peter Smithfield on her own. *Before* MacLaren did.

After all, a girl had her pride.

Rae hurried home, the puppy in one hand, shopping bags in the other. She wanted to do some disappearing on her own before MacLaren came back on duty.

This other officer, now, wasn't nearly as competent. She'd managed to lose him twice already without hardly trying.

She'd let him find her again quickly, so that he didn't suspect a thing.

As she stood in the hallway, fumbling with her keys, Barbara opened the door. The kids came swarming past her.

"A puppy!" they cried.

"His name is Tom the Dog," Rae said, handing him over. It was love at first sight, and the whole crew gamboled their way into the living room.

"Is something wrong?" Barbara asked.

"No. But I've got a line on your ex-husband, and need to shake this surveillance long enough to get to him. Do you mind puppy-sitting for a while?"

"Not at all." Her brow creased with concern, Barbara put her hand on Rae's arm. "This isn't dangerous, is it? Because if it is, I don't care about the money. I'll manage some- how—"

"It's not dangerous," Rae said. "Just complicated. Now, I'm going to stay at the Tropical Breeze under an assumed name. I can carry my makeup and a change of undies in my purse, but I'll need more. So I'm fixing up a package to be FedEx-ed to the hotel. Can you take care of that for me?"

Barbara nodded.

"Now, there's some money in the drawer of my nightstand. Use it for food or whatever."

Rae stuffed her makeup, a change of underthings, a hair- brush, toothpaste and a toothbrush into her purse. "Barbara, there's a FedEx shipping form on the desk. Hand it to me, will you?"

As she filled the form out, Rae came to the line marked Recipient. A crazy, powerful impulse caught her, and she found the pen moving before she had a chance to think about it.

"Mrs. G. MacLaren," she wrote.

For a moment, she thought about tearing it up. But it really was a great smoke screen. MacLaren would never, but *never* think of looking for her under his own name.

"They call it poetic justice," she murmured, as pleased with herself as the proverbial cat that had eaten the canary. This, she thought, was good.

Chapter 8

"Find her, MacLaren," Captain Petrosky growled.

"You're awful damned cranky today, sir," Gabriel said.

"Cranky my...eye. This case is one hot potato. The moment this breaks, I'm gonna have bureaucrats coming out of the walls like cockroaches. I don't need complications."

"Understood."

"Rae Boudreau is a complication. I need for you to make her not a complication."

"We've been on her like glue, sir. If she finds him, we'll pull him out from under. But I'd like for you to consider letting me tell her something about the case. Maybe then she'd back off."

"No." Petrosky emphasized that by chopping the air with the edge of his hand. "Now, I've got Eddy teamed up with DeZuniga for the gambling houses—"

"Eddy's my partner," Gabriel protested.

"For now, he's DeZuniga's. Rae Ann Boudreau scammed Wilson like he was some green kid, and it'll take him years to live it down. As far as Rae Ann goes, you're the man."

You're the man.

Gabriel knew better than to argue with Petrosky in his current mood. He left the captain's office and walked down the corridor toward the street.

You're the man.

It was slang, street talk. It didn't mean anything more than that he was the one who'd been tapped to deal with the problem.

One side of his mouth lifted in a cynical smile. He wanted to be the man—but he wanted to be *her* man. A primitive notion, that. Had anyone told him a month ago that he'd feel like this, he would have laughed.

The man. Her man.

She'd conned him. The minute he'd turned surveillance over to Brett Wilson, she'd disappeared. No one would call it Gabriel's fault. But he sure as hell was taking it personally. If he could get his hands on her, he'd…he'd…

He'd kiss her, taste her, touch her. He'd possess her as completely as a man can possess a woman. There in the cool starkness of the bathroom, on the bed, the floor, the back seat of a car, anywhere.

Damn her. He was going to find her. And when he did, there'd be hell to pay.

Rae sat in the lobby of the Tropical Breeze hotel, watching the entrance of the condominium building across the street. She'd been here for two days now, and hadn't seen any activity in 4B. But she would. Certainty coiled through her like the breathless anticipation in the air just before a storm.

Something was going to happen, and soon.

"I wonder," she murmured, leaning into the shaft of light streaming through the glass. "Did Sylvia really rent that place, or did somebody else? Somebody who has an interest in keeping Peter Smithfield away from the cops?"

It was an intriguing prospect. But also one that would interest Gabriel more than it would her. Still, she liked solving puzzles. Naturally, she'd turn whatever she discovered over to MacLaren. Purely as a public service, of course. And to gloat.

Her reverie vanished as someone crossed her peripheral vision.

There was something familiar about that movement, something...

MacLaren.

He sat in the chair opposite hers. Rae swiveled to face him, her breath suddenly too swift and shallow. Oh, he was mad. The rugged planes of his face had settled into grim lines, and the set of his mouth promised trouble.

Angel Gabriel, she thought, come down to exact retribution. She pushed the thought away hastily. Besides, no angel could possibly look so aggressively male, so...tempting.

"Hello, Rae," he said. "Or should I say, Mrs. Mac-Laren?"

"I thought it was a nice touch."

His mouth thinned. "I've got to give you credit, honey-child. You're good. You made that other detective look like a complete fool, and it'll be years before he lives it down."

"Gee, I'll take that as a compliment," she said. "How did you find me, by the way?"

"Remember your lovely neighbor, Marlene Britton?"

"How could anyone forget Marlene?"

He grunted, remembering the way the woman had all but thrown herself at him once he'd gone into her apartment. "She happened to see your houseguest carry out a large Federal Express package. I called FedEx—"

"Pulled rank. Again."

"—and got the address of this hotel. You lied to me, Rae." She gaped at him. "I never did."

"You led me to believe that some guy was staying with you. Instead, I find out it's Barbara Smithfield and her kids."

"I led you nowhere, MacLaren," she said. "You went there all on your own. You jump to conclusions, and it's *my* fault?"

Gabriel considered a number of answers, but all ended with him kissing her senseless, and that would only distract him. Besides, his time was coming. Soon. Very, very soon.

"It's almost dinnertime," he said, glancing at his watch. "Why don't you join me?"

Rae studied him with narrowed eyes. Logic told her to run, and run fast. But crazy as it was, she just wanted to be with him for a while. That was her heart talking. She knew better than to listen to her heart. But knowing better did her no good. Simply, she needed to be with him. The need was powerful and raw, whirling through her with hurricane force. It overwhelmed her rationality and her willpower, leaving her adrift in his eyes.

"Sure," she said at last. "Why not?"

He rose with lithe power. She turned toward the hotel dining room, overly aware of his presence beside her. Other women seemed to be aware of him, too; she noticed a few heads turning as he passed. And why not? she told herself sternly. He was a supremely arrogant male, and that always attracted women who didn't know better.

She did know better. She just didn't know how to keep from letting him get to her.

The dining room echoed the hotel's tropical theme. The maître d' obviously mistook them for a couple, ensconcing them in a palm-shrouded booth. She noticed that Gabriel maneuvered so that he sat facing the door. It was a cop thing.

"I don't want my back to the door, either," she complained.

"Bet I've got more enemies than you do," he countered.

"Now that, I wouldn't dispute."

"You could sit by me," he offered, patting the seat beside his. "Nice and cozy."

Rae shook her head. Cozy was not the ticket, definitely, absolutely. "Uh-uh."

"What's the matter, Rae? Don't you trust yourself?"

He'd hit it straight on the head, but she would have died before admitting it. "Just be sure you yell something before everybody starts blasting, so I can get out of the way."

The waiter came to take their drink order. Rae watched Gabriel as he scanned the wine list. Her heart hadn't settled down yet. Maybe it wouldn't. Maybe she'd spend the rest of her life with an accelerated heart rate and an overactive libido where he was concerned.

"What would you like?" he asked, glancing up at her.

Their gazes met. Rae felt a jolt down to her toes, and saw a matching reaction in his eyes.

This was bad.

"Mmm, just some mineral water," she said.

He handed the wine list back to the waiter. "A cup of coffee for me, thanks. Black."

That disturbing crystalline gaze returned to Rae. She tore hers away with an effort, concentrating on her silverware instead.

"Barbara Smithfield wouldn't talk to me," he said. "Any reason why?"

"She's smart," Rae retorted. "She knows that once the police find her ex-husband, she won't have a chance of collecting the support she needs."

He was silent so long that Rae looked up at him. He'd leaned back in his chair, his long legs stretched out in front of him, his expression thoughtful.

"Why did you take her in?" he asked.

"Well, she'd been kicked out of her apartment. What was I supposed to do, let her and those kids sleep on the street?"

"A lot of people would."

"A lot," she agreed.

Gabriel winced inwardly. Her tone implied that *he* would, and that hit a sore spot. Barbara Smithfield hadn't even opened the door to him, but he hadn't missed the hostility in her voice. And he couldn't help but think she had a right to it.

"Is that a criticism?" he asked.

"Take it any way you want."

They glared at each other for a long, frozen moment. But beneath the annoyance in his eyes, Rae saw desire simmering, ready to break free at any moment. She realized then that she should never have agreed to spend time with him. Anger would not be enough to keep her safe. Her instinct for self-preservation seemed to have deserted her the moment she'd laid eyes on him.

The waiter appeared, depositing a basket of soft bread sticks and a tray of butter pats on the table. Apparently unaware of the tension in the air, he flipped open his order pad. "Are you ready to order, miss?" he asked.

Rae nodded. "A steak, thick and rare," she said. "Baked potato, plain. Salad with Italian dressing." Pinned by a vivid, visceral memory of the last meal she'd shared with Gabriel MacLaren, she added, "And no dessert."

"How do you know you don't want dessert already?" the waiter protested. "We have the most delicious chocolate—"

"No chocolate," she said. "Chocolate is dangerous."

The waiter's brows soared. "Dangerous?"

"That stuff will kill you," she said.

After a moment of helpless indecision, the waiter turned to Gabriel. "And you, sir? What will you have?"

"Ptomaine," Rae muttered.

That got her another startled look from the unfortunate waiter. Gabriel's teeth flashed in a grin a wolf would have envied.

"I'll take another steak, thick and rare," he said. "And don't worry about her. She's taken her medication today."

The waiter shot them a look over his shoulder as he scurried off. Obviously, he thought they were both crazy.

They probably were.

"Now," Gabriel said, "tell me why you're here."

"I'm on vacation," she replied. "Stress."

"You've got a lead on Peter Smithfield."

She batted her eyelashes at him. "Don't be silly, Officer. How could I have found a lead when all you smart, powerful policemen haven't?"

Ordinarily, that remark would have infuriated Gabriel. But he still had his proverbial ace up his sleeve, and smart as she was, she hadn't figured it out yet.

"Have a bread stick." Taking one himself, Gabriel leaned back in his chair and studied her. There was something beneath the defiance and sassy mouth, something that bothered him. If he had to guess, he'd say that she was nervous.

Of course, that might be because he'd found her. He hadn't gotten the impression, however, that Rae had ever been intimidated by anyone or anything, including the police.

So it had to be personal.

Maybe he'd gotten to her just a little. He was surprised not to feel more triumph. Instead, however, he simply wanted her. He hungered for her, passionately and with his soul. He hungered to know her, to be allowed past the steel-hard fortress she'd built around herself.

"Is that how you keep people away?" he asked.

"Huh?"

"The wisecracks. It's your way to build walls around yourself."

She made a face. "That's pop psychology, MacLaren."

"Really? You've been divorced how long?"

"Nearly three years," she said.

"And how many relationships have you had since then?"

"I'd think it would be worse to have a lot of ephemeral relationships."

"Worse than what?" he asked.

Rae was sorry she'd let herself participate in this conversation. He was too quick, and he saw too much. Time to divert. "I've decided to have wine after all," she said.

"Later," he said, smiling. "Have you been involved with anyone since your marriage?"

"That's none—"

"Of my business. Right. Answer the question, Rae."

She glared at him, resenting his intrusion, resenting her lack of defense against him. The past three years had been an emotional wasteland for her, as though her life had been on hold until Gabriel MacLaren entered it. She resented that, too.

"Why do you want to know?" she countered.

"Because."

"That's a childish response," she said.

Completely exasperated, Gabriel reached across the table

and captured her hands. "There's nothing childish about the way I feel about you. Make no mistake about that."

Desire burned in his eyes, a need hot enough, wild enough, to consume them both. Rae wanted to look away, to escape. But there was no escaping, because his passion matched hers. Her heart began to pound so fast she thought surely it would beat its way right out of her chest. No man had ever looked at her like this, as though he wanted to eat her up, devour her body, mind and soul.

"Excuse me," the waiter said.

Rae glanced up. The young man stood beside the table, a large metal tray balanced in his hands. Aromas of steak and potatoes and fresh asparagas assailed her nostrils.

Relieved that the tense moment had been shattered, she disengaged from Gabriel and sat back. With a flourish, the waiter set her plate in front of her.

"Steak, thick and rare," he said.

She wouldn't have noticed if it had been shoe leather. Her senses were consumed by Gabriel. Her opponent. He tilted his head as he looked at her, and her heart did a curious, almost painful flip-flop.

"Are we going to do the normal-conversation thing now?" she asked.

He cut a juicy red slice of beef. "I've decided that there's nothing normal about you, and there's no point in trying. At least you haven't stooped to telling doughnut jokes."

"You get a lot of those?"

"All cops do," he said. "Goes with the territory."

"Like risking your life."

He shrugged. "Serving summonses on folks who don't want them isn't all that safe, either."

"True." Rae poked at her baked potato for a moment, then set her fork down. "Every day, I do something different. I have to cope with new circumstances, new people. It's exciting. When I'm heading out to what looks to be a difficult service, I get this adrenaline surge that's like nothing else on this earth."

"Yes," he said. "I know exactly what that feels like."

Rae swallowed hard. Of all the things she didn't want to feel toward him, kinship neared the top of the list. "It can create problems for relationships," she said, and nearly clapped her hand over her mouth. Hadn't it listened at all to what her mind was saying?

"Are you asking if I've ever been married?"

"No," she said. Yes, whispered her heart, treacherous thing that it was.

He smiled, and she knew how badly she'd betrayed herself. "I've never been married. But the job has messed up a couple of relationships for me. They couldn't handle the hours, the distraction and, most of all, the danger."

"It's even worse with men," she said. "The protective thing, you know."

"It's natural for a man to want to keep his woman safe."

His woman. It was a powerfully evocative phrase, and sent tingles running up her spine. "How primitive," she said, striving for sarcasm.

"Yes," he said. "It is. A man can be as rational as he wants about many things, but when it comes to a threat to those he loves, his reaction is anything but rational."

"Instinct over intellect."

"Never underestimate instinct," he said softly.

His eyes held the possibilities of many things that were primitive, suggested men and women and sensuality. And those things compelled her at the most basic of levels.

She'd thought herself immune. She'd made the mistake of thinking she could be an island, and, like so many other fools who'd thought the same, she had fallen. Love had won.

"I've got to go," she said, pushing away from the table.

"What the hell—"

She walked out. It took all her willpower to keep from running. Evidently, Gabriel got caught up in paying the dinner tab, for she managed to get on the elevator without him.

Once safely in her room, she took a long, hot shower. But there was no escaping what she'd learned about herself today.

She scrubbed herself dry, then stared at her reflection in the fog-shrouded bathroom mirror. Her eyes had changed.

They held awareness now, a woman's acknowledgment of desire. She made a face at herself. A bad marriage should have taught her better. A bad marriage to a *cop*, she reminded herself sternly.

"Instinct, hah!" she muttered. "All it takes is a little will-power."

Willpower, right. At least she'd managed to get a room overlooking the condos across the street. She could watch for Peter Smithfield, leaving Gabriel to cool his heels downstairs, primitive instincts and all.

She wrapped one bath towel around her head, the other around her body. It was a tight fit; the Ritz, this wasn't. Whistling under her breath, she opened the bathroom door.

And saw Gabriel lounging on the sofa.

He dangled a key between thumb and forefinger. "The room is registered to Mrs. MacLaren," he said. "I'm *Mr.* MacLaren, remember?"

Rae scowled at him, trying to hide the hammering of her heart. "Okay, buster, you've had your fun. Out."

"Uh-uh."

He smiled at her, a crooked, gosh-ain't-I-something grin that made every nerve in her body tingle. His gaze drifted downward, and she had the uncomfortable feeling that he could see right through her towel.

Even as she stood there damning herself for her weakness, reaction spurred through her.

"You heard me," she said, low and strained. "Out."

"Make me."

"That's it," she snarled.

Hitching her towel a notch, she strode across the room to him. He rose from the sofa to meet her, his mouth still curved in that infuriating, inveigling grin.

She stopped directly in front of him. Toe-to-toe, Rae jammed her hands on her hips. "Get out of my room," she said.

"Sorry, sweetheart. My orders are to stick to you like glue, and that's what I'm going to do."

With a hiss of indrawn breath, Rae laid her hand flat in the center of his chest and shoved. He didn't budge. She planted her feet more firmly and shoved again. Damn him, he stood there smiling at her as though she hadn't put any pressure on him at all.

And then it happened.

The world took a shift. Anger turned to arousal; frustration turned into passion hot enough to singe her soul. If it had happened only to her, she might have been able to regain a measure of control. But as she stood there looking up into Gabriel's eyes, she saw it happen to him, too.

Oh, this was bad. And so very, very good.

Against her will, her fingers spread out over his chest, feeling the swift, strong beat of his heart against her palm. Slowly, he reached up to cover her hand with his.

Her breath went out all at once, and she felt as though someone had punched her in the stomach. The world vanished; the only reality for her was Gabriel MacLaren, and the storm he'd caused in her soul.

Gabriel reached up to caress her cheek. He wasn't surprised to find that his hand was shaking. Everything shook. This woman had stirred him so deeply that he wasn't sure he'd ever be right again. He had to have her. Body and soul, mind and heart and indomitable will, he wanted her.

"Rae," he said.

"I—"

"Never mind," he interrupted, his voice harsh with arousal. "Talking never works for us."

She opened her mouth to protest. Before she could get a single word out, he claimed her lips in a kiss that rocked her to her toes. He swept in like a conqueror, tasting her, exploring her, taking every heated response she had to give. Rae could deny him nothing, nothing. Sinking her hands into his hair, she let herself fall into a yawning well of sensation.

He dragged the towel off her head and discarded it. Her wet hair came tumbling down around her shoulders, a cool touch against her overheated skin. Gabriel's hand felt callused and very warm as he slid it to the back of her neck. He tilted her head back, gaining still more access to her mouth.

Rae moaned, a soft, breathy sound of pure arousal. She slid her hands along his wide shoulders and then down his arms, reveling in the hard maleness of his body. She explored the long, strong line of his back, his taut waist and, finally, the washboard-ridged plane of his abdomen.

"Damn, Rae," he gasped, tearing his mouth from hers. "You feel like heaven, and taste like it, too."

"I thought you didn't want to talk," she said.

He smiled, his eyes raging with need and desire and a tender yearning that upped her heart rate still more. "I just didn't want *you* to talk."

"I see. And what else do you want from me?"

His smile vanished. Utter seriousness darkened his eyes as he stared right into hers. "Everything," he growled.

Rae trembled. It should have been outrageous, impossible, terrifying. But his eyes promised as much as they demanded, and more. The lure of it was more than flesh and blood could resist.

And oh, boy, was she ever flesh and blood. Her skin was so sensitive that she thought she could feel every loop of the terry-cloth towel as he slid it slowly off her body.

Gabriel laid his hands on her waist, immobilizing her. He'd become one great heartbeat. He'd never been so tuned to a woman before. He'd never felt such desire or such tenderness.

Slowly, with exquisite care, he slid his hands up her ribs until the lush undercurve of her breasts brushed his fingers. Then he stopped, just looking at her.

He'd never seen a woman more beautiful. And naked...she was everything he'd ever wanted in a woman, everything he'd ever dreamed of. Her breasts were full and round, crested with rose brown nipples that begged for his mouth. He let his gaze rove downward, taking in the sweet curve of her hips, the sleek, silken lines of her belly and thighs.

"You're so much woman," he muttered. "So beautiful."

Had anyone else said such a thing, Rae might have scoffed. But she could see that he truly believed what he'd said. And strangely, instead of making her feel silly, it made her feel...well, beautiful.

She'd never felt beautiful before. As he framed her face between his big, hard hands, she felt her heart contract with love for him. It was a huge, powerful thing, that love, almost painful in its intensity. At another time, she might have been frightened of it. But now she could only tremble, and wait, and want.

To her surprise, she found herself leaning toward him, her rib cage pressed against his hands. He smiled at her, holding her for a moment. Then he gathered her in, pressing her naked body against his. He was hot, even through his clothes. Her skin took up that fire. Man and woman, woman and man, they seemed to meld, merge, their separateness burned away by passion.

Rae gasped as he slid his hands down her back to her buttocks, his touch infinitely possessive. She understood then. This would be no simple, civilized lovemaking. Gabriel MacLaren intended to claim her in a way that was as compelling as it was primitive. He really did want everything.

And she would give it to him. This was their time, a magical rift in the reality of what they were and what they had to do. For this brief, precious interlude, there would be no holding back between them, no subterfuge, nowhere to hide.

His hot breath brushed her ear. That ephemeral touch became more as he nibbled the upper curve of her ear. She drew her breath in with a hiss as sensation ran in waves from that contact point.

"You like that," he murmured.

"Ah," she gasped as he sucked her sensitive earlobe, "I like everything you do."

"That's good," he said.

This was too one-sided. He was slowly driving her bats and enjoying every moment of it. The time had come to make things a bit more even.

She slid her hands along the hard swell of his pectorals, seeking his nipples. Finding them already tight and hard, she ran her thumbs around the small male nubs. He didn't move, but she felt him exhale sharply against her ear.

"You like that," she whispered.

He lifted his head and gazed deeply into her eyes. "Are you playing games, Rae?"

She stilled, pinned by the emotion she saw in his eyes. She could hurt him now, stab straight to the heart with the right answer. Or wrong. She rejected the possibility.

"Does this feel like I'm playing?" she asked, moving so that her right leg slid between his.

He was fully aroused, hot and hard beneath his jeans. Reaction shot through her, and she had to hold on to his waist to maintain her balance. His eyelids drifted downward. He slid his hands along her back to her buttocks, tilting her so that she could feel him where she ached the most.

"Oh," she whispered, stirred beyond all hope of rational thought. "Oh."

Things got a little hazy then. She tore some buttons getting his shirt off him. She wasn't clear on who actually got his jeans off, but once she had access to his skin, nothing else mattered. Her hands seemed to have a mind all their own. She reveled in the feel of him, the differing textures of skin and hair and muscle, the steel-in-satin hardness of his manhood.

The world tilted and spun as he lowered himself to the sofa, bringing her with him. She sprawled across him, kissing him with an abandon that would have astonished her had there been room for anything but desire in her, then sliding downward to explore the rest of his body with her hands and tongue.

He arched, calling her name in a voice gone hoarse with need. She didn't stop. His voice began to shake, and still she didn't stop. Couldn't.

"Rae," he said. "Look at me."

She obeyed. He brushed a few damp strands of hair back from her face, and the tenderness in his hands made her tremble.

"It's my turn," he murmured.

Slowly, yet with a shaky urgency that excited her still more, he shifted, placing her beneath him. For a moment, he lay poised above her, looking at her with eyes that had gone hazy with sensuality. Then his eyelids lowered, and his lips parted.

His kiss was torrid, unbridled, untamed as a thunderstorm. Rae gave herself up to it, to him. The world had turned to fire and passion and the feel of his mouth, his hands. A bomb could have gone off in the room, and she wouldn't have cared. She shifted her hips, trying to ease the ache between her thighs.

He left her mouth to kiss his way along her jaw. Then she felt his tongue, warm and wet as he delved into her ear. Her breath went out in a long sigh as he moved to straddle her. The satin weight of his arousal slid against her belly, a sensation that soon had her shaking with need.

"Gabriel," she gasped.

He laughed, a deep male note of triumph. "Do you know that's the first time you've called me by my first name?"

"Which do you prefer... Ah!" she gasped as he licked his way along her neck.

"Darlin', you can call me anything you want," he said against her skin. "As long as you love me like this."

Love me, he'd said. Oh, yes.

His mouth was hot as he trailed a wet path along her collarbone. Slowly, oh, so slowly. Rae thought she'd go crazy wanting more. She shivered with anticipation as he licked downward along the outer curve of her breast.

He let go of her hands finally, but all she could do was sink them into his hair and hold on. He kissed the full undercurve of one breast, then the other. Her nipples swelled into taut peaks, needing his hands, his mouth. He would get there, she knew. But she'd passed the point of waiting.

"Please," she whispered.

Gabriel looked into her eyes. They were glazed with passion, heavy lidded and sultry. *Please,* she'd said. *Please.* It stirred him immeasurably to know he'd brought her to this.

"Anything you need, Rae," he said. "Anything you want."

Beyond reticence, beyond shame, Rae slid her hand beneath her breast, offering it to him.

With a muttered exclamation, Gabriel took it. Her hips swayed beneath him as he suckled her, until he thought he'd go crazy from the feel of all that heat and silken skin rubbing against him.

He rose to his knees so that he could look at her. Her face had gone soft with passion, and her lips were parted, giving him a glimpse of the lush wetness within. Ah, hell, she looked just like heaven. Her breasts were swollen with arousal, the areolae deep pink and glistening.

The time for waiting had passed. He got to his feet beside the sofa and scooped her into his arms.

"What...?" she began.

"We're going to bed," he said.

He laid her on the bedspread. Then he paused, one knee on the cover, and looked at her. Oh, woman! he thought. She was as sumptuous as a banquet against the dark blue fabric, and he wanted nothing more than to lose himself in her. Maybe forever.

He'd intended to hold back a while longer. But her arms came around him, she parted her legs and that was it.

"Rae," he groaned. "Oh, *Rae*."

She cried out in pure, sensual abandon as Gabriel slid deep into her. He felt so good, so very good. She felt complete, as though something in her soul had been crying out for his possession.

Time seemed to end. Her passion spiraled up and up and up as she met his driving thrusts. She wrapped her arms around him and held on tight, for he was her only anchor in a spinning maelstrom of sensation.

Higher and higher they strove. Together, always together they moved, hearts pounding in unison, breaths mingling, sighs and soft moans of pleasure taken, pleasure given.

The first tremors caught her. Gabriel watched it happen to her, saw her eyes lose focus, felt her clench around him. He held out until she called out his name. Pressing his face into the hollow of her throat, he let himself go. He was flung up high, then slammed down into a climax so powerful that stars pinwheeled across his vision.

"Rae," he groaned.

They held tightly to each other as they spiraled back down to earth. Gabriel rolled onto his back, bringing her with him. She laid her cheek on his chest, melded to him as though she'd been a part of him forever.

Soon, her breathing slowed. He ran his hand along the tumbled mass of her hair, smoothing the wild curls against her shoulder. She murmured his name. Even asleep, he thought, she'd known his touch. His heart contracted.

Again, he remembered how he'd begun this thinking he'd work her out of his system. But now, with Rae lying warm and lush against him, he knew he'd been wrong.

Oh, hell.

Chapter 9

Rae stared up at the velvet blackness of the ceiling. Gabriel slept beside her, his arm around her waist, but her mind wouldn't relax. She kept replaying the night, over and over and over. And still she found no answers.

Simply, making love to Gabriel MacLaren had been the most stunning, beautiful thing that had ever happened to her. He'd been fierce and tender, passionate and incredibly sensual all at once. She felt new and strange, as though she'd been taken apart and put back together a whole new way.

It scared her. She didn't want to be vulnerable. She'd found that Rae Ann Boudreau, process server extraordinaire, was simply a woman. No more, no less.

Gabriel MacLaren had made her feel cherished. He'd made her feel loved.

And it wasn't real.

Reality was Peter Smithfield, and those three kids who'd be desperately poor until they got some support. Reality was that Gabriel had spent half a lifetime in a heart-breaking, spirit-souring job, and cynicism had no place in love.

And reality was that he hadn't offered her love. Sensation,

sensuality, pleasure so hot there'd been times when she thought she'd surely be consumed by it, but not love.

"Oh, damn," she muttered.

Gabriel stirred, reaching for her in an automatic gesture of possession. She laid her hand on his chest, and watched, fascinated, as his body reacted to her touch, even in sleep.

Temptation whispered in her ear, seductive as the devil himself. Almost of its own volition, her hand slid downward, tracing the line of hair that ran from his chest to his sex.

She stopped at his navel. Breath suspended, she fought her own arousal.

Hoo, boy, you've got it bad! Yes, she did. She wanted to awaken him and make love to him all over again. All she had to do was let her hand drift downward a few inches....

"Easy, girl," she whispered. "Time to engage brain."

The only way to do that, she knew, was to get out of this bed. Moving slowly and carefully, she slid free and got up.

She needed a walk. A good, free-swinging mile or so to get her mind functioning on a useful level again, and she might be able to decide exactly what to do with Detective Gabriel MacLaren.

And herself.

She glanced at the lighted dial of her watch—2:45a.m. Perfect. Moving swiftly and silently, she got dressed and grabbed her well-stuffed fanny pack. It had to weigh five pounds, but she didn't think it would be a good idea to leave it, just in case Gabriel woke and got curious. It wouldn't do for him to see her locksmith tools or the little .380 she carried with her.

The night clerk eyed her curiously as she trotted through the lobby. "Miss, I'm not sure it's safe for you to go out at this hour," he said.

"I'll be fine," she assured him.

At least a mugger would only steal her money. Gabriel MacLaren had slipped in and stolen her heart right out from under her, and she hadn't even seen it coming.

The night air was cool and humid, and here near the waterfront, tinged with the sea. Rae turned left, toward the beach. Nothing like a breeze off the water to scour cobwebs from the mind.

Headlights bloomed as a car turned the corner in front of her. The duty light on the roof tagged it as a taxi. Rae crossed the street with a casualness born of years of process serving.

A man got out of the cab. A thrill of anticipation ran up Rae's spine. She knew that body language, the set of the narrow shoulders, the way the man carried his head.

Peter Smithfield. Even in the dark, he looked smarmy.

She slid into the entryway of a nearby souvenir shop and watched as Smithfield retrieved a gym-type bag from the back seat of the taxi and paid the driver.

"Gotcha," she muttered.

She touched the fanny pack, feeling the crinkle of the papers inside. Just like the Boy Scouts, Boudreau Professional Process Service was always prepared.

Peter Smithfield walked swiftly inside. The condo building was one of those with a minuscule lobby, unlocked at night because the elevator and the stairs had to be accessed with a key. Once Smithfield got on that elevator, he'd be a much tougher target.

Rae sprinted down the street. Pushing the lobby door open, she saw the elevator doors just closing.

"Damn," she muttered. "Damn, damn, *damn*."

Then she shrugged. It paid to be philosophical about such things—especially when there was another way. She pulled her locksmith's tools out of the fanny pack and started working on the stairway door. First, she slipped the slender pick into the keyhole, then a moment later followed with the tension wrench.

She bit her lip, concentrating on the delicate job of manipulating the cylinder. It took finesse to pick a lock.

Keeping the lightest possible tension on the wrench, she slid the pick in and out an almost infinitesimal distance as she fiddled with the pins inside the cylinder. A little more…just… Click.

"Yes," she whispered.

A shadow fell across the lock as someone stepped between

her and the light. She whirled. And found herself staring into a pair of furious ice blue eyes.

"Hello, Rae," Gabriel said.

There was no trace of the man who'd made love to her so tenderly such a short time ago. This was all cop, and an annoyed cop, to boot. His gaze flicked to the lock. Her picks still stuck out of the key opening, mute betrayal of her actions.

"Hi," she said.

"When were you going to mention that Peter Smithfield was staying here?" he asked.

"Never," she said.

Gabriel stared at her for a moment, assessing her defiance. "Tell me something, Rae. Do you have the summons with you?"

"Don't leave home without it—that's my motto."

Gabriel's expression didn't budge. No matter how deeply Rae searched, she could find no softness in him, no chink in that smooth, hard cop's face.

A strange empty feeling settled in her chest, unbidden and most unwelcome. For one blinding moment, she wished she were still up in that hotel room with his arms around her and none of this had ever happened.

Then she remembered who she was and what she had to do. Her chin came up automatically. "I'm just doing my job, MacLaren," she said. "You ought to know that score."

"Oh, I know it, all right," he growled, reaching past her to pluck the picks from the lock. Eyeing her speculatively, he slipped them into his pocket.

"Hey!" she protested. "Those are mine."

"I'm impounding them."

"Oh, yeah? When can I have them back?"

He smiled without any humor at all. "When they've finished going through channels. You know how channels are."

"I've got to admit, you really are one dedicated woman," he continued. "No rain or snow or dark of night is going to keep you from doing your job. And especially not—"

"It wasn't like that," she said.

"I suppose you just had to go for a walk, hmm?"

"Well, yeah."

Gabriel was furious. Making love to her had touched his soul in a way he'd never experienced before. He'd wanted it to be as special for her. Instead, it had just been another of her games. She'd intended to distract him, and she'd done it damned well.

She'd used him.

It shouldn't matter. He'd come into this ready to use her. In vice, he'd been used, he'd been conned, he'd been betrayed every way there was. But Rae had left his bed to pursue Smithfield, and that didn't sit well at all.

With a growl of frustration, he took out his cellular phone and flipped it open. "MacLaren here," he said to the detective who answered. "I need to talk to Eddy."

"What are you doing?" Rae asked.

"As you've said to me on more than one occasion, mind your own beeswax." Hearing his partner's voice, he switched conversations. "Eddy, I've got our friend Smithfield down here at the Garden Towers Condominiums."

His gaze drifted to Rae, and memories began to slide through his head. Soft memories. Sensual memories. Memories he had no business having. He gave himself a mental shake and returned to Eddy. "The condos are right across from the Tropical Breeze Hotel. Right. I need you to come pick him up. No, can't bring him in myself. Complications."

Damn, but Rae was beautiful, he thought. Her mouth was still swollen from his kisses, and her hair gleamed like rich chestnut silk beneath the light. She had been the most incredible lover, the wildest, most responsive woman he'd ever known. And even at her wildest, she'd engendered such tenderness in him that his heart felt as though it might not be big enough to contain it all.

Tenderness, however, had been misplaced. He'd been a fool many times in his life, but never like this.

"Got a place to put him?" he said to his partner. "Good. See you in fifteen minutes." He closed the phone.

Rae saw her chance slipping away. "You're putting him in protective custody," she said.

"Yup."

"Come on. Just let me serve papers on the guy, and then I'll be out of your hair forever."

Everything inside him rose up in protest at the thought of losing her forever. He didn't like it. If he could have cut this weakness out of his heart with a knife, he would have done so. And despite that, he wanted to take her back to that hotel room and make love to her all over again. Instead, he had no choice but to hold tightly to his anger as a shield against his feelings for her.

"Honey-child," he drawled, "until I have orders otherwise, you're not going to get near Peter Smithfield for five seconds, let alone five minutes."

"Damn it, MacLaren—"

"A couple of hours ago, I was Gabriel," he said.

Rae didn't want to remember the exquisite lovemaking. She didn't want to remember how he'd made her feel things, do things, she'd never imagined before. "That's not an issue here," she said. "Peter Smithfield is."

"You're really something, you know that?" he said, laughing in spite of himself. "Absolutely one-track. Just sit tight until my partner gets here, and then I'll decide what to do with you."

Rae crossed her arms over her chest and glared at him resentfully. The tense silence seemed to go on forever. Finally, two men came into the building. One was tall and skinny, with a hangdog face and shark's eyes. The other was short, wiry and Latin, with eyes the color and hardness of obsidian.

"Hey," the tall one said.

"What's shakin', MacLaren?" the Latin one said, his gaze traveling over Rae like a pair of overbold hands. "Peter Smithfield looks a hell of a lot better in person than in his mug shots."

"Yeah, yeah," Gabriel said, scowling because he didn't like the way DeZuniga was ogling Rae. "Rae, meet my partner, Eddy Drake, and this is Saul DeZuniga. Gentlemen, Rae Boudreau.''

Eddy nodded. DeZuniga gave Rae another once-over, then shifted his black gaze to Gabriel. "You are in trouble, man."

Gabriel grunted ill-naturedly. "Peter Smithfield is upstairs. Apartment... Which apartment, Rae darling?''

"Three-C,'' she said without hesitating.

Eddy bobbed his head and jerked his thumb at DeZuniga. Both men loped upstairs.

Rae leaned one shoulder against the wall and watched Gabriel. His eyes were impenetrable. Search as she might, she couldn't find the slightest clue as to what he might be thinking.

The two detectives came back down.

"He's not in 3C,'' Eddy said, pinning Rae with a hard stare.

"Oh,'' Rae said. "Two-C?''

Both men looked at MacLaren. After a moment, DeZuniga shook his head. "You are *really* in trouble,'' he said.

They went back upstairs. Gabriel moved so that he was out of sight of the stairway door, yet still blocking the path to the outer door. She wasn't sure if he were making sure Smithfield didn't run—or she didn't.

Actually, he had a right to be cautious, for her insides were jumping like a cat in a camp fire. She'd clung to her defiance because that was the only way she knew how to do things, but in her heart, where it really counted, a cold dread had begun to grow.

She didn't like this reality. She preferred the world she and Gabriel had created up in that hotel room, a place of tenderness and caring, of pleasure shared. And that scared her. She'd managed to keep her head above the sea of emotion that plagued so many people. Now she'd fallen off the lifeboat, and she found she'd forgotten how to swim.

She found herself watching Gabriel. He looked like a tiger standing there, she thought, all lean, powerful muscle and masculinity. When he hooked his thumbs in his belt, making the muscles writhe on his forearms, her mouth turned dry.

When he shifted to one side, pulling his shirt tightly against the ridged hardness of his abdomen, her pulse began to race.

Oh, boy, she had it bad.

Finally, Eddy and DeZuniga returned. Each had a grip on one of Peter Smithfield's arms. Rae came up on her toes, tempted almost beyond reason to serve Smithfield then and there. But she glanced at Gabriel, and the look on his face convinced her to stay where she was. She wasn't afraid. Deep in her soul, she knew Gabriel wouldn't actually hurt her. But a cop had a lot of ways of punishing someone without flailing a rubber hose, and she was sure Gabriel knew most of them.

There was also the fact that he'd caught her breaking and entering. He hadn't mentioned it, exactly, but she was sure it had occurred to him that he could arrest her right here and now. She shot him a glance, and found him looking at her with a self-satisfied expression on his face. He knew exactly what she was thinking, the rat. Rae had to struggle against the urge to challenge him, to see if he'd really do such a thing to her.

Of course he would. He was a cop.

Better to wait and hope for another chance at Peter Smithfield. But oh, it was hard! She wasn't used to backing off. Her chest heaved with frustration as Drake and DeZuniga led the gambler toward the street door.

"He was in 4B," DeZuniga growled as he passed Gabriel. "We had to knock on every damned door in the place."

They hauled Smithfield out. Rae crossed her arms over her chest and waited to see what her lover would do next. He smiled at her. It wasn't a very nice smile.

"It's just you and me now, Rae," he said.

That surprised her. "What do you mean?"

"Peter Smithfield is no longer an issue between us, so it's time to stop playing games."

"No longer an issue?" she repeated incredulously. "I've got his wife and kids living with me because he doesn't give a tinker's damn whether they have a roof over their heads or not, or whether they've got enough to eat—"

She broke off as he strode toward her. For a moment, she

considered bolting up the stairs, but after one glance into his eyes, she realized he'd only come after her. She had the feeling that he'd come after her if she ran to the ends of the earth.

A daunting thought. And a stirring one.

He loomed over her, all hard-honed muscle and icy blue eyes. As always, his presence sent shock waves of reaction through her body. She felt her breathing change, her blood heat.

"Now," he said, his voice low and intimate, "let's make sure you don't find a way to interfere until they've got Smithfield safely stashed."

"Huh?"

Without looking away from her, he reached to flip the inside latch on the stairway door. It swung closed with a soft snick Rae felt down to her toes. If there'd been any hope of escape, it was gone now. She had the feeling, however, that escape had been closed off since the moment she'd first met this man's gaze.

Still, no one controlled Rae Ann Boudreau. No one made her back down. With a defiant smile, she offered her wrists for the handcuffs. Instead of the cold touch of steel, however, she felt his warm, callused hand close around her wrist.

"I'm not going to arrest you," he said. "I'm just going to keep you out of trouble for a couple of hours."

Her nostrils flared. "What do you mean?"

"Come on, Rae," he said.

"Come where?"

"Back to the hotel room."

No. Uh-uh. Not there. She resisted his tug on her wrist. Before she quite realized what was happening, he tossed her over his shoulder and carried her out into the street. By the time she'd gotten her wits back, they were nearly at the hotel entrance.

"MacLaren!" she barked. "Put me down!"

He ignored her. Rae was not about to give him the satisfaction of struggling, so she hung there quietly and resentfully, plotting a variety of ways to get revenge.

The night clerk's mouth dropped open as Gabriel bore her past the desk. Rae was glad her hair covered most of her face.

"Sir—" the clerk began.

"We're newlyweds," Gabriel growled.

Rae drew her breath in, ready to protest. But his long strides had already carried them to the elevator, and the moment was lost. As soon as the doors closed, he eased her to her feet.

She might have been relieved, except for the fact that he slid her down along the front of his body, and the contact strummed every nerve she possessed. Everything in her focused on him, and the feel of his big, hard body against hers.

Her balance seemed a little off. Maybe it was because all the blood had rushed from her head when he'd set her upright. And maybe it was because of the sweltering rush of desire that coursed through her. Whichever, she found herself leaning against him, her left hand spread out across his chest.

His arm came hard around her waist, a gesture rife with possessiveness. It was not the touch of an adversary. No, indeed. This was the touch of a lover.

Startled, she tipped her head back to look at him. At that moment, the cold, impenetrable cop's facade cracked, and she found herself looking into a seething maelstrom of emotion. It was all laid out for her, hot and hard in his eyes. Anger, betrayal, razor-edged desire and...triumph.

He'd beaten her again. And he was enjoying it. Damn him.

It wasn't until the bell rang to announce their floor that Rae realized that she didn't *have* to stand pressed up against him. She pushed against his chest.

He held her a moment longer, his hand spread out across the small of her back. She found herself pinned in his blue crystal gaze, her very soul captured like a moth in a flame. Then his mouth lifted in a cynical half smile, and he let her go.

Silently, she waited as he unlocked the door to her room and pushed it open. Rae went in ahead of him. Her gaze immediately went to the bed.

The covers were rumpled, the pillows tossed wildly against

the headboard. They had made such beautiful love there, turning the impersonal hotel bed into their own personal Shangri-la.

Would those sheets smell like him? she wondered. The thought crept treacherously through her, bringing a wealth of memories with it. Memories of his urgency as he'd laid her on that bed, the feel of his hands, his mouth, his body. Her heart remembered, and her flesh. She could almost feel again the exquisite sensation of being joined with him, impaled on his passion and hers.

In that bed, she had trusted him implicitly. She had given herself up totally, without restraint, borne by the faith that he would keep her safe.

Girlfriend, things have sure changed. The cynical thought seemed out of place here in this room where they'd shared so much. Then she looked at Gabriel, and revised that judgment.

Trust had vanished. All that remained was the cop and the process server, and an unmade bed. Warily, she watched as Gabriel closed the door behind him and leaned against it. His eyes had once again become cold and unreadable.

"What's the matter, Rae?" he asked. "No wisecracks, no sassy remarks forthcoming?"

"Would you laugh if there were?" she countered.

"Not when the joke's on me."

"What joke?"

He pushed away from the door and walked toward her. Rae found herself backing up instinctively. Not from fear. From self-preservation. That little scene in the elevator had been proof enough that she couldn't trust herself around him.

"How long do you think you can keep me here?" she asked, sidling to the left.

He sidled with her. "Long enough for Smithfield to get stashed somewhere nice and private."

She changed directions. So did Gabriel.

"Long enough for me to get some sleep," he continued. "It's business as usual in just a few hours."

"You want to sleep?" she demanded incredulously. "You want to sleep here?"

With me. The words, although unspoken, seemed to hang like fire in the room.

"Sure," Gabriel said. "Is that a problem?"

He'd managed to back her into a corner by now.

"Back off, buster," she snapped. "I don't know what's got you on your high horse, but between the two of us, I think I've got more cause for grievance."

His brows rose. "Because I ended up with Smithfield?"

"Why else?" she demanded.

"Tell me something," he said, his voice dropping to a near-whisper. "Why did you make love to me tonight?"

Once again, she saw raw emotion churning in his eyes, emotion so fierce and unbridled that most men would have hidden it away.

Why did you make love to me tonight? It was a dangerous question, one that left the respondent much too vulnerable. Rae didn't want to be vulnerable. Not to him. Not to anyone.

And because she didn't dare tell him that against her will, against all sense of self-preservation, she'd fallen in love with him. Good Lord, she might as well hand him the sacrificial knife!

"That isn't a fair question," she said.

"Still sidestepping?" he countered.

"As I recall, you've sorta got me trapped in this corner."

"I wasn't speaking in the physical sense. Do you want to know what I think, Rae?"

"Do I have a choice?"

"No." He closed the distance between them. She moved back the last few inches left to her and found herself with her back against the wall. Damn. Damn him.

"I think you made love to me to keep me distracted," he said. "And it worked big time, didn't it? The minute I was asleep, you sneaked out to grab Peter Smithfield."

"That isn't the way it was," she said.

He propped his hands on either side of her head. His gaze

bored into hers, an icy cold rage turning them flat and pale. "I don't like being conned, Rae."

"I could say the same," she countered. "There were two people involved in that lovemaking, you know."

"I'm not the one who left," he growled.

"So I went for a walk!"

His brows rose. "A walk? At 2:00 a.m.?"

"Yes."

"Come on, Rae," he said. "You can do better than that."

She took a step forward, intending to get out of this corner any way she could. But he didn't move back, and she either had to stop or walk straight into his chest.

"Let me out," she said.

"No."

They glared at each other for what seemed like forever. Then something new came into his eyes, and her adrenaline went into a jagged upward surge.

Desire.

She hadn't expected to see it in him. Not now, with such bitter conflict between them. But there it was, leaping like a flame in those gorgeous ice blue eyes.

It hit her like a physical blow, igniting a slow burn deep in her belly. Her gaze drifted to his mouth, which was achingly sensual despite the hard-cut line of his lips. Instinct drew her hand up, laid it against the beard-roughened curve of his cheek. She watched the heat in his eyes flare higher, hotter.

If this were an illness, at least they were both infected.

Deliberately, she let her fingers trail down the strong column of his neck. His pulse throbbed beneath her hand, revving perceptibly as she slid her thumb into the hollow at the base of his neck.

He reacted instantly, leaning toward her until their mouths nearly touched. She knew it was a ploy; she could see that in his eyes. Even so, her body thrilled to his nearness. Her skin felt hot and too sensitive, her breasts and nipples tingling in awareness. She could almost feel his hands on her. Touching her. Loving her all over again.

"What do you want, Rae?" he asked, his voice low and harsh.

"I..." She trailed off, not having the slightest idea of what she wanted to say.

His eyes slitted nearly closed. Until then, she hadn't realized just how much danger she was in. Now it was too late.

His mouth covered hers. Although the kiss was butterfly light, butterfly soft, she reacted instantly. Desire torched through her, settling in an ache deep in her belly. Her breasts swelled and sensitized, as though her very flesh craved his hands.

Slowly, almost imperceptibly, he deepened the kiss. Anger, resentment, caution—all drained from her mind like water from a sieve. Rational thought flew away, leaving only passion. She opened her mouth, accepting the touch of his tongue to hers.

A wild, rushing wave crashed through her. Gone were the problems between them, the anger, the mistrust.

He made a hoarse sound deep in his throat. She echoed it as he moved closer, slowly fitting his body to hers. Breasts, belly, thighs—sweet fire ran from every contact point, desire so hot it made her legs weak.

There was nothing civilized about their passion. Nothing civilized in the way he plundered her mouth, or the way she sank her fingers into the dark wealth of his hair. This was as elemental as the sea, as fathomless and untamed. And like the sea, it conquered, overwhelmed, overcame.

He slid his hands down her back, his fingers spread as if to encompass as much of her as possible. Then he dipped lower, cupping her, bringing her up against his aroused body.

She cried out, a soft sound of arousal that made him surge against her. Sensation swirled like wine through her veins, driven by every beat of her heart. He slid one hand to the back of her neck, the other beneath her sweatshirt. Shifting position to allow him access to her breasts, he slid his palm upward along her ribs. Helplessly, Rae arched to meet his hand.

His skin felt hot against her nipple, but she knew his mouth would be hotter. She yearned to feel his mouth there, right there. She ached for it. Just as she thought she might go crazy with the wanting, he dragged her shirt upward.

Rae shivered with anticipation. The air felt cool on her overheated skin, and she couldn't wait for him to warm her. Suddenly, her sweatshirt snagged on her fanny pack. With an impatient hiss, Gabriel unhooked the pack and tossed it away.

It landed with a solid clunk.

Gabriel stilled, and Rae's heart did a swift, hard dive into her stomach. He pulled away from her. It took every bit of self-control she possessed to keep from drawing him back.

"What have we got here?" he asked, retrieving the pack from the floor.

He unzipped it and peered inside. His brows went up as he spotted her gun.

"I have a permit for that," she said.

Gabriel let his breath out in a long sigh. He'd almost allowed her to con him again. Hell, it had been easy enough. One look, one touch, and he was on a roller coaster to nowhere.

Well, the sight of the gun had brought him crashing right back to sanity, that was for sure. He hefted the .380 in his open palm. With any other woman, he would have considered the gun a contradiction. After all, who'd think that a creature of lush curves and warm, silken skin would possibly have anything to do with a deadly little semiautomatic? Rae, however, didn't seem to fit any mold save her own.

"Nice gun," he said.

Cautious, she nodded.

"Packs a kick, though," he continued. "Not enough mass to absorb the recoil."

"I can handle it."

Her matter-of-fact statement sat like lead on his heart. He dropped the pistol back into the fanny pack. "I bet you can. Better see if you can get a couple of hours' sleep."

"Where?" she asked, then instantly regretted the question.

He lifted his brows in supercilious inquiry. "Don't worry. I'll crash on the sofa."

With a sigh of frustration, she turned away. She was far too old, too cynical and too busy to have regrets for what might have been. Still, she couldn't keep from watching Gabriel out of the corner of her eye as he wrestled the sofa over to the door. After positioning it to block the exit, he settled into it as though it might have a prayer of being comfortable.

"Serves him right," she muttered.

Conned him, indeed, she thought huffily. She'd given herself to him in a way she'd never done before, even during her marriage, and he thought it a con? Cops were too cynical for words.

She'd known it. She'd known it all along.

There had never been a chance for them. She'd allowed herself to get trapped by a fantasy of her own making, a fantasy without a chance of coming true. She'd known it.

She lay on top of the covers, unwilling to snuggle into the bed where she and Gabriel had shared so much pleasure, and stared up at the ceiling. There'd be no sleep for her. Judging from the amount of wiggling he was doing on the sofa, he wasn't going to get any sleep, either. It was some consolation, but not much.

"This is stupid," she announced to the room in general.

"What is it now?" Gabriel asked.

"I'm not going to get back to sleep, and neither are you."

"Ah. Do you have an alternate suggestion?"

His voice was arid and harsh, and she decided that answering him would be a waste of time. She sat up and switched on the light.

"Hey," he growled, shielding his eyes with his hand.

"I'm going to take a shower," she said.

With a growl, he sat up. Her pulse stuttered as she took in the picture he made. He'd put on the same shirt he'd worn earlier, which ought to be fine, except that it was missing the top two buttons. A V of curly chest hair was visible in the opening, as well as some very hard, sculpted male chest. With his hair tousled and his eyes shadowed with fatigue, he looked…he looked like a man who'd spent the past week making love to some lucky woman.

Oh, brother. She had to get some space, some objectivity, and some coffee. Alone. She went into the bathroom, closing the door behind her. Then, after a moment's hesitation, she locked it.

Gabriel wondered if she were locking him out or herself in. After the way she'd looked at him a moment ago, he couldn't be sure. But oh, man, she had *looked* at him. He was surprised the sofa hadn't burst into flame beneath him.

The sound of running water came through the bathroom door. He lay back down and closed his eyes, trying not to think about Rae in the shower. He might as well have tried to fly. His imagination conjured up the vision of Rae naked, water sluicing down her delectable body. Enticing. He'd wash her, his hands gliding over her glistening breasts. Her skin would be soap slick, hot from his touch.

In his fantasy, he walked into that bathroom. Naked, he'd step into the shower. He'd put his arms around her and pull her wet, naked body against his. There would be no Peter Smithfield, no damned summons to be served, nothing but skin and passion and heat.

His body had reacted powerfully to the fantasy, becoming so hard it was actually painful. Gritting his teeth, he turned face down. It wouldn't do for her to come traipsing out here and find him ready to celebrate the Fourth of July in a big way.

"Damn," he growled.

The bathroom door opened a crack, nearly startling him out of his skin. Rae peered out the narrow opening, steam curling out from around her.

"Excuse me," she said. "Would you mind handing me that bag over there? The blue one?"

He closed his eyes, willing self-control. After a moment, he was able to get up off the sofa to fetch the bag. She had to open the door wider to take it from him, and he got an eye-searing glimpse of her shapely derriere in the mirror. Steam fogged the glass, making that pale, curvy image seem to float.

Reality, at that moment, seemed a hell of a long way away.

Gabriel knew he was staring, but he couldn't have looked away if his life depended on it. Arousal swept through him in a wild rush, and it was all he could do to keep from pushing that door open and claiming her all over again.

Sure, his cop's mind whispered. And get used all over again. But damn, she was more woman than the law ought to allow.

"Here," he growled, holding the bag out.

Rae noticed that Gabriel's gaze seemed to be focused on a point behind her. Then she stiffened. She'd forgotten the mirror. A glance over her shoulder confirmed her suspicion. Oh, yes, she'd really slipped up this time. She'd taken great pains not to reveal more than her neck and face to Gabriel, while leaving her naked behind exposed in the mirror.

"Men are toads," she said.

Gabriel didn't pretend to misunderstand. "A man would have to be crazy not to look," he said. "I might be a fool sometimes, given the proper motivation, but I'm not crazy."

"That's a matter of opinion," she countered.

He put one hand on the door, exerting enough pressure so that she had to lean against it to keep it from swinging open. Her heart started to pound with fear. Not because she thought he might force his way in. He wouldn't.

She was afraid that she'd let him in.

"Are you going to pretend that nothing happened between us?" he asked. "Can you honestly think you can forget what happened in that bed over there, what we did and what we shared?"

Never. "Yes."

"Then why haven't you covered up?"

Rae's face went hot, and she wished she could crawl in a hole. Of course, there was no answer to his question. She hadn't covered up because it simply hadn't occurred to her.

"It's okay," he said. "I like looking at you."

Her gaze strayed down his body, and she realized just how much he liked looking at her. She jerked her gaze back up to his face.

"As you can see, I can't seem to hide my feelings very well," he said with a self-deprecating smile.

Somehow, she had to get a handle on things. Her libido was zinging almost out of control, and making love to him now would be the biggest mistake of her life.

"You call those feelings?" she inquired.

He shrugged. "I can sure feel them."

Rae thought she detected a note of disdain colored his voice. She swallowed hard, hoping she was mistaken. Disdain would turn the memory of that beautiful lovemaking into something less. Something...well, tawdry.

"Let go of the damned door," she ordered.

He did. But he smiled when he did it, taking away any hope of triumph for her. Rae closed the door and locked it, then stepped into the shower. Grateful for the comfort of the heat, she turned and let the water beat against her back.

"These things happen," she said, moving so that the shower peppered her front. "You made a mistake. Deal with it."

Gabriel didn't matter. He didn't.

Strange, though, that the water running down her face tasted suspiciously like tears.

Chapter 10

Rae didn't say a word as she stuffed her gear into the soft-sided suitcase she'd shipped with her clothes. Her eyes felt heavy and sore, but she told herself it was fatigue.

Gabriel leaned against the door, watching her. He looked big and sexy and as arrogant as ever. Rae wondered if anything could puncture that cynical self-confidence. Probably not. People who dared to try would just find themselves at the wrong end of a pair of handcuffs.

"I'll drive you home," Gabriel growled.

"No, thanks."

"I'm going that way, anyway," he said.

She shot him a look that should have dropped him where he stood. "Oh, so the surveillance is still on?"

"Until I hear otherwise."

"Why don't you call and ask?"

One corner of his mouth went up. "Anxious to get rid of me?"

"Detective," she said, tilting her head back to meet his gaze, "you have no idea."

She zipped the bag closed and headed for the door. She

wasn't exactly sure what she'd do if Gabriel didn't get out of the way. But he did, and with a smile.

That smile was full of cynicism, like the man himself. But it also contained a megawatt-voltage of sensuality, and she registered it in places she didn't even want to admit she owned.

Of course, he followed her out into the hall. She walked along, head high, looking neither to the right nor the left— and certainly not toward him.

"Seems a shame to waste money on a cab when there's a perfectly good car waiting downstairs for us," he said.

"No," she said with finality.

"It would make following you a whole lot easier."

"I bet."

She jammed her thumb onto the Down button for the elevator, and held it there.

"That's not going to make it come any faster," Gabriel said.

"MacLaren, go away," she snapped, completely exasperated.

"I can't."

"You won't, you mean."

"Can't," he corrected. "Orders, remember?"

The elevator arrived. Rae put her nose in the air and walked on. Gabriel came with her. Clasping his hands behind him, he rocked back and forth from his heels to the balls of his feet. Rae kept her eyes forward and her temper under tight rein.

Only a few more minutes, she thought.

The same clerk was still on duty. His brows rose as Rae marched up to the desk and slapped her key on the counter.

"I hope you folks enjoyed your visit," he said.

"Best honeymoon I ever had," Gabriel said.

Rae was getting some definite homicidal impulses. She signed the charge slip with a slash-and-dash approximation of her signature, then ripped her copy off and headed for the door. She wasn't surprised that Gabriel followed her; she was only surprised that she'd managed to stay sane this long.

A taxi idled outside. She started toward it, but Gabriel caught her by the arm and pulled her to a stop.

"Is that for you?" he asked.

"I called while you were in the bathroom."

"Sneaky."

"Sneaky would have been leaving the room," she countered.

"I'd only find you again," he said cheerfully.

"Why do you think I didn't walk?" she snapped.

Removing her arm from his grasp, she got in the taxi. As it pulled away from the curb, she glanced out the back window and saw MacLaren getting in the Taurus.

After that, she kept her face turned forward. She wasn't going to shake Gabriel, much as she'd like to. Some day she'd like to peel off a twenty and growl at a taxi driver, "Ya get this if you lose him."

She leaned forward and tapped the driver on the shoulder. "If I offered you a twenty and asked you to lose someone, what would you do?"

He shot her a glance. "Are you kidding, lady? Think I'd risk my license for a lousy twenty bucks?"

"So, how much?"

"Who do you want to lose?"

"A cop."

He gave an explosive snort. "You ain't got enough."

"I need to buy a car," she complained. "Taxi drivers have wimped out."

"No joke," he retorted. "This is the nineties, lady. Everybody's gotta be politically correct."

Thoroughly disgusted with her morning so far, she sat back and pouted. Not that she pouted where anyone could see her, but there were times when it felt good.

She saw the welcoming committee the moment the taxi turned onto her street. Her mouth dropped open as she saw the receiving line. Other than little Sarah, who clung to her mother's hand, the receiving line went from largest to smallest. Including the dog. Rae shook her head in mingled amusement and chagrin. She'd only called Barbara to warn her that she was on the way home, and hadn't expected anything like this.

"That yours?" the taxi driver asked.

"Yeah, I guess so," she said.

"Cute."

Ordinarily, Rae would have had a rejoinder for that. But she was moved by the sight, more than she would have expected. She didn't have much family, only a few cousins with whom she had only a Christmas-card acquaintance. Her parents had died long enough ago that she'd almost gotten used to them being gone.

Typical Rae-is-an-island mind-set. It had worked well for her, making loneliness seem to be her choice and her preference.

Until now. Now she had four people—and a dog—who were actually happy to see her. It felt good. She had the door open the moment the taxi reached the curb.

"I bet you wish you had that twenty now," she said as she paid him.

"I wish I was Richard Gere, too," he said. "But I ain't."

"Everybody's a comedian," she muttered.

The kids rushed her the moment she stepped out onto the sidewalk. So did the dog. She gave the kids a hug, swinging them around, then bent to pet the whining, impatient puppy.

"Hello, mutt," she said, only half trying to avoid the wet, slapping tongue. "I wasn't sure if you'd remember me."

"Sure, he would," Joey, the younger boy, said. "We showed him your picture all the time."

Rae ruffled the boy's hair the same way she was ruffling the dog's. Both responded about the same, although the puppy, having a tail, had better body language. She filed that away for future reference. And wondered if men responded similarly to the hair-ruffling thing.

She glanced down the street where a dark Taurus idled at the curb. Then she scooped the child up in one arm, the puppy in the other, and turned to Barbara.

"I'm starved," she said. "Any Froot Loops left?"

"How about bacon and eggs?"

Of its own volition, Rae's gaze drifted back to the Taurus.
"I'd kill for bacon and eggs."

"Do you want to invite your friend?" Barbara asked.

"Huh?" Startled, Rae looked at the other woman. There
was a knowing look in Barbara's eyes that made Rae very
uncomfortable. She was going to have to spend a lot of time
getting Gabriel MacLaren out of her system, and she didn't
want to have to do it under scrutiny.

"Your friend," Barbara said. "Do you want to invite
him?"

"He's not my friend," Rae replied, perhaps more force-
fully than was necessary.

"What is he, then?"

"A cop," Rae said, turning away. "Only a cop."

Rae got to her office about noon that day. She'd intended
to go right after breakfast, but the kids had wanted to tell her
about all their adventures, and Tom the Dog had latched on
to her. Literally. He'd gotten a grip on her sock with those
needle-sharp puppy teeth, and hadn't let go until he fell
asleep.

And Rae, feeling like a heel because she'd left him for two
days, had resisted everyone's attempts to disengage the
puppy. If he wanted her that badly, well, who was she to
deny him?

"Cute," she muttered, echoing the taxi driver's comment.
It had been cute. Cute and heartwarming, and more welcome than she'd have believed.

"You're getting soft, Boudreau," she muttered.

She turned her computer on and waited for it to run through
its warm-up. I Am Lobo, I Hunt Alone flashed up on the
screen, mocking her. Once, it had seemed to be the perfect
statement of her attitude, the bold marquee of her life. Now
it seemed as empty as her life had been. As her life would
be.

This Smithfield case had ruined her. Gabriel had made her
want things she couldn't have; Barbara and those three kids
had given her a feeling of belonging she hadn't known since

she was a kid herself, and made her wish she could keep it forever. But they had lives of their own. They'd move on, find their own place, maybe a nice stepdad who'd love them as much as they deserved.

Rae Boudreau would be alone again. Of course, she'd still have Tom the Dog. But deep in her heart, her guts, her soul, she wanted Gabriel. As long as she lived, there would be a MacLaren-shaped emptiness in her.

"Damn you, MacLaren," she said. "Smithfield is mine."

She punched in her access code to the Realtors' MLS program, and started looking for properties that had been bought by the city during the past few years. After a few hours of digging, she came up with eleven prospects that were currently owned by the city, and nine that had passed into other hands within the past six months. Those would have to be checked out, too.

With a sigh of satisfaction, she leaned back in her chair. MacLaren had miscalculated. It wasn't over yet, by God.

Something fell through the mail slot on her door. One swift glance showed her a fat white, #10 envelope. No address, no stamp. Rae shot out of her chair as though it had burst into flames. Snatching the door open, she looked out into the hall. Empty. Then she saw the door to the stairway shudder, as though it had just swung closed. She ran toward it, but found only an empty stairwell.

"Interesting," she murmured.

Returning to her office, she picked the envelope up and hefted it thoughtfully. Thoughts of mad bombers aside, it felt heavy. Paper heavy. She closed the door behind her and locked it, then slit the envelope open with her fingernail.

"Holy smoke!" she breathed.

Money. A whole stack of hundred-dollar bills. She took it to her desk and spread the money out. Then she began to count. Finally, she let her breath out in a huge sigh and sat back.

Twenty thousand dollars.

"Too weird," she said. "No note, no thank-you-for-being-so-wonderful-that-we-couldn't-resist letter? Uh-uh."

She spotted a small folded piece of paper in the envelope. Swiftly, she opened it. In neat, block, laser-sharp print, it said, "A prudent woman knows when to back off."

"Prudent?" she asked. "An educated bribe, huh?"

She fanned the bills out and held them up to the light. They were used, not worn-out, exactly, but obviously not new, and the metallic coding strip had been pulled out of every one of them.

"Hmm. Somebody's got deep pockets," she mused.

There were two possibilities here. First, it could be exactly what it seemed. On the other hand, it could be a setup by the cops. Then she shook her head. The cops wouldn't bother tying up twenty grand bribing a process server when they already had Peter Smithfield in custody.

So it had to be a real bribe. And a real threat. With a grimace of disdain, she tossed the money on her desk. Rae Ann Boudreau didn't take bribes. And she didn't back off.

But this meant that maybe, just maybe, Gabriel MacLaren's case was as important as he seemed to think it was. And maybe, just maybe, she ought to discuss this with him. But that would only work on a quid pro quo basis: something for something, an even trade, tit for tat. She wondered if he'd understand the concept.

Someone knocked at the door, nearly startling her out of her chair. Hastily, she stuffed the money back into the envelope and shoved it into the center drawer of her desk.

"Open the door, Rae."

Her pulse jumped at the sound of that deep voice. "Speak of the devil," she muttered. Then, raising her voice, she called, "What do you want?"

"To talk to you."

Rae's initial impulse was to ask him if he had a warrant. But that would only nip the negotiating process in the bud. With a sigh, she leaned forward and cleared her computer screen.

"Come in," she said.

"It's locked."

That meant he'd already tried the door. Her mouth curled in a cynical smile. Cops. She got up and let him in.

He'd changed into a pair of khakis and a polo shirt a shade darker than his eyes. Despite the fact that he'd shaved, he looked tired, brooding and very, very sexy. Her stomach dropped down to somewhere around her knees.

That razor-sharp cop's gaze darted around the room, taking everything in. She knew the layout was now printed in his memory, and that he could catalog her office down to the paper clips.

Unwilling to accept the psychological disadvantage of sitting down, she eased up onto the edge of the desk. "What can I do for you, Detective?"

"I came to give you some bad news."

"Which is?"

"You're not going to be able to get rid of me for a while," he said. "Seems you made the powers-that-be nervous when you slipped away from surveillance a couple of days ago. They want you watched until this case breaks, and they want me to do it."

"You came all the way up here just to tell me that?" she inquired.

Gabriel crossed his arms over his chest and regarded her from beneath his brows. He didn't know why he'd come up here. He'd cursed himself with every step, telling himself that only a fool would expose himself to temptation—and betrayal—again. But he'd come. He'd made each of those steps despite the lash of common sense and even self-preservation.

Simply, he had to see her again. Parting the way they did had left a hole somewhere in the region of his heart, a yawning, empty place that would nag him until he patched it somehow. And the only way he could think to do that was to resolve things with Rae. He'd live without that, sure, but he didn't want to spend the rest of his life bleeding inside like this if there were another option.

"We need to talk," he said.

Rae raked her hand through her hair. "You're right."

"I am?" he asked, surprised that she'd agreed with anything.

"Sure," she said. "There's no need to let our personal conflict keep us from doing business."

His cop's mind gave a hoot of derision. Resolve things, eh, MacLaren? Might as well deal with a Waring blender. She's a player, and if you aren't careful, you're gonna get burned just like her ex-husband did.

"Exactly what kind of business did you have in mind, Rae?"

"The Smithfield case." She held up her hands, forestalling any protest. "Just hear me out, will you?"

"Okay," he said. "Shoot."

He was more distracted than he'd like to admit. She wore jeans and a burnt orange sleeveless top, which would have been unremarkable on another woman. But Rae had curves another woman would have sold her soul for, and filled that top out so well it made his mouth water. The sunlight struck ruddy sparks in her hair and gilded the tips of her long eyelashes. She looked like the woman who had burned him with passion the night before, the woman who had cried out his name as she'd carried him to heaven with her.

He wondered what would happen if he touched her. Would reality stand between them, or would the world go away again in a searing wash of passion?

"Are you still with me?" she asked.

He smiled. "More than you know, honey-child."

Rae studied him suspiciously. He didn't have a businesslike expression in his eyes. In fact, he had the look of a man who'd just imagined something delicious and very naughty, and was in the process of elaborating on the fantasy.

The rat. Now he had *her* doing it. She didn't want to remember how he had made love to her with a tender male intensity that even now sent heat pouring through her veins.

"MacLaren," she snapped. "Business."

He ripped off a sardonic salute. "Aye-aye. Business."

"I'd like to propose a situation and get your reaction to it," she said. "On a strictly theoretical basis, of course."

"Of course," he replied, his tone dry.

"Let's say that someone knew something about Peter Smithfield that might be, ah, significant."

His brows went up. "I'd advise that someone to tell the police immediately."

"Mmm. What if that someone had his or her own interest in Peter Smithfield, and wasn't inclined to give that information to the police without knowing the nature of its importance?"

"Let's stop pussyfooting around, Rae," Gabriel said, suddenly out of patience with the game. "If you know something about Peter Smithfield, spill it now."

"Why should I?"

"Because this is an important case—"

"Why?"

"You know I can't tell you."

She nodded. As she'd expected, they'd run up against the same roadblock there had always been between them. "Unquestioning adherence to rules can be dangerous, Detective. It can blind you to things that can bite you."

"*You* bit me," he said softly.

Rae drew her breath with a gasp. "I did not!"

"Yes," he said, "you did."

Unbuttoning his shirt, he pulled it aside, showing her a small red mark on his shoulder. Rae stared at it in consternation. She didn't remember doing that. But there had been times when passion had pulled her outside herself, when instinct had swept restraint away. Who was she kidding? she thought. There hadn't been any restraint from the moment he'd touched her.

And if she didn't watch it, the same thing would happen again.

"Business," she reminded him.

"Right. Now tell me what you know about Peter Smithfield."

She could see a wedge of dark chest hair in the V of his unbuttoned shirt. The sight of his throat fascinated her, the long, smooth muscles, the rapid thrum of the pulse beneath his skin. Her hands twitched because she wanted to touch him, and it wasn't allowed. Oh, definitely not allowed.

"No can do," she said. "You see, I have no way of knowing whether or not my information really is significant, or if I'm just bowing to the usual bureaucratic baloney. I really dislike bureaucratic baloney."

She shifted position slightly. "Now you, Detective MacLaren, embrace bureaucratic baloney. Your boss tells you not to talk, and you're determined to cling to that order no matter what the cost."

"Rae—"

"Ethically," she continued, "my first concern must be the interests of my client. Unless, of course, you can give me a good reason otherwise. Even then, I'd have to discuss the situation with my client before I could help you out."

"Rae—"

"If you were to tell me *why* my client should forego pursuing her own legal matter, then maybe we can work together."

Gabriel let his breath out in a long sigh. He agreed with her, damn it. But he'd been specifically ordered not to tell her anything about the case, and his opinion simply didn't matter.

"I've got no flex on this," he said.

Rae nodded; it was only what she'd expected. That didn't mean she wasn't disappointed. "Then neither do I."

"You're playing with something real hot here," Gabriel said. "I just hope you don't get burned."

"I've already been burned," she retorted.

The words dropped like ten-ton boulders into the suddenly silent room. Never, never, *never* had she intended to say something so revealing.

And Gabriel, damn his eyes, hadn't missed a thing. His mouth curved in an infuriatingly self-satisfied smile. She felt as though she'd flung her heart, naked and quivering, out there to get stomped on. Then his smile faded. A new look came into his eyes, an almost unbearable flare of pure sensuality.

He started toward her. Frozen by desire and dismay, she

watched him come. This wasn't a cop. Nor was he her opponent. For this moment, he was simply a man. Her man.

Gabriel stopped so close in front of her that their knees touched. His eyes raged with things he wanted, she wanted. He propped one hand on either side of her hips. She felt as though her nerves were going to jump right through her skin.

"I think both of us got singed in that fire," he said.

His tone was intimate, his eyes even more so.

"Stop it," she whispered.

"I can't." He bent and feathered a kiss along the curve of her cheek. "Don't you think I would if I could?"

His mouth moved downward, seeking. Rae parted her lips, seeking, too. They met, merged. She dropped into a deep, dark well of sensation. Somehow, she'd become tuned to him, mind, heart, spirit and, of course, body. Every nerve, every cell, every inch of skin, recognized him, and responded.

"Why is it like this with you?" she gasped as he left her mouth to make a hot, wet trail along the line of her throat.

"I don't know," he murmured. "Maybe we were just made for each other."

"You've got to be kidding. I tick you off every time I open my mouth."

"Not true," he said. "There are times when your open mouth is anything but annoying."

He claimed her mouth again, parting her lips with gentle aggression to delve deep inside. Rae moaned softly. It surprised her, that soft note of arousal. She hadn't intended it. She hadn't intended any of this.

She raised one hand with the vague intention of pushing him away. Instead, it landed on his shoulder, and insinuated itself to the back of his neck. All on its own, she'd swear.

She arched her back, fitting herself to his hard torso. It felt...it felt as though she'd come home. He kissed her, a gentle reaffirmation of passion. Rae didn't want gentleness. She didn't want a chance to think. She'd already fallen way, way off her self-made pedestal. Her interest had been conflicted, her isolation breached, the barriers around her heart shattered.

She had nothing more to lose, except this moment. So she wound her arms around his neck and pulled him still closer. His reaction was instantaneous and purely male. With a muttered groan, he deepened the kiss. His hands slid to her hips, claiming them, spreading out over her curves as though to hold her forever.

"Rae," he muttered against her open mouth.

"Don't talk," she whispered. "Just kiss me."

Gabriel obeyed. His pulse roared in his ears, and for a moment he felt as though he'd fallen off a cliff. Then she moaned deep in her throat, and his whole being centered on her. Oh, my, he thought. She was sweet and hot and incredibly responsive, and he'd never met a woman to compare.

Rae slid into a swirling haze of arousal. She ran her hands along his back, tracing the ridges of his ribs, the long, strong line of muscles along his spine. She couldn't stop. Didn't want to stop. Sensation rippled along her nerves as he pressed his open mouth to the wildly throbbing pulse beating beneath the skin.

She wanted him there, everywhere. Sinking her hand in his hair, she urged him downward. He slid his tongue into the hollow at the base of her throat. With his forefinger, he traced the edge of her top, leaving fire in his wake. Then he drew the fabric down, revealing the beginning swells of her breasts.

"Ah, that's pretty," he breathed.

Rae felt no embarrassment as he smoothed the top over her breasts, delineating the proud jut of her erect nipples. There was something reverent about his gaze, and the sight of it tore away all possibility of shame. Simply, he found her beautiful. The knowledge of that aroused her immeasurably, and she arched her chest, offering herself to the man she loved.

Bending, he explored her flesh, nibbling, sucking, licking.

Rae couldn't move, couldn't do anything but hang on. She gasped with pleasure as his hands shifted to her thighs, spreading them. Her gasp turned to a sigh as he moved to stand between her legs, pressing hot and hard just where she wanted to feel him most.

She didn't know he'd moved his hands until she felt cool

air on the skin of her back. Then she realized he'd pulled her shirt out, and had deftly undone her bra. Heat replaced coolness a moment later as he spread his fingers out across her back.

The phone rang, and the shrill electronic tone stabbed deep into the passionate haze that gripped Rae. She slid her hands down to Gabriel's chest and gave a push.

"Ignore it," he growled.

"I can't."

He heaved a sigh. Then he bent once more, kissed her with gentle intensity and let her go.

Rae felt abandoned, bereft. Her hands shook as she stuffed her top back into the waistband of her pants. But the phone rang again, reminding her that reality truly did exist, and that she had a role in it.

She picked the receiver up. Gabriel went to look out of the window, ostensibly giving her a modicum of privacy, but she knew better. The cop had returned. With a mental grimace, she thumbed the Speak button.

"Boudreau Process Service," she said. "Rae Boudreau here."

The caller was a lawyer, one of her regulars. "I've got a job for you," he said.

"Who are you abusing this time?" she asked. "Did I tell you that the last guy started to cry when I gave him the papers?"

"Very funny," the lawyer retorted. "Meet me at my office at five."

"You're on," she agreed, and hung up.

That left Gabriel to deal with. As though he'd read her mind, he turned and met her gaze. Her heart did a flip-flop before dropping into her stomach.

"I guess the mood's broken," he said.

"I guess so."

He raked one hand through his hair. "Things got a little out of hand there."

"Yes, they did," she agreed. "But it wasn't all your fault. I got carried away, too."

His brows went up. "I never said it was all my fault, Rae. Passion like that is a two-way street. Even if it weren't, I'd have to be crazy to be sorry for it."

"Now just a minute—"

"We've got a real thing on our hands," he growled. "You can stick your head in the sand and pretend you don't see it, but I guarantee it's going to burn you anyway."

Her temper kicked in. Jamming her fists on her hips, she scowled at him. But oh, he was a lovely man, standing there with the sun shining off his thick dark hair. Too bad he had such stiff-necked male arrogance.

"So we made a mistake last night," she retorted. "And another one today. I look at this like getting pregnant—if you know what causes it, and you don't want it to happen, then it ought to be very clear what you have to do."

"Right," he snarled, his own brand of temper flaring in his eyes. "I agree."

"Great," Rae snarled back. "Fine."

"Fine!"

He stalked out, slamming the door behind him. Rae stood stiffly, buoyed for a moment by indignation. Then her breath went out all at once, and she let herself sink back against the desk.

Her heart had betrayed her, making her want something she couldn't have. Gabriel MacLaren was too hard, too honed by his years as a cop. He couldn't bend. He couldn't *see*.

She couldn't have him. Of course, she'd known that from the beginning.

Hadn't she?

Chapter 11

Rae pushed her chair away from the computer and glanced over at the clock——4:33. She'd better get over to the lawyer's office. No matter how much satisfaction she might get out of finding Peter Smithfield, bills had to be paid. She had five extra mouths and a tail to feed these days.

She retrieved the bribe envelope and thrust it into her purse. Just in case. She wouldn't put it past the cops to sneak in here and go through her things. Now for the computer. She encrypted everything on her hard drive, left a cyber-raspberry for anyone who might be tampering and turned the machine off again.

The Taurus was waiting outside, of course. Gabriel looked gorgeous in sunglasses, and her heart did another of those almost painful flip-flops. She reined herself in sternly. The time had come for a new philosophy as far as Gabriel MacLaren was concerned.

Tough love, she'd call it. If she was tough enough, she'd get a handle on her love for him.

"Going somewhere?" he asked.

Tough love, baby-cakes, she told herself. She made a detour toward the car. He smiled, his eyes hidden beneath the dark glasses. Reaching into her purse, she took out her own sunglasses and put them on. There. They were even.

"Does it matter whether I tell you or not?" she asked.

"No. But it would be a lot less trouble if you'd just give me the address."

She repressed the urge to tell him to go straight to hell. Instead, she gave him her sweetest smile. "Nine-oh-one Gilchrist Lane," she said. "Then I'm going home for a while. We're having hot dogs for supper. I love hot dogs. Done to a crisp, so they swell up and split. Barbara calls them Chernobyl dogs."

"That's disgusting," he said.

Possessed by a crazy impulse too powerful to resist, she reached into the car and ruffled his hair just the way she'd ruffled the puppy's earlier.

"What the hell are you doing?" Gabriel demanded.

"An experiment in behavior," she replied. "The dog wagged his tail when I did that. And drooled."

One corner of his mouth went up. "Darlin', I'm perfectly willing to wag my tail for you. But drooling is out. Now, if you want to experiment with a judicious application of my tongue to—"

"Taxi!" she called.

A passing taxi screeched to a halt. She strode around the front of Gabriel's car, determined to escape. She did *not* want to think about his tongue, which he surely did know how to use. In fact, there had been one time when he'd—

"Stop it," she snarled, jerking open the taxi's door.

"I am stopped," the driver said.

"Sorry. I was talking to myself," she replied.

After giving him the address, she leaned back against the seat and watched the city go by. She didn't need to look to know that Gabriel was following. Crazy as it seemed, she could actually feel him there, as though her body had a special MacLaren-radar.

The taxi turned a corner, and her interest perked up. This

was the street on which Mike Doukas's deli was located. Mike was a peach, and she decided to stop to say hello.

"Stop at that deli, would you?" she asked, pointing. "Wait for me, please. I'll only be a minute."

The driver pulled over. Rae slid to the curb side of the taxi and got out. The deli's front window sparkled, and an enticing aroma of freshly cooked pork wafted out. Even at this hour, the place was crowded. Someone else might have been harried. But Mike beamed at everyone with indefatigable good humor and worked like three men, waiting tables and manning the counter, too.

A light bulb went off in Rae's mind. She found a space at the edge of the counter and waved to attract his attention.

"Hello, beautiful Rae," he said without stopping work.

"Hi. You're drowning."

"But cheerfully."

"You need help. I know somebody."

His mustache quirked upward. "Reliable?"

"Salt of the earth," she said. "She's got three kids, one preschool age, and an ex-husband who doesn't like to pay support. She's broke and can't afford child care."

Maybe she'd just ruined Barbara's chances. But Mike had the right to know exactly what he was getting.

"Good kids?" Mike asked. "They could occupy themselves here while Mama works during the rush?"

"Yes."

He pointed at the phone, which hung on the wall behind the counter. "Call her."

Smiling, Rae obeyed.

Barbara answered on the first ring. "Hello?"

"Do you have any objection to schlepping food?" Rae asked.

"I've got three kids," Barbara said. "What do you think I do several times a day anyway? What is it?" Excitement crept into her voice. "Do you know of a job for me?"

"Can you start now?"

"Can you pass up hot dogs for supper?"

Rae eyed a mile-high barbecue sandwich that Mike was

making for one of his customers. "I'll try. Look, bring the kids."

"What?"

"He needs you to work certain hours, and is willing for you to bring the kids while you do it. Now, get over here. He's got people standing in line." Rae gave her the address.

"Give me fifteen minutes," Barbara said, and hung up.

Rae turned back to Mike. "She'll be here as soon as she can. Hey, what are the odds of me getting one of those sandwiches?"

"Can you make your own?"

"Honey, just hand me a roll."

A few minutes later, she had one of those mile-high feasts tucked into a bag ready to go. She even figured out how to ring her own sale on the cash register.

"Hey," Mike said. "You don't have to pay for that. Consider it a finder's fee."

"Don't be silly." On impulse, she looped her arm around his neck and kissed him on the cheek. "You're a doll. And don't worry, I won't ruin your reputation by telling anybody."

The taxi was still waiting for her outside. She glanced down the street and spotted Gabriel's Taurus parked against the curb. She'd half thought Gabriel would have paid the cabbie off and sent him away, but he hadn't. She wasn't sure if she felt relief or disappointment. Something primitively female in her wanted to be desired, pursued, claimed. But self-preservation was a powerful instinct, too, one she intended to listen to more often.

Glancing out the window as the taxi started forward again, she saw the Taurus follow about a block behind. Gabriel stayed at a distance while she got her summons from the lawyer and then headed for home. But as she walked into her apartment building, she saw Gabriel's tall, lean reflection in the glass door.

She waited for him at the elevator. He looked as tempting as sin itself as he strode toward her. She felt her nostrils flare in pure physical reaction.

"Don't waste your time coming upstairs," she said. "I'm only going to be here long enough to collect the dog."

Gabriel smiled. Her eyes were flickering with desire and dismay, and he knew she didn't have a handle on herself at all. Well, that wasn't a surprise; he was feeling rather inside out himself. "I don't mind."

"I'd think you'd want to take the chance of running into Marlene Britton again," she said.

"Can't I count on you to protect me?"

"I left my ruby slippers at home," she said.

His brows went up, and laughter sparkled in his blue crystal eyes. Of course he'd get the Wicked Witch connection; no dust settled on this vice detective's shoulders.

"Of course, you'd like this opportunity to ask Barbara Smithfield a few questions," she said.

"I hadn't thought of that," he said with complete false innocence. "But it's a good idea."

"Too bad," she said with relish. "She's not here."

"Then I'll just talk to you," he replied.

The elevator doors opened, and Rae stepped inside. He came with her, his vitality all but overwhelming the small space. Needing a diversion, she opened the bag from the deli. A powerful waft of barbecued meat filled the elevator.

"Wow," Gabriel said.

"It's mine," she growled.

"When did Mike start doing barbecue?"

She shrugged. "I don't know. But the word has gone out, and half the city wants one of these."

"Me, too," he said. "Come on, sweetheart. Share."

"In your dreams, MacLaren."

The elevator stopped. Gabriel accompanied her to the apartment, then waited while she fished for her keys. Inside, she heard a bark, then the sound of claws scrabbling at the wood.

Rae smiled. Tom the Dog had had time to become territorial about the apartment and those in it, and it was possible he might object to Gabriel's presence. She looked forward to finding out.

The puppy came pouring out the moment Rae opened the door. He did not attack Gabriel. He launched himself at Rae's legs and all but climbed her pants, trying to get to the food bag.

"Traitor," she said. "Ouch!"

Laughing, Gabriel scooped the puppy up from the floor. Tom wriggled madly, trying to lick the detective's face. Gabriel gestured for Rae to precede him inside.

"I knew I was safe," he said. "When I started in vice, my first partner was this craggy old guy who knew every trick in the book. Know how he managed to get into places where we knew there were mean dogs?"

"How?" Rae asked, unable to resist.

"He'd buy a pizza. Pepperoni or sausage. By the time the dogs finished the pizza, they thought he was God."

Rae shook her head and went into the kitchen. Cops, she thought. She divided the sandwich evenly, plopped each half onto a paper plate, then opened the refrigerator to see what liquid offerings were inside.

"What would you like to drink?" she called. "We've got milk, Kool-Aid, ah, Juicy Juice." She glanced up at the doorway. "What the devil is Juicy Juice, anyway?"

"I don't know," he said. "Read the label."

"Food labels scare me. How about some good, old-fashioned cola stuffed to the gills with caffeine and refined sugar?"

He chuckled. "Sounds like heaven."

She filled two tall glasses with ice and cola, balanced a plate carefully on each one and headed for the living room. On the way, she stopped to pick up a bag of sour-cream-and-onion potato chips with her teeth.

"Ah, domesticity," Gabriel said, taking the bag of chips from her with one hand, his meal with the other.

She sat down in the recliner, giving him no chance to get close. Gabriel gave a mental sigh. Maybe it was for the best. He sat on the sofa and looked around, cataloging his surroundings. The kitchen was cramped, but the living room was big and sunny, and the parquet-tile floor gave it personality. The furniture didn't look used at all.

"You don't spend much time here, do you?" he asked.

Rae shrugged. "I'm trying to make a living."

"Is it working?"

"Well enough," she said. "I'm working toward getting my private-investigator's license, and then I can expand my horizons, so to speak."

He sat back, regarding her thoughtfully. "I'm surprised you didn't go into law enforcement."

"I don't like—"

"Cops," he finished for her. "I know."

"I was going to say 'authority,'" she said.

"Ah. Sorry."

They lapsed into silence then. But it was a companionable silence, which surprised Rae. So much of their time together had been spent in feint-and-parry conversation. She might even have enjoyed her meal if the dog hadn't kept staring at her.

She'd never been stared at in quite that way before. Those big blue eyes watched every bite; that pink-brown nose quivered as though he might be able to actually inhale the sandwich from a distance. She felt as though the very air had become thick with doggy desire. Every bite became more and more of an effort.

Gabriel couldn't help but enjoy this. Tough, tenacious Rae Ann Boudreau had been laid low by a wagging stub of a tail. It showed him a new aspect of her. Dogs, kids... She'd gone way above and beyond the call of duty in trying to serve Peter Smithfield. Failing that, she had taken Barbara Smithfield and her kids into her home, apparently without a hope of being repaid.

Obviously, Rae wasn't quite as tough as she'd like everyone to think. A generous heart beat beneath that tough exterior, a heart capable of kindness, loyalty and love.

Try as he might, he couldn't reconcile that woman with the one who'd ruined her husband's career. Things didn't add up. He'd learned long ago that when things didn't add up, he'd better start looking for some new numbers to plug into the equation.

But that could come later. Right now, he was enjoying the sight of her trying to eat in front of that poor, pitiful, master manipulator of a dog, and failing miserably.

"Ignore him," he said. "If you let him start with that stuff now, you'll be dealing with it for the rest of his life."

"How can I ignore him?" she asked. "Look at him."

Gabriel scratched his jaw, eyeing the puppy. He had to admit that the little beast had talent. "You've got to be strong, Rae."

"Yeah, right." She peeled a strip of pork out of her sandwich and held it up. "Is that what you want, you mooch?"

It was. The meat vanished so fast she had to look to make sure her fingers were still there. Great. She'd soothed the savage beast, so to speak. With a sigh, she took another bite.

And realized that those blue eyes had zeroed in again.

"Hey," she said, "you got some."

"Told you so," Gabriel murmured.

Rae nodded. "I get it now," she said. "You've got to resist until the last bite, and only then offer the bribe."

He smiled. "That's one way of looking at it."

Rae smiled back. Then she realized that it had happened again. She was having fun. With Gabriel MacLaren. *Detective* Gabriel MacLaren. This wouldn't do, wouldn't do at all.

She peeled off another strip of pork. "Sit," she said.

Receiving only an ice blue stare for her trouble, she gently pushed the puppy's behind to the floor. "Sit," she said again. The moment she lifted her hand, however, Tom snatched the pork.

"Hey!" she yelped.

Gabriel's deep laugh caught her somewhere in the midsection, taking her breath with it. Against her will, her gaze dropped to his mouth. She wanted to kiss him. Badly.

"You ought to enroll in obedience classes," MacLaren said.

"His or mine?" Rae countered.

"Obviously, he doesn't need classes to train you."

"Very funny," she retorted, rising to her feet, glass in hand. "I need a fill up. What about you?"

Gabriel's gaze traveled the length of her, beginning from her feet and ending at her eyes. It was worth the trip. His hands actually itched, he wanted to touch her so badly.

"Sure," he said, reaching blindly for his glass.

Naturally, he knocked it across the coffee table. He lunged for it, grazed it, juggled it madly for a couple of seconds, then lost it again. It crashed to the floor, sending shards of glass spraying across the wood. Momentum carried his arm downward, and his palm landed squarely in the broken glass.

"Oh, hell," he growled.

Rae reached for him. "Let me see."

He lifted his hand. For a moment, all Rae saw was blood. Her heart lurched crazily.

"It's okay," he said.

"Come here," she ordered, grasping him by the wrist and hauling him toward the bathroom.

She turned on the cold water and held his hand under it. Soon, the bleeding eased. He had several cuts on his palm, but none seemed to need stitches. Her heartbeat steadied.

"It doesn't look too bad," she said, carefully extracting a small, wedge-shaped sliver of glass.

He peered at the wounds. "I told you it was okay."

Reaction set in then. She let his hand go, not wanting him to feel the tremor that had begun in her arms. He'd really gotten to her. She'd never been a squeamish woman, but the thought of him getting hurt had truly upset her.

She reached up to open the door of the medicine cabinet. "Let's see what kind of disinfectant I have up here... Ah, here it is!" she said, spotting the hydrogen peroxide.

"I'll do it," he said. "You'd better clean up that glass before the puppy gets into it."

That got her out into the living room at top speed. But she found that Tom the Dog hadn't bothered with the glass. He had, however, polished off the remains of both sandwiches.

"Everything okay out there?" Gabriel called.

"Yes," she replied.

In one encompassing glance, she took in both the room and the situation. This was her chance. She needed space from Gabriel, time to get her emotions back into some sort of balance. If she stayed, if he looked at her, touched her...she'd be lost.

This wasn't rational, for she knew Gabriel would find her. But it was a powerful instinct, and she'd learned long ago to listen to such things. She picked the puppy up and tucked him under her arm like a football. Then, retrieving the leash and her purse, she slipped out of the apartment.

"Let's go for a walk, baby," she crooned to the puppy.

For once, luck was with her. The elevator was on the floor below, and headed up. She stabbed the Call button just in time.

The doors opened, and she found herself face-to-face with her worst nightmare: Marlene Britton.

"Rae, sweetie, how have you been?" Marlene gushed in her smarmiest voice as she stepped out.

Rae hustled onto the elevator and hit the Lobby button. "Got to run, Marlene." Sudden inspiration hit then, and she held the door to keep it from closing. "Oh, by the way, I left Detective MacLaren all alone at my place. You wouldn't mind looking in on him for me, would you?"

"Not at all." Marlene preened like a cockatiel.

"Thank you *so* much," Rae cooed. "Bye, now."

She didn't start smiling until the elevator doors were safely closed. Oh, this was good! On a scale of ten, it had to be at least a twelve and a half.

"Mommy's good," she told the puppy. "Mommy's very good."

She took the summons out of her purse and slipped it into her pants pocket. The address it gave was only a few blocks from here, so she thought she'd mosey over and see about serving it.

Quickly, she hooked the leash onto Tom's collar. He instantly darted out to the extreme end of the lead, tugging against the restraint. Since he took the direction she wanted to take anyway, she let him pull her along.

"Looks like I'm going to have to consider getting a pair of Rollerblades, huh?" she asked. Then, as he stopped to investigate a nearby tree, she amended. "Or maybe not."

In the end, she carried him. Every bush, every tree, was a distraction. So were lampposts, parking meters, benches, street signs and, most especially, garbage cans. Tomorrow was trash pickup day, so there were a lot of garbage cans.

Finally, however, she reached her destination. Perhaps as consolation for the vagaries of the trip over, she arrived just as her quarry pulled up in his driveway. This was too good. Rae walked right up to him as he got out of his car.

"Mr. Dillard, I've got some legal papers for you," she said, thrusting them into his hands.

With a curse, he tossed the summons onto the driveway. Then he took a swing at her. Rae ducked, actually feeling a breeze as his fist just missed her face.

"Hey, if you've got a problem, take it up with the judge," she said.

His face creased with fury, and he cocked his fist again. Rae backpedaled, shielding the puppy with her body. She was willing to forgive and forget, but also willing to kick Dillard's kneecap into the next universe if he kept coming.

Suddenly, Gabriel appeared out of nowhere. Slamming into the man, he bore him backward against the car. "Police," he snarled. "Put your hands on the back of your neck. Now!"

Dillard slowly raised his hands and clasped them on the back of his neck. Gabriel slapped handcuffs on him. Once the man was immobilized, Gabriel glanced over his shoulder at Rae. "Are you all right?"

"Yes," she said.

Tom the Dog growled, and Rae realized he'd been growling since Dillard had first thrown the papers. She lifted the puppy up to comfort him. Tom, however, wasn't upset. He was mad. The hair on his back stood straight up, making him look twice his size, and those ice blue eyes were fixed on Dillard's throat.

Actually, now that she'd noticed, the dog's expression was

awfully similar to Gabriel's. She'd better get them both out of here before something happened to Dillard.

"I'm not going to press charges," she said.

Gabriel struggled to contain his anger. Something had clicked in him when he'd seen the guy take a swing at her, something powerful and very uncivilized. Simply, he'd wanted to tear the other man's arms out of the sockets.

"Are you sure you want to let this go?" he asked.

"It goes with the job," she said.

A muscle jumped spasmodically in his jaw. He made a very dark and brooding guardian angel, she thought, but he'd certainly been that tonight. She went to him, laying one hand on his forearm. It was iron hard beneath her palm, every muscle taut and ready.

"Let it go, Gabriel," she said.

He let his breath out in a long sigh. "All right," he growled. "But only because you asked. If I had my druthers, I'd use his face to put a nice shine on that car."

Sheesh, Rae thought. Men! Get that testosterone pumping, and they reverted to regular caveman status. She rolled her eyes. Now that she'd served Dillard his summons, he was no longer her concern. And she wasn't interested in dealing with primitive male posturing and chest beating.

Gabriel took the handcuffs off Dillard. He didn't want to. He wanted Dillard to pay for trying to hurt Rae, and he wanted to be the one to collect the debt. Because of the extreme violence of his emotions, he sternly controlled his temper.

"This is your lucky night, pal," he growled.

"Go to hell," Dillard snarled.

MacLaren reached for him. Rae smoothly stepped between them, easing Dillard back with a deft bump of her hip. If she didn't get these two apart, there'd be a fistfight for sure.

"Forget it," she said, stiff-arming Gabriel toward the road.

"I don't want to forget it."

"Look—"

"*You* look," he snapped. "I see that bastard take a swing at you and you expect me to be Mr. Sweetness and Light?"

She scowled, her own temper flaming to high. "I expect you to let me mind my own business. Before you came in, flexing your muscles and beating your chest, I had things under control—"

"Under control?" he echoed incredulously.

"Yes, under control," she retorted. "I'd already done what I needed to do here. I'm not some hormone-laden male who thinks it's fun to get dragged into a fight by some two-bit jerk—"

"Right," he growled. "But you think it's fun to sic that razor-clawed female on me—"

"Oh, so *that's* what's really bugging you," she said.

His eyes narrowed. "You conned me."

"Did I promise not to leave?" she countered. "Did I promise you a cozy night watching sitcoms?"

An engine roared to life behind them. Rae got one pulse-thumping glance at two glaring red taillights hurtling toward her. Then Gabriel flung her out of the way. She clutched the puppy to her chest as she reeled, off balance, then went down backward over a nearby trash can.

Tires screeched and squealed. Then she heard the sickening crunch of metal as the car hit something.

"Gabriel!" she shrieked.

Chapter 12

Still clutching the puppy to her chest, Rae leapt to her feet. Terror ran in icy torrents through her veins. There was only one thought in her mind, one concern: Gabriel. If anything had happened to him, she'd…she'd…

Dillard had backed his car into the lamppost opposite his driveway. Even as she registered that, the man smoked his tires as he slammed the car into Drive and took off down the street. The open trunk lid flapped with every bump, looking for all the world like a wide-open, laughing mouth. There was no sign of Gabriel.

"MacLaren," Rae screamed. "Gabriel!"

A dark silhouette darted out from the bushes across the street, and her heart gave a huge leap. Gabriel. Light glinted off the gun in his hand. But Dillard was already fishtailing around the corner, and a moment later disappeared.

Rae's breath went out all at once. He was all right. Oh, God, he was all right.

He worked the slide on his gun, ejecting the chambered round, and catching it in midair with a deftness that spoke of long practice. Watching him, so big and lean and capable,

Rae was possessed by a wash of joy almost too big for her to contain. She took a deep breath, then another. She had to get this under control. But it grew bigger and more powerful with every beat of her heart, and there was nothing she could do to stop it. It shook her, possessed her, made her tremble.

She loved him. So much, so much.

He turned to look at her. Their gazes locked for a long, frozen moment, and she found herself trapped in his eyes. Those pale blue depths burned with anger, frustration, concern...and something else, something that made her legs turn weak.

Then he strode toward her. Her heart twisted from side to side as though it wanted to tear free of its moorings. He stopped in front of her, running his hands along her shoulders and down her arms as though to reassure himself she was really there. Rae understood. Adrenaline raced in hot spurts through her body, reaction to the danger, or perhaps only to the man.

"You're all right?" he asked.

She nodded. "You?"

"Yeah. I tore my shirt jumping into the bushes, though."

Smiling crookedly, he hooked one finger into a triangular tear right over his breastbone. Rae's nostrils flared. She didn't know what came over her then. It was reckless and stupid, and would surely cost her dearly. But she had no choice. She slid two fingers into the tear and laid them on his chest. His skin was hot. The heavy thump of his heart seemed to enter her through her fingertips, and her own pulse rate quickened to match his.

Even in this tricky light, she saw his pupils dilate. Heat licked along her limbs, pooled deep in her body. A now-familiar ache settled at her core, an ache she knew he could ease.

"Rae," he said, "I don't know what this is between us, but I'm upside down and dizzy with it. I can't get my balance."

She smiled up at him. There was nothing complicated in her feelings just now, nor was there any confusion. She'd almost lost him tonight. No loss, no pain, could possibly be worse. And at least for now, nothing less frightened her.

For once, everything seemed simple. She wanted him. Needed him. Tomorrow would come soon enough. But tonight, she wasn't going to think about anything but touching him and being touched.

"Please," she whispered. "Hold me."

He gathered her in, shifting the puppy so that he wouldn't be squashed between them. Rae leaned into Gabriel's hard strength, absorbing his warmth, letting herself be comforted by the strong, steady beat of his heart against her cheek. For the first time, she didn't feel as though she'd be giving up something of herself in order to be with him. Simply, this was the man she loved. In the aftermath of almost losing him, nothing else seemed to matter.

"Gabriel..." She let her voice trail away, not knowing quite what she wanted to say. Maybe the right words didn't exist.

"What?" he murmured, his breath hot against her temple.

"I..." Still unable to find the right words, she leaned her forehead against his chest. His skin smelled of soap and musk, an excitingly male aura that was uniquely MacLaren. She knew that scent, reacted to it as though it had become imprinted in every cell in her body.

Gabriel gently combed his hand through her hair. Whatever else she might be, Rae Ann Boudreau was unique. From the moment he'd met her, he'd been an emotional spinning top. Desire and fury, tenderness and frustration... She'd wound him up, whirled him around, and he didn't think he'd ever be the same again.

Even when he'd been angriest at her, during that black moment when she'd conned him into bed to distract him from Peter Smithfield, he hadn't been able to keep from admiring her spirit. All right, he amended, sheer gall.

He'd been so mad at her for setting him up like that. And he would have done exactly the same had he been in her shoes. He couldn't laugh then. But he could now, and did.

"What's so funny?" she demanded.

Still chuckling, Gabriel let his hand drift along the line of her jaw. She tried to be so tough, but a moment ago, her eyes had held such emotion that it had stunned him. He tilted her chin up so that her face was turned more fully into the light.

"You know, I haven't been afraid for a long time," he said, curving his hand around the smooth column of her neck. "But tonight, when I thought you might get hurt, I learned what it was like to be frightened again."

Rae closed her eyes against a sudden upwelling of tears. A day ago, an hour ago, she wouldn't have been able to admit those feelings. But he'd had the courage to face it, and to tell her.

And because of that, she found the courage to do the same.

"I was afraid, too," she whispered. "I ah, I..."

"Say it," he said. "I need to hear it from you."

She opened her eyes. There, in the face of his honesty, she could hold nothing back. "I was afraid for you. If anything had happened to you, I...I don't know what I would have done."

There. She'd said it. She'd laid herself bare, and in doing so had given him a power over her she'd never given another human being. It frightened her, but it also set her free. It was a reckless sort of freedom, but infinitely exciting.

"Come home with me," he said.

There was such need in his eyes. Open, honest, naked. Desire so deep and hot it made her tremble inside. "Yes."

Nothing more needed to be said. He put his arm around her waist and turned her toward home. She let Tom the Dog investigate anything that interested him, since Gabriel tended to kiss her during any pause in their walk.

Finally, they reached her street. Rae picked the puppy up and ruffled his ears. "I hate to leave him alone again—"

"So bring him along," Gabriel said. "Anybody who growls at...what was that guy's name?"

"Dillard. Stanley Dillard."

Gabriel's brows went up. "Stanley? Well, anyway, Tom showed remarkable good judgment in wanting to bite that bastard, and I consider him a friend for it. The dog, not the bastard.''

"He's not exactly housebroken—"

"I don't care. I want you, I want you now. No, I want you ten minutes ago, and I'm gonna die if I don't get you alone soon.''

"Are you sure—?"

"Get in the car, Rae."

She gazed up at him through her eyelashes. "You know, this conversation is beginning to sound awfully familiar—"

"Get in the car."

There was something very compelling in being desired so very much, Rae thought. This was a woman's ultimate power over a man, and it was a heady thing. She bent down to pick Tom up. Then she straightened, looked directly into Gabriel's eyes and smiled.

He drew his breath in with a hiss. Sliding his hand around to the back of her neck, he pulled her against him. She felt as though an ocean wave had hit her from behind, tumbling her end over end until she didn't know up from down. For a moment, she was actually afraid of losing her balance.

"Come with me," he whispered.

She'd have gone anywhere. "Take me," she said.

He let his hand slide from her neck to her shoulder, then down her arm. She shivered as his fingers curled around her wrist in a hold that was both erotic and possessive. Her heart slammed against her ribs as he drew her to the car.

The puppy curled up on the seat beside her and went to sleep. Gabriel put the Taurus into gear. Rae found herself leaning toward him, her body drawn to him as though tugged by a string.

"You're beautiful," he said.

"I'm not," she replied. "But I'm glad you like me."

He turned his head to look at her, and kept his gaze on her so long she became concerned.

"Don't you think you ought to look at the road occasionally?" she asked.

"Once in a while, it would help," he agreed, shooting a

brief glance at the traffic. "How can you say you're not beautiful?"

"Come on. I've got eyes and a mirror."

He smiled at her, another of those crooked, tender grins that made her insides leap and quiver. "Ah, darlin', you have so much to learn."

"About men?"

"About yourself."

He steered around a parked delivery van, apparently by ESP since he didn't appear to be watching the road. Rae turned his head so that he was facing forward.

"Am I making you nervous?" he asked.

"Very."

"That's good," he said.

Rae held her breath as he reached over, laying his hand on her knee. She hadn't realized that the knee was an erogenous zone. But then, when Gabriel touched her, her whole body became an erogenous zone. She reached across with her right hand and twined her fingers with his.

Of its own volition, her thumb began to move, caressing the side of his thumb. Up and down, lightly, seductively. She liked the friction, the contact and the way his breathing changed. The temperature of his skin went up. Oh, boy.

He moved his hand upward, spreading his fingers so that they slid along the inside of her thigh. His touch seared her, and for a moment she thought she might slide right off the seat.

"Oh," she breathed.

Gabriel was really having trouble keeping his attention on the road. His whole being was centered on Rae, her responsiveness, her heat, the tiny, aroused movements her body was making. He loved the way she felt under his hand.

A few minutes, he told himself. Just a couple of blocks more.

He'd always prided himself on his iron control over his emotions and his actions, but now, under the lash of his desire for this woman, he was losing it. And he wasn't going to be satisfied until he'd brought her to an equal state of recklessness.

Holding his breath, he let his hand drift farther up her thigh. She made a small, constricted sound deep in her throat, and it sounded just like heaven. Her leg quivered beneath his hand. Then she shifted, spreading her legs apart to give him access to what he wanted.

"Oh, woman," he muttered.

And then he cupped her, possessing her heat. Her hips bucked, pressing her more firmly against his hand. It was all he could do not to stop the car and take her right here, right now.

He didn't know what to call this thing between them. But it was powerful, stirring, more intense than anything he'd ever felt. The moment he'd met her, he'd stepped into an emotional whirlwind, a jolting, uncontrolled roller coaster of the soul.

Rae let her head fall back against the seat as Gabriel caressed her. Some kind of madness seemed to have claimed her, making her feel hot and cold, reckless and frightened all at the same time. This was too big to be contained, too crazy to be understood or explained.

"I'm going to taste every inch of your skin," he said, his voice hoarse with arousal. "I'm going to love you, touch you, take you, make you scream."

Rae drew her breath in with a hiss, unbearably aroused by his words. It was no idle threat. During that sultry, magical night at the hotel, he had loved her, touched her and taken her until she had screamed his name.

She made a soft sound of protest when he pulled away, and reached out to bring him back. Instead, he captured her hand and brought it to his mouth. He licked her fingertips slowly, one by one, his tongue hot and excitingly rough against her skin.

"Do you like that?" he murmured.

"I like that. I like everything you do."

Rae took his hand and brought it to her lips. He rubbed the pad of his thumb along her upper lip, then her lower. She opened her mouth, letting him slip his forefinger in. Out. In again.

"Ah, Rae," he groaned.

He swung the car in a tight left turn, and hit the button on the garage-door opener strapped to his visor. The headlights spotlighted a white paneled door sliding up out of the way. Rae registered a standard cookie-cutter town house: two story, brick-and-vinyl-siding construction.

Gabriel pulled the Taurus into the garage and hit the remote again, sealing them into privacy—and the magic of the night. Rae turned toward him. He stroked her face with gentle fingertips, then reached across her to scoop the sleeping puppy off the seat.

"If we don't go in now, we'll never get out of this car," he said.

Rae got out in a hurry. Gabriel followed her inside. The door opened directly into the kitchen, which was as bland and conventional as the outside of the town house. It was tidy, however, so unlike her own haphazard housekeeping. An antique oak table occupied the eating area, its much-polished surface gleaming in the light from the overhead lamp.

"Nice," she said.

Gabriel cupped her cheek in his hand, his thumb straying to slide across her lower lip. Reaction jolted down to her toes, and her eyelids began to drift downward. Then Tom the Dog woke with a snort, and whined to get down.

Chuckling, Gabriel set him on the floor. "Go get 'em, tiger."

Tom went exploring, his nails clicking on the floor. Gabriel filled a bowl with water, and set it down for the dog. Then he came to Rae, reaching out with one long arm to pull her against him.

"Now," he said, "you're mine."

"Got a bill of sale?" she countered.

"Yeah. Right here," he said, claiming her mouth.

The kiss was tempestuous, thorough and not the least bit gentle. It was as elemental as nature itself, as untamed as a thunderstorm, as devastating as a Class 4 hurricane. Rae clutched him, holding on as though he were the only thing anchoring her. Finally, when her limbs had gone rubbery and her breath went swift and shallow, he raised his head and gazed straight into her eyes.

"You're mine," he said again.

Rae wasn't inclined to dispute his claim just now. Her emotions were as tangled as her thoughts, and her body seemed to be agreeing enthusiastically with everything he said. So she just smiled and slid her hand into his hair, making a claim of her own.

His eyes darkened as he reacted to her touch. He pulled her top off, flinging it over his shoulder to land in a tawny pool on the linoleum. Her bra followed a moment later. Crazy to get to his skin, she tugged his shirt up over his head.

He stilled for a moment, his gaze burning into hers. Then, slowly, exquisitely, he fitted her to him. Skin to skin, softness to hardness, they matched. His hands seemed to be everywhere, leaving fire wherever they went. Rae cried out softly with arousal, and he drank the sound in as though it were wine.

"Yes," he rasped. "Rae."

She arched her back as he deftly unbuttoned her pants and eased the zipper down. His hands were hot as he slid them beneath her panties. He caressed the smooth curves of her behind, cupping her. Then he dipped lower, sliding two fingers into the secret heat between her legs. For a moment, Rae felt completely molten, even her bones melting into the sweet, liquid heat of passion. She was so aroused that she hardly registered movement as he picked her up and carried her to the kitchen table.

The wood was cool against her back, but Gabriel's hands were hot as he claimed her breasts. He caressed her knowingly, excitingly, running his thumbs around her nipples until they swelled into tight peaks. Rae wanted more, more. She ran her hands down the hard-muscled length of his arms and up again.

"Come here," she pleaded.

But instead, he straightened. For a moment, she thought he

planned to leave her, and dismay landed hard in the pit of her stomach. Then he met her gaze, and the tenderness in his eyes washed away all her fears.

Still holding her gaze, he slowly worked her pants down her legs and tossed them away. He held her hips for a moment, just looking at her. Again, he made her feel beautiful. Again, he made her feel sexy and desired, and she wanted only for him to keep touching her forever.

He worked her panties down, kissing every inch of skin as it was exposed. Finally, she lay naked before him. His mouth was demanding as he kissed her, a man's primitive claim of a woman. His woman. In accepting it, she became his. Completely, totally. And he became hers. She could feel it in his kiss, the tension in his body, the way his hands trembled when he touched her.

He licked a hot, wet path down her neck, pausing to dip his tongue into the hollow at the base of her throat. His hands roved her body, stroking her hips, her belly, caressing her breasts until they swelled. And still she wanted more. With a soft moan, she sank her hands into his hair.

He raised his head and looked at her.

"What do you want, Rae?" he murmured against her skin.

"Everything," she said.

He laughed softly, cupping her breasts in his hands, mounding them as he lowered his head. Rae rolled her head from side to side in extravagant arousal as he laved her nipples, first one, then the other. Teasing her. Preparing her for more. She couldn't stand it, couldn't wait. Slowly, he drew one nipple into his mouth. Rae cried out in sheer voluptuous pleasure.

Ah, but he had more for her, much more. He played with her breasts until she writhed helplessly. Then he moved lower, sliding his tongue into her navel, then claimed the core of her. Rae could only gasp, and respond. He took her higher, higher, seeming to know everything she wanted, everything she needed.

And then the exquisite rushing pleasure swept her away. She cried his name, completely lost in the shuddering climax.

As she drifted in the aftermath, he entered her. She didn't question how he'd gotten rid of his clothes, or how he knew exactly the right moment to claim her. She only knew that he was there, and she wanted him more than anything else in the world.

His eyes had narrowed to ice blue slits. This was no civilized lover, one ruled by technique. No, Gabriel MacLaren made love with all the wildness of a tornado. His passion was uncontrollable, irresistible.

Rae wanted it all. This was passion as she'd never experienced before, and it set her free. Her world narrowed to encompass him, only him. He would take her to the heights, and he would keep her safe. His movements grew deeper, stronger, and Rae could only hold on as he drove them both straight up toward heaven.

They reached it together, an incredible sharing of passion that left them both gasping and stunned.

He collapsed against her. Rae closed her eyes, enjoying the feel of his strong shoulders beneath her palm. He shuddered, pressing his open mouth against the skin of her neck.

"Rae," he muttered hoarsely. "Rae."

She stroked his hair back from his face. He lifted his head to gaze down at her with eyes hazed with satiation, then leaned down to kiss her tenderly.

"I—" she began.

"Shh." He laid his hand over her mouth. "This was magic. Don't question what's happening here. Just accept it. Even if just for tonight."

"Is that enough?" she asked.

"This is more than I've ever had before," he said. "More than I ever expected. More than I ever imagined."

Stirred by his words, she reached up and traced the hard, sensual line of his mouth. Maybe he was right. Maybe they could have this precious, magical time, and use it to carve something still more precious for themselves.

Because she loved him, she let herself believe. Only because she loved him.

"The table was nice," she murmured, "But—"

"But it's time we moved upstairs," he finished for her.

She put her arms around his neck. "Yes."

The phone rang at five the next morning. Gabriel answered groggily, but roused quickly when he heard his partner's voice.

"Get to down to the station ASAP," Eddy said. "Smith-field got away. Slithered out the bathroom window and climbed two floors down a damned drainpipe."

With a muttered curse, Gabriel flung his covers aside. "I'm on my way."

"Wait, there's—"

"I'll meet you in Petrosky's office," Gabriel said, tossing the receiver into the cradle.

Rae sat up. "What is it?" she asked.

"Work," he replied. "Go back to sleep."

"You can turn on the light," she said.

"Don't need it." He got out of bed and instantly stubbed his toe on the dresser. "Damn," he muttered.

"You don't need the light," she said.

He chuckled. "Another woman would have said 'I told you so.'"

"I'm not another woman."

"Darlin', that was the first thing I noticed about you. Maybe it was the belly dancing costume."

Still chuckling, Gabriel limped over to the closet and flicked the light switch. He found Rae quite a delectable sight first thing in the morning, curved and feminine and infinitely desirable, her hair sleep tousled, her skin gleaming like smooth ivory satin. Then she opened her eyes, and looked at him. His heart did another of those curious flip-flops.

Damn. Whatever this thing was between them, he'd fallen fathoms deep. And he didn't think he'd ever come up again.

Quite a revelation for a guy who'd managed to stay emotionally remote for most of his adult life. But Rae—tough, stubborn, infuriating, beautiful, passionate Rae—had shaken the very foundations of his soul. Simply, he was a goner.

"Damn," he muttered.

"What's wrong?" she asked.

"Nothing's wrong," he said, pulling his clothes on with efficient haste. "It's just that I'd rather stay here with you, and I won't be able to."

"Hey, look on the bright side," she replied. "Maybe they'll tell you not to follow me anymore."

"Darlin', I'd follow you to the moon and back again, and not because of orders," he said.

He sat down on the bed to tie his shoes. That was nearly his undoing, because it put Rae within arm's reach. Of course, he had to kiss her goodbye. Of course, the kiss lasted about ten minutes and got him so aroused he thought he might die of it.

"I've got to go," he groaned. "I'll see you later."

"At the office," she said. "I've got a job to do, too."

Gabriel felt as though he were floating as he drove down to the station. Morning traffic was still fairly light at this hour, and he made good time.

He knew something was wrong the moment he walked into vice. Nobody insulted him, nobody called out ribald jokes. As he passed the desk of one of the other detectives, he quirked one eyebrow questioningly.

"Petrosky's in the hospital. Appendix," the man said, keeping his voice low. "We've got—"

"MacLaren!" someone else called.

Gabriel couldn't place the voice. The other detective scribbled something on a notepad and held it up.

"Roth," Gabriel growled, recognizing the name of an up-and-coming lieutenant from the next precinct. "He's subbing for Petrosky? Oh, brother."

The other detective nodded. Roth had the reputation of being a real political hack. He'd probably go far—on the backs of better men.

"MacLaren," Roth called again, "I want to talk to you."

"Wish me luck," Gabriel whispered to the grinning detective.

Roth sat behind Captain Petrosky's desk as though he owned it. Gabriel disliked him instantly. The man had a weasel-clever look and a weak chin, and didn't offer to shake hands.

"Detective MacLaren," Roth said.

"That's me," Gabriel replied.

Roth's dark eyes turned as hard as pebbles. "Put your gun on your badge there on the desk—"

"*What?*"

"You're suspended." With obvious satisfaction, Roth added, "Without pay, pending investigation."

"What the hell are you talking about?" Gabriel demanded.

"We've had a complaint about you, Detective. Now, I don't mind if a fellow strays from the straight and narrow once in a while, but when I get a call that you've been sexually harassing the subject of a police surveillance, I'm forced to act."

Gabriel struggled to make his mind work through a haze of numbness. "Rae Boudreau?

"Rae Boudreau."

Something cold and hard and very heavy dropped into Gabriel's stomach. "I should have known," he muttered under his breath. "I should have known. With this, she took me right out of the game."

Roth pointed to the desk. "Internal affairs will be in touch. The gun and the badge, Detective."

Gabriel laid them down on the desk gently, barely repressing the urge to throw them both through the window. Without another word, he turned and stalked out of the office.

She'd done it again, he thought. Rae Ann. She'd sabotaged him just the way she'd sunk her ex-husband. Damn her. *Damn* her!

Brett Wilson came in just as Gabriel went out, almost getting himself mowed down. "Hey, MacLaren, what's up?"

"I just got myself suspended."

"Let me guess," Brett said. "Rae Boudreau."

"In spades."

Brett Wilson shook his head. "That woman is poison. You get between her and what she wants, she'll ruin your life."

With a wordless growl, Gabriel turned and strode away.

The other man called something after him, but he was in too much of a hurry to listen.

Damn, he'd been stupid. To Rae, feelings were just another token in the game. Something to be used. Something to be spent to gain advantage. And she'd done it twice. How did that saying go? "Fool me once, shame on you. Fool me twice, shame on me."

"Never again," he said.

This time, two people were playing. And he intended to win.

Chapter 13

Rae worked at her computer while Tom the Dog chewed an old tennis shoe nearby.

"I'm going to have to train you to serve subpoenas," she said. "Make you earn your keep."

The puppy looked up at her. His long pink tongue lolled from the side of his mouth, and his pale eyes danced with happiness.

"Gawd," she muttered. "I have to work my fanny off to make a living, and all he's got to do is look cute, and I'm willing—no, *eager*—to feed him and house him and pet his head. Oh, brother."

She stiffened suddenly as someone tried the door. Ordinarily, she didn't lock herself in. But after receiving that bribe, she wasn't inclined to leave her back unprotected. Taking her .380 out of her purse, she slid it into the back waistband of her jeans and walked noiselessly to the door.

"It's me," Gabriel said.

She unlocked the door and swung it open. He stood in the hallway, looking as lean and dangerous as a leopard. Her heart leapt, and for a moment she thought she might float away on a swift-running river of happiness.

Then she looked into his eyes. They were as flat and unemotional as glacial ice. It had happened again. The man who had made love to her with such tenderness and passion was gone, leaving only MacLaren the vice cop. Cold. Hard. Unreadable.

Last night, he had given her everything. Now, in the hot, hard light of day, he was going to take it all away again. She didn't know why; she only knew that her joy shriveled like cotton candy in a hailstorm.

As always, she only knew one way to deal with things: straight on. "What is it?" she asked.

He walked past her into the office. Tongue lolling, Tom the Dog bounded to meet him. Gabriel bent and picked the puppy up, then turned to face Rae again. His hands were very gentle as he petted the dog, but his eyes were savage.

"I've been suspended."

"What?"

"What part of 'I've been suspended' don't you understand?"

"None of it," she said. "Why would they suspend you?"

His brows contracted. "Let me explain it to you. This morning when I reported in, the acting captain demanded my gun and badge pending investigation."

A great wave of relief washed through her. *That* was why he seemed so fierce this morning. Not her, not them.

"I'm sorry," she said, taking a step closer to him. "But it has to be okay. You're a good cop, and they know it. This has got to be some kind of misunderstanding—"

"Oh, they understand," he said. "And so do I."

His voice held a note of icy disdain she'd never heard before, and her stomach clenched with sudden dread.

"What do you mean?"

"Come on, Rae. I'm tired of playing this game with you. Someone called in a complaint, saying that I was harassing you. Now I'm off the case. Very convenient, don't you think?"

"You…" Rae took a deep breath as a stunning wave of pain stabbed through her. "You think I did it."

"You're a smart girl, honey-child. You always take the most direct route to get what you want, don't you? As your ex-husband can testify."

Rae's breath went out all at once, and she felt as though someone had punched her in the stomach. She didn't want to believe this. She *couldn't* believe it. "Wh-what did you say?"

"I know what you did to your ex-husband," he said. "Did you think somebody wouldn't tell me? Hey, from what I heard, he loved being a cop. Now he's selling insurance somewhere."

"And of course it was my fault," she said.

He spun away from her and went to look out the window. His shoulders were stiff, the line of his back completely uncompromising. Not that Rae would have asked for it. Not now.

"You think that I made love to you as a ploy," she said. "And once you were lulled, I called in and sabotaged you."

"Is there a reason why I shouldn't think that?" he asked.

Rae could deny the charge. He might even believe her. But would it matter, really? "No reason," she said. "No reason at all."

Her heart congealed into a tight knot. He hadn't believed in her. He hadn't even suspended judgment long enough to ask for her side of the story. No, he'd believed the worst, simply because another cop had told him, and cops always stuck together.

Well, she'd given Gabriel MacLaren more of herself than she'd ever thought she could, and he'd *missed* it. He'd made love to her, explored every inch of her body and captured her heart, and he had no idea who she was.

There was no point in loving a cop. Ever.

And MacLaren, blind, arrogant MacLaren, stood with Tom the Dog comfortably cradled in one big hand, and the puppy had fallen sound asleep. Rae's treacherous heart went bouncing all over her chest. The man had such capacity for kindness, for gentleness. But no faith, at least in human beings.

Somewhere in his tenure in vice, he'd lost the capacity to believe in people.

"Is that all you have to say?" he asked.

"Yes!" she cried.

Tom the Dog woke, blinking eyes so nearly the color of Gabriel's that Rae's heart lurched again. But she wasn't about to give in to lurches of the heart—or anything else.

"You woke him up," Gabriel complained.

"That's okay. You woke *me* up, and that's a good thing."

Gabriel knew she was angry. No, not angry—furious. And she wanted to fight. Fine. He could use a good argument. Anger was good. Anger, he could deal with.

"Come on, Rae," he growled. "Get it out."

She wasn't sure for a moment whether she wanted to scream or throw something. "You're an arrogant ass, MacLaren," she said. "You're so damned sure you're right that you don't bother to look at what's around you."

"I know a bad deal when I see one," he retorted.

"Maybe, but you wouldn't know a good one if it bit you."

Gabriel couldn't believe her. She stood there in front of him bold as brass, acting as though her feelings had been hurt. This was incredible, absolutely incredible. Hell, *he* was the one who'd gotten conned all along the line. If anyone had the right to a little indignation, he was.

"Don't come off all huffy and hurt," he growled. "I'm the one who got suspended."

She looked him up and down. "Let me ask you something, MacLaren. Did somebody actually say that I was the one who called in that complaint?"

"Who else had a motive to get rid of me?"

"Just about everyone who knows you, I'd say," she snarled.

"Well, did you?"

"Wrong question," she said. "And really, really wrong time."

"Answer it anyway."

Rae wasn't going to give it to him. She wasn't about to

give him the tiniest little thing. "Uh-uh, Mr. Jump To Conclusions. I don't give a rip what you think of me."

"No?"

"No!"

They stood without speaking, just glaring at each other. Rae's anger ebbed and died in the silence. She wanted to keep it, for it kept the heartache at bay. Now she only wanted to cry.

"This is going nowhere," she said, her voice shaking just a little. "You think what you think, and you know what you know. I see no point in continuing this conversation."

"You listen to me, Rae Ann—"

"I'm through listening." She stalked to the door and wrenched it open. "You can go straight to hell, and take your bloody conclusions with you."

His mouth curled in that cold, cynical cop's grin. She didn't know why he couldn't *see* her. Yes, she did. He was a cop. He'd seen the worst of humanity every day, year after year, and he no longer had faith in people. He couldn't trust her. He probably never would. And without trust, there was no hope for them.

"It would be best for us both if you'd just go," she said.

Gabriel nodded, acknowledging that point. To be honest, at least with himself, he had to admit that he wasn't absolutely sure he *could* walk out that door knowing he'd never see her again.

Fortunately, there was another reason for him to stay. A reason that didn't put his feelings on the line. Or his pride.

"Peter Smithfield walked away from protective custody early this morning," he said.

Aha! Rae thought, instantly sifting the possibilities. And not liking any of them. "I expected he might do that."

"And that's why I had to be out of the way."

Damn you. "So you figured I called in the complaint."

"It adds up better than anything else," he replied.

I love you. Probably always will, because I'm the biggest fool around. She studied him with narrowed eyes. "And?"

"I no longer have official sanction to investigate this case."

"So take a vacation."

He smiled again, a razor-swift flash of teeth that made her instantly suspicious. She had the sudden, skin-prickling feeling that this was going to cost her.

"This is my case, and I intend to work on it. They can take that suspension and put it where the sun don't shine."

"What's that got to do with me?"

"Right now, you've got much better resources than I do."

She blinked in sheer astonishment. And then surprise turned to dismay, and she nearly bolted out of her chair. "No. Uh-uh. No way, not in a million years—"

"You stuck it to me, honey-child. And now you're going to help me out of the mess you put me in."

"You're out of your mind."

He nodded. "Absolutely."

"I won't do it."

"Sure, you will," he said with a smile she didn't like at all. "Or else you'll never get rid of me. I'll be your constant companion morning, noon and night. Hey, I'll even sleep in front of your door, like a loyal servant. You'll have to step over me to get your newspaper in the morning."

He meant it, she knew. He meant every word. She had to swallow against a sudden tightening of her throat. It could have been so very different...if he'd had any capacity for trust.

But he didn't.

"You can follow me all you want," she said. "It doesn't mean you can stay with me all the time."

"Sure, you can lose me," he agreed. "But remember, I was able to find you again. And I always will."

Rae didn't want to be with him. She didn't want to lay her heart out every minute of every day, and have him step on it because he simply didn't notice such things.

"Maybe I should just shoot you," she said.

"You wouldn't be the first person who wanted to."

"Now that, I believe."

He smiled at her again. Rae crossed her arms over her chest and studied him from under her lashes. Her feelings had betrayed her too often. The time had come to stop listening to her heart and start listening to her head. And her head told her the best way to be rid of the heartbreak was to find Peter Smithfield.

With the case closed, Gabriel would vanish like smoke in a hurricane. Then she could get on with her life.

Without him.

She felt the loss in her heart, her flesh and in her soul. "Time heals all wounds," or so the saying went. She hoped so. But she'd been given a glimpse of what might have been. For a brief, magical time, she'd experienced true love, romantic love, the sort that captures the spirit and makes the blood sing. She would always remember that, and wonder. If things had been different, if she'd met him under other circumstances, if, if, if...

Then she gave herself a mental shake. *Ifs* didn't get people through life. Guts did. Guts and determination. She'd find Peter Smithfield. But this time, she'd do it on her terms.

"Okay," she said. "But only under certain conditions."

"What conditions?"

"First, you let me serve my summons before you make him disappear again."

"Okay. Now—"

"Don't start giving orders, MacLaren," she snapped. "Or you can spend the next twenty years sitting in your car staring up at my windows."

His brows soared. Rae didn't give him a chance to start talking. If he started in with that bureaucratic baloney again, she might lose her temper and do something they'd both regret.

"I found Smithfield twice," she continued. "But things are harder now. I've got to fight city hall, too. If I'm going to find him again, you have to tell me what's going on."

"I'd planned to," he said amicably enough.

"Huh?"

"When they suspended me, they suspended my orders, too," he explained.

Surprise held her speechless for a moment. His eyes had turned hard and grim, but the grimness was self-directed.

"I followed orders because I believed in the man who gave them," he said. "But that man is in the hospital now, and his replacement doesn't know his butt from a hole in the ground."

Mutiny was the last thing she'd expected from him. "You're quite the rugged individualist all of a sudden, aren't you?"

He crossed his arms over his chest. "You had me pegged as some goose-stepping robot who didn't have the brains to think for himself, eh?"

"'Goose-stepping' is a good word for it," she agreed.

He studied her from beneath his brows. She had to admit he looked devastatingly dark, handsome and brooding, and that every cell in her body registered that fact.

"You've got a hell of a lot to learn about men," he said at last. "And especially about me."

Rae put her hands up to ward that one away. "Uh-uh. I've learned all the lessons I can stand."

"What do you mean?"

"I mean that sleeping together was a big mistake—"

"Tell me about it," Gabriel said, scowling. Of course it had been a mistake. He knew that. He just didn't know why it annoyed him so much that she thought so, too.

Rae couldn't keep her temper from sparking again. Damn him, he didn't have to agree! "So," she said through gritted teeth, "I'll help you. But this is a business arrangement, nothing more. You keep your distance, or the deal's off. And afterward, we never have to set eyes on each other again."

"That's fine with me," he growled.

"Good. Then we understand each other."

"Right."

She turned away. It irritated her that he'd agreed to her terms so readily. What do you expect, idiot? that sensible-

Rae voice whispered in her head. Did you think he'd get down on one knee to beg for your love? Sheesh!

Heck, she ought to be relieved that he didn't care. That way, she'd have less temptation.

Sure, right. Look at him, the feminine-Rae voice whispered. Look at the way the light sheens in his hair and the way all those gorgeous muscles ripple when he moves. She ought to have better control of herself. But even after his accusations, his lack of faith in her, she still loved him. It was a visceral, primitive thing, that love, and it wasn't going to leave her alone.

Business, she reminded herself. Strictly business.

"Have a seat," she said, sliding into the chair in front of the computer. "Give me everything you know about Peter Smithfield, no matter how inconsequential it might seem."

Gabriel took one of the armchairs and set it down beside her chair. She swiveled to face him, and they were so close that their knees touched. His chest constricted, and it was all he could do not to reach for her. Only business, his— With a muttered expletive, he pushed his chair back a couple of inches.

"This case is political," he said, after clearing his throat. "Real political. That's why everyone is so edgy. One wrong move, and all of us will be out selling insurance."

The last was an oblique reference to her ex-husband. Of course, she got it. For one startling moment, he thought he saw the sheen of tears in her eyes. But it was gone so fast he thought he must have imagined it.

He ran his thumbnail along his jaw. "We've had illegal gambling houses cropping up like mushrooms in this city. We find one, we close it down, and another one pops up a week or two later. You were in one, remember?"

She nodded.

"You saw the setup. A nice house, expensive furnishings, good-quality dealers, high-rolling clientele. Exclusive. You've got to have an invitation to get in. Friends of friends only."

"And Peter Smithfield has a lot of friends?"

"Yup. We busted him on some minor stuff, and found out he had a rap sheet from a few years ago—"

"And used it to coerce him to help you get into those exclusive clubs," Rae said. "Cops!"

"Hey, those are the bad guys, Rae."

"Sure, I believe you. And I also believe that your whole case hinges on some two-bit compulsive gambler just because he can get you invited to the best parties. Not good enough, MacLaren. Tell me something that makes sense."

Gabriel inclined his head, silent compliment to her quick mind. "We think he either knows who's behind the gambling, or knows someone who can lead us to him."

"Did you give him money to gamble with?" she asked.

"That was the deal."

She rolled her eyes. "He conned you. He took your money and had a good time gambling it away, knowing from the beginning that he wasn't going to give that guy up."

"That appears to be the case."

"Hmm." Lost in thought, she gently chewed her bottom lip. "Something doesn't add up. I can't quite put my finger on it, but I've got this itch at the back of my neck that tells me so."

Gabriel watched her mouth in fascination. He'd like to run his tongue along that red, lush flesh. He'd like to— Grimly, he forced himself to think about the business at hand.

"I know that itch," he said. "I get it whenever I'm on a troublesome case. I've learned to pay attention to it."

She nodded, only briefly acknowledging the sudden kinship she felt. She had no business feeling anything for him. "Have you been able to trace who owns any of those houses?" she asked.

"We keep running into dead ends."

Rae cocked her head to one side and regarded him for a moment. Then she smiled. "There are no dead ends, MacLaren. Other than the ones you accept."

"Agreed."

"Okay," she said, turning to the computer and turning it on. "There might be something in the case file that could help us, maybe something you didn't see because you were looking for something else.''

"Happens all the time. Plus, in a case this complex, my partner and I divide up tasks, which also divides our attention. There are times when I'm so busy I don't have time to do more than glance at reports he's written.''

"Is there anything you can think of now?''

Gabriel cast back through the jumbled files of his memory. Most space seemed to be taken up by a woman named Boudreau, who'd seared him to his soul with her fire and her passion. Damn. Then he recalled something in one of his partner's reports that had nagged at him. He'd made a mental note to talk to Drake about it, and had forgotten amid the chaos Rae had brought into his life.

"I had a hunch on one thing, but I can't remember exactly what it was. I'd have to take a look at the file again.''

"Hunches work for me,'' Rae said. "So let's get that file. Will your partner put himself on the line to help you out?''

"He's my partner,'' he said, looking shocked at the question.

Cops always stuck together, Rae thought, her gaze carefully focused on the computer screen lest she give herself away.

"Drake will do anything he can to help,'' MacLaren continued, adding, "if he isn't under suspension, too.''

Rae swiveled to look at him. Her temper spiked heat through her veins, making her reckless. She no longer cared about the deal, or anything but the anger that made her blood burn. "Gee, maybe somebody called in to say he slept with me, too.''

"The complaint wasn't that we slept together, Rae. Only that I harassed you. The blame was only on one side.''

"I don't want to talk about it,'' she snapped.

"You're the one who brought it up,'' he growled.

"Now I'm the one who doesn't want to talk about it.''

With a look that should have scorched his eyebrows, she turned back to her computer, shutting him out. He grabbed the arms of her chair and swung her back around.

"Hey, look,'' he said. "If we're going to work together

effectively, we can't keep snarling at each other about things you don't want to talk about."

"I did not snarl."

"You did."

"And we're not exactly working together," she snapped. "I'm working with you under duress."

His jaw tightened. "I'm the one who got suspended. If anyone's got the right to be upset, it's me."

"Right. Fine."

She tried to swing her chair back toward the computer, but he clamped his hands on the arms, pinning her in place. Her breath hung up somewhere around her diaphragm, and there didn't seem to be anything she could do to free it.

His eyes looked impossibly clear and blue, and he was so close she could see the tiny dark hairs that were beginning to show on his chin and jaw. His mouth was tight with annoyance, but nothing could hide the sensual curve of that lower lip.

She could tell him what had happened. She could show him the same evidence that had convinced the commissioner to take action. He'd believe her then.

But it wouldn't be enough. She wanted the one thing he apparently couldn't give her: faith.

She planted her feet on the floor and pushed, trying to ease her chair away from him. His hands curled around the chair arms, holding her in place despite her efforts.

"Let go," she said.

"I thought we'd called a truce."

"There was no truce," she retorted. "Only coercion."

"Damn it, Rae, it doesn't have to be this way."

She loved him. Damn him. "Yes," she said, "it does."

"You're the most aggravating woman I've ever met," he growled.

"I try hard," she retorted.

Gabriel opened his mouth to retort, but she put her hands on her hips, pulling her black cotton vest tightly across her breasts. Suddenly, he found himself having trouble remembering why he was angry. Simply, she was too desirable for words, and his soul yearned for her.

So did his body. Everything that made him a man desired her, a hunger as strong and primitive as a thunderstorm. But that hunger was less profound than the heart hunger he felt for this woman. She was a player. Games within games within games. She'd betrayed him, sold him out simply to win, and still he wanted her.

Was this love? Hell, he didn't know. Love was supposed to be a good thing, not something that ached and raged like this.

As a vice cop, he'd seen love bought and sold; he'd seen it used and abused and thrown away. He didn't believe in love. Never would. And if he changed his mind, it would be with a woman who could love him back. Not a player.

He cupped Rae's chin with one hand and tilted her face more fully into the light. What was really there? he wondered. Were there any feelings for him at all? Had the passion, that fiery, incredible passion…had that been all a game, too?

He had to know.

Even though he told himself to be cold, to keep his emotions in check, he couldn't keep his hand from trembling as he slid it from her chin to the back of her neck. He claimed her mouth softly, gently. He could feel reluctance in her for one breathless heartbeat. His whole being was suspended between heaven and hell, waiting for her to reject him. Then her lips softened, and all the tension drained out of her body, and relief raced through him as bright and warm as sunlight.

This, at least, was real.

It was magic. It always had been. He curved his other arm around her waist, pulling her up out of the chair. She felt like heaven against him, warm and lush and erotic. Her breath went out in a sigh he felt down to his toes. As if it had been his. As if, with that kiss, they had lost their separateness, their confusion and conflict, and had become one.

"Wait," she gasped. "Stop."

He didn't want to stop. But he did, and every cell in his body protested. "Rae—"

"Don't." She pulled away. "Why did you do that?"

"I had to."

Her lower lip trembled. "Well, next time, don't have to."

"Strictly business," he agreed.

"Yes."

But her eyes were stark with the knowledge that it *would* happen again. They couldn't help themselves.

"The trick," he said, perhaps talking more to himself than to her, "is not to resist it, but to make it not matter."

"How very...astute of you," she replied, her tone arid. "Why don't you go get that case file? The sooner we get this over with, the better."

"I agree," he said. Coolly, as though it didn't matter.

Gabriel watched her throat move as she swallowed convulsively. This time, he knew he hadn't imagined the tears in her eyes. Ah, damn it, he thought. Of all the reactions he might have imagined, this was the least expected.

And the most dangerous.

Gabriel rang the bell at Eddy Drake's apartment. The door swung open, revealing Eddy's narrow hawk's face and, behind it, a slice of bachelor-messy living room.

"Oh, it's you," Eddy said, opening the door wider.

Gabriel stepped into the apartment. Eddy hadn't cleaned the place since his wife left him six months ago, and things were getting pretty bad. Pizza boxes littered the coffee table, and a veritable forest of empty two-liter soda bottles had sprouted on the floor beside the sofa. Gabriel had seen this before—too many times. The job was as tough on the wives as it was on the men. Maybe tougher. They had to send their husbands off to work not knowing if they'd ever come home again. Not many could handle it.

I bet Rae could. He thrust that thought away quickly. Sure, Rae could probably handle anything. If she cared enough to put the games aside.

"Hey, why do you look so sour?" Eddy asked. "It's not like you've never seen the place before."

"Yeah, and I still get nightmares," Gabriel retorted.

"It's just me, and I don't seem to care. How are things going with that sexy, sassy process server?"

"Things don't 'go' with that process server," Gabriel said. "They sort of sweep you up and away, and before you know it, you're not in Kansas anymore." With a sigh, he raked one hand through his hair. "Look, I need another favor from you. See what you can find out about Rae Boudreau's ex-husband. He used to work at the Stiller Street Precinct a few years ago."

"Yeah, I heard the story," Eddy said. "Brett Wilson gave me all the gory details."

"I don't want gory details. I want the truth."

Eddy grunted. "All right. But if you were smart, you'd leave this the hell alone."

"If I were smart, I wouldn't be a cop."

"Yeah. Here's your file," he growled, thrusting a manila folder into Gabriel's hands.

Quickly, Gabriel thumbed through the folder's contents. He frowned, then went through the papers again. And cursed.

"What's the matter?" Eddy asked.

Gabriel slapped the folder shut. "Something's missing."

Chapter 14

"**W**hat do you mean, something's missing?" Rae demanded.

"Just that," MacLaren replied, tapping the case file. "I know there was more in here a few days ago. Somebody's gotten into it and pulled something they didn't want me to see."

Rae leaned back in her chair and studied him. Bright early-afternoon light poured through the windows of her office, slashing with unremitting harshness across his face. He looked grim and tired, his mouth set in a hard line.

"Of course they pulled something," she said. "If it's political, and as high-placed as you think, then they've got somebody, probably several somebodies, in their pockets."

"No kidding."

"Your partner?" she asked.

He shook his head. "I trust Eddy implicitly."

"Who *don't* you trust?" She couldn't keep herself from adding, "Besides me?"

"Damn it, Rae..." His breath went out with a hiss, and he

swung away from her to look out the window. His big, lean body cast a sharp-edged shadow across the floor.

Rae watched him for a while. He didn't move, nor did the line of his back become less uncompromising. But she knew that inside, where no one could see, he was struggling with himself.

Of all the people in the world, she understood. She'd gone through the same struggle, the same violation of her trust in the system. She didn't know what to say to make it right. She didn't know *why* she wanted to say something to make it right, but she did.

"Look, MacLaren—" she began.

"They're not going to get away with this," he growled. "I'm a cop. I became a cop because I believed in the law. And I'm not about to let some sleaze break the law with impunity just because he's got political connections. I'm going to get him."

"That's going to be hard when you're on suspension," she countered.

He swung around with a suddenness that startled her. Before she had a chance to get her breath back, he'd clamped his hands on the arms of her chair again.

Too close, she thought, every cell in her body registering his presence, his scent, his maleness.

"I'm taking this guy down if I have to bring the whole city government down with him," he growled.

Idiotic, she thought, but on the whole, rather magnificent. His eyes looked like cracked glass, and held a most exciting ferocity. He'd fight the Devil himself for what he thought was right, and he wouldn't care what happened to him as long as he brought his enemy down with him. Full speed ahead and damn the torpedoes. Her pulse beat a swift, heavy tattoo in her ears. Whatever else Gabriel MacLaren might be, he was much man.

Much man, her heart told her. On a personal level, as well. She remembered how he'd leapt into the path of Dillard's car to get her to safety, and her heart did one of those steep dives again. How many women could say that their man would die for them? If only, she thought, he could have loved her.

"You can let go of my chair now," she said.

He blinked, and some of the fierceness left his eyes. But not all. For a moment, he pinned her there with that blazing blue crystal gaze, then straightened.

"Sorry about that," he said. "I get a little intense sometimes."

"I remember," she murmured.

He drew a sharp breath, and she instantly regretted her words. It was much too dangerous to remind him of their lovemaking. But it seemed the damage was already done, for those memories lay stark and vivid in his eyes.

She turned hastily around to the computer. If he touched her now, if he said something tender and funny, she'd be lost. Sudden tears fractured the light into a million multicolored specks.

"Earth to Rae," Gabriel said.

Strangely, the sound of his deep voice steadied her. Taking a deep breath, she managed to shore up her collapsing resolve.

"I'm here," she replied. "I'm just thinking about the best way to go about this." Absently, she tapped her fingertips on the edge of the keyboard. "How much can you remember about the case?"

"Maybe enough, if you're as good as I think you are."

The compliment surprised her. She glanced over her shoulder at him. "Thanks," she said.

Their gazes met and locked, and a tense silence fell for a moment. Then Rae gave herself a mental shake and forced herself to disengage. Just before she turned back to the computer, she thought she saw a flash of regret in his eyes.

"Names first?" he asked.

"Any and all," she replied. "We don't know what will connect up, so everything is equally important right now."

He started pacing the room. "I'll start with anything connected to Peter Smithfield. First, there's Applegate—"

"His girlfriend," Rae interjected.

Gabriel's brows rose. "Then there's Walsh, the—"

"Cousin. Johnstone, the alias."

"*One* alias," Gabriel corrected, pleased to know something she didn't. "He's been a real busy boy lately."

Rae called up the Smithfield file. "Give."

"Peter Jarvis, Paul Sheridan—"

"Steal from Peter to pay Paul," Rae murmured.

Gabriel stopped pacing for a moment. "That's almost as bad as a doughnut joke."

"I've got some of those, too," she said. "Been saving them for the right opportunity. Is Sheridan a family name?"

"No. He lived on Sheridan Place Drive for a while."

"Mmm. That means I've got to check the name of every street he's lived on. Sheesh. Hasn't the guy figured out that if he put this much time and energy into an honest enterprise, he'd probably be a millionaire by now?"

"Guys like Peter Smithfield never figure anything out," Gabriel said.

Rae rolled her eyes. "I'm not sure *any* man ever figures anything out."

"How flattering."

"You're welcome. Any other aliases?"

"Yeah. P. Michael Duncan—another street name, before you ask—and Peter Elliston."

A shiver of recognition raced up Rae's spine, the nose-twitching awareness of a fresh trail. "Hold it a minute. I know that name." Quickly, she called up the Smithfield file and scrolled through it. "There," she said, stopping the cursor. "Remember the condo where…" With a lift of her eyebrows, she glanced over at Gabriel. "You *do* remember the condo?"

"How could I forget?" he asked. "Four-B."

Suddenly he grinned at her, and the smile was so full of devilment that her mouth nearly dropped open. Oh, he was a sexy, sexy man!

"I thought you were mad about that," she said.

"I wanted to strangle you," he admitted. "You stood there and lied with the straightest face I've ever seen. And I would have done exactly the same thing in your position."

"Well, hallelujah," she breathed.

"Don't get cocky, Boudreau. That doesn't mean I won't arrest you again," he countered.

"Do you want to hear my wonderful revelation or what?"

"Speak."

"Elliston Enterprises is the owner of the condo," she said. "Four-B. Maybe his girlfriend really rented it, or maybe she doesn't know anything about it."

"She doesn't," Gabriel said. "She broke up with him. The relationship cost her several thousand dollars, she told me."

"What a jewel he is," Rae murmured.

Gabriel grunted. "So we have one thing that at least seems to be a fact. Someone allowed Smithfield to use that condo, and that someone didn't want him being found by the police."

"I'm willing to assume that for now," Rae said. "It also explains why he's dropped completely out of sight. See, he knows that as long as you think he's useful, he's dangerous to the other side. He's got a lot of incentive to keep them from finding him."

"Yeah, like breathing," MacLaren said. "Your point?"

"Why not go right to the source?" she asked.

He grinned, a smile of pure, unholy devilment that sent a shock wave of reaction crashing through her. "Why not? Start with Elliston and see where it takes us."

She got on-line, using the Internet to access certain of the information services to which she subscribed. One thing led to another, then another, and soon she was in so deep she lost all track of time. She was conscious of Gabriel moving close to watch over her shoulder.

Things were getting more interesting by the minute. Elliston Enterprises was owned by another corporation, which was headquartered out of state. It would take time to research that, she knew. And Elliston in turn *owned* three other companies, all of which were out of state, as well.

"Who owns that parent company?" Gabriel asked.

Rae nodded, acknowledging his quickness in following the information flashing onto her screen. She accessed another information server. Then another, and another.

"There," Gabriel said, pointing to a line on her screen.

"Robert Harding-Scott," she said. "Let's check him out."

She slid to still another server. In less than an hour, she'd found Mr. Harding-Scott's social security number, his credit history, driving record, marriage license...and death certificate.

"Holy cow," Gabriel said.

"Right. Somebody's using his name as a front. Interesting."

Rae went back to work. Instead of finding more answers, she just found more questions, more leads to follow up. She had the names of eight corporations to research, and a possible eleven more. And that wasn't counting the names of officers and agents-of-record, all of which would have to be run down.

"I've never seen anything like it," she muttered, leaning back in her chair.

She leaned her head first to one side, then the other, trying to work some of the kinks out. Her back felt like one solid knot. With a groan, she put her hands on the small of her back for support as she arched forward.

"Here, let me," Gabriel said.

He started rubbing her shoulders. Rae opened her mouth to protest, then closed it again. What was she going to say to him, anyway? *Don't touch me because I can't trust myself?* *That* would be true disaster. Besides, his hands were warm and strong, and he knew exactly where the worst of the tension was located.

With a sigh, she let herself drift off into pure sensation. Heat ran from his palms to her knotted muscles, then coiled away in a hazy tide throughout her body. Those talented fingers moved to her neck and worked pure magic there. No matter how hard she tried to keep her eyes open, they kept drifting to half-mast.

"Oh, that feels good," she murmured.

Her words went through Gabriel like lightning. She'd whispered those words to him during lovemaking; she'd gasped them in the throes of passion so hot it had burned his soul.

Oh, yes, he remembered. Arousal swirled through him. Of their own volition, his hands moved downward to her back.

His breathing slowed and deepened as he traced the line of her backbone with his thumbs. Down, up, down again. She sighed, and he felt her pleasure down to his toes. Quite the sensual creature, his Rae Ann.

He spread his fingers out over her back, feeling the firm female musculature beneath the skin. Despite that, there was something fragile about her, a vulnerability that made him want to put his arms around her and hold her tight. And more.

This had to stop. It took an effort of will for him to take his hands from her, but he managed. He wasn't able to keep them from shaking, however, or stop himself from wanting to put them back on her. So he jammed his fists into his pocket.

"I... That seems okay now," he said, hardly knowing one word from the next.

Rae opened her eyes. To her surprise, she saw that the light had turned ruddy as afternoon waned into evening. She didn't know whether work had swallowed the time, or that back rub. Suddenly, she caught sight of Gabriel's reflection in the computer screen, and even with lines of text across his face, his expression held such hunger that her heart began to race wildly.

It had happened again. Lulled by fatigue and the companionable way they'd worked together, her mind had somehow passed control over to her heart and her body, both of which wanted Gabriel MacLaren more than was wise.

"I need..." she stopped, having no idea what she'd intended to say. So she returned to the relative safety of her computer screen. "I'm e-mailing some people I know. Call in a favor or two. This is going to be very complicated to access, and some of those folks have networks I would kill for."

Gabriel nodded. "Good thinking. While you're at it, will you print me out a copy of that list of corporations? I'll take it home tonight and see if I can sort through the tangle. Oh, and if you can, I'd like a list of minority stockholders, too. I want to know how many dead guys are running companies these days."

"Printing," she said, making it happen. "And by the way, what does a cop know about minority stockholders?"

"O ye of little faith," he said, one corner of his mouth curving up. "I'm going for my B.A. part-time, I'll have you know."

She turned to regard him thoughtfully. "Why?"

"Why not?"

Rae had to concede the point. So much of her life had been lived by the concept of "why not?" that she could see no reason to fault anyone else for it. But it sparked a feeling of kinship she hadn't expected, and didn't welcome. So she returned to the safety of her computer screen.

Unfortunately, safety didn't last; Gabriel leaned over her and put his hand over the mouse. "We need a break," he said. "Why don't we grab something to eat and come back to this later?"

"Let me guess. You want to go to Mike's deli."

"Unless, of course, you want to go to one of those yuppie places with the etched glass and hanging plants, and eat microscopic portions of something you can't even pronounce."

She stood up. "You make it sound so appetizing."

"I really want barbecue," he said. "Please?"

At the mention of barbecue, Tom the Dog went to sit at Gabriel's feet. The two males, their expressions identical, gazed at Rae with pleading eyes.

Crossing her arms over her chest, she met those twin ice blue stares levelly. She wanted barbecue, too. Much as she'd like to be uncooperative, she couldn't get past that fact.

"Oh, all right," she said.

"Well, dog, she fell for it," Gabriel said, glancing down at the puppy. "Want to go eat barbecue?"

Tom wagged his stub of a tail. Gabriel tore the printout from the printer, tucked it under his arm, then snapped the leash onto the puppy's collar. The two of them waited by the door while Rae closed the blinds and collected her purse.

"Let's go," she said.

Gabriel opened the door. She strode past him, trying not to notice that his gaze swept her from head to toe and back again. But she noticed. Oh, yes, she noticed. His eyes turned hot, and a stunningly sensual smile curved his mouth.

This was bad. Arousal smoked through her, a response as automatic as breathing. And she was supposed to work with him, close quarters, and stay sane? She stopped to lock her door, then turned to look at him. Bad. Very bad.

"This is nuts," she said. "Us. Working together."

"This isn't as crazy as you think," Gabriel said. "Don't you watch talk shows? Guys in love with their girlfriends' mothers, guys dressing up as girls and vice versa—now, that's nuts. What we have is a good, all-American disagreement. Perfectly healthy."

"Are you trying to start another fight?" she asked, scowling.

"Uh-uh. I'm just trying to get you moving toward the elevator before I starve to death."

"That's supposed to be incentive?"

He chuckled. "The dog is starving, too."

"I'll do it for the dog," she said, stalking toward the elevator, nose in the air.

They didn't talk much on the way to Doukas's. Gabriel parked in front of the delicatessen, and the delicious aroma of roasting pork nearly floated Rae right out of the car.

Gabriel heaved a sigh. "God. Get me in there."

He came around to open Rae's door, and laid his hand on the small of her back as he escorted her in. It wasn't an overtly sensuous gesture, but she felt his touch like fire through her clothes. Her body responded as it always did to him, running hot and fast with desire.

The rush-hour crowd had already come and gone, and the deli had the air of a tired housewife. Mike waved at them from behind the counter, but Rae saw no sign of Barbara and the kids. Maybe they'd already gone home, she thought.

"Hey, MacLaren!" Mike called. "Where have you been hiding?"

"Don't talk to me," Gabriel retorted good-naturedly.

"You gave Rae, almost a stranger, one of those barbecue sandwiches, and didn't send so much as a taste for your good buddy."

Mike snorted. "If you ever become as beautiful and nice as Rae, then you can expect the same treatment."

Gabriel laughed. "She's beautiful, all right."

"Don't forget nice," Rae added.

He lowered his voice. "And sexy," he whispered, gloating at the chance for revenge. "Very, very sexy."

Rae didn't want to think about sexy, sex or anything that might remind her of the two soul-searing nights she'd spent with him. So she waggled her fingers at Mike, then went to sit at one of the Formica tables at the front of the store.

Gabriel followed her, watching the unconscious swing of her hips as she walked. Truly, she was delectable. He leaned back in his chair and studied her from beneath his brows. She sat demurely, her legs crossed, looking as serene and innocent as a Botticelli angel. But sensuality lurked beneath that placid surface, and it was all he could do to keep his hands off her.

Whatever faults she might have, he found her completely fascinating. Or maybe *captivating* might be a better word, he amended. She'd certainly captivated his heart, his soul and his body, and he didn't seem to be able to do anything about it. Being involved with Rae was kind of like slapping a saddle on a tornado, and all other women paled in comparison.

He sat up in surprise as he saw a blond woman walk out of the back storeroom. A little girl tagged after her, carrying a clear plastic bag full of kaiser rolls. Then two boys followed, and the family resemblance among the four was obvious.

"That's Peter Smithfield's wife," he said.

Rae nodded. "She works here."

He shot a glance at Rae. "Your doing?"

"Mike needed help, and Barbara needed a job," she replied.

Gabriel folded his arms over his chest. Mike was too nice for his own good, and it would be too easy for someone to take advantage of him.

"What's the angle?" he asked.

She scowled at him. "Barbara and I have a nefarious plan to con him out of his hidden millions, what else?"

"Very funny," he growled.

"Mommy, there's Rae," Sarah cried, her sweet childish voice cutting the thick tension between Rae and Gabriel.

The girl ran to Rae and flung her arms around her. The boys followed with a tad more dignity, although Joey zeroed in on Gabriel as though pulled by a string.

"You're the cop," he said.

Rae cleared her throat. "Officer MacLaren, meet Mike, Joe and Sarah Smithfield."

"Hi, kids," he said.

"Can we see your badge?" Mike asked.

"I—" Gabriel began.

"He had to leave it at the office," she said. "But maybe he's got a nice scar to show you."

"Cool," Joey said, his face expectant.

Gabriel shot Rae an indecipherable look. Then he pulled up his sleeve and displayed a scar on his biceps.

"Cool," Joey said again.

They crowded closer to Gabriel. He started telling the story of how he got his scar. Rae thought the outrageous tale of a drug bust that turned into a Wild West shoot-out complete with blood and bodies everywhere just a tad too dramatic for belief, but who was she to rain on somebody else's parade?

Mike's and Joey's eyes got bigger and more avid the wilder the story became, and Rae knew that from this day on, Gabriel MacLaren had become better than any superhero in their minds.

Rae couldn't take her gaze from Gabriel. He looked years younger, and delight made his eyes sparkle like cracked glass in sunlight. Her heart did a crazy flip-flop in her chest. She'd never seen this side of him, never thought it existed. What would it be like to have a child with eyes like that? she wondered. For a moment, she yearned for such a child, a child born of her and him and their love. Crazy. Crazy and impossible. Oh, God.

When the story ended, the boys sat frozen in awe. Sarah, ever the practical female, pursed her lips and said, "Gross."

"What's gross?" Gabriel demanded.

"All the blood and stuff. I don't know why boys like blood."

Gabriel slid a sly glance to Rae. "It's because we haven't come all that far from our caveman days, precious."

"You're telling me," Rae muttered, lifting Sarah onto her lap. "What about you, sweetie? Do you have a story to tell?"

The child nodded. "I'm gonna get to put the napkins on the table," she said. "An' Joey and Mike get to take stuff out of the boxes for Mr. Mike. We all get a dollar." Then she aimed one short, dimpled finger at Gabriel. "Is he your boyfriend?"

Rae wanted to melt into the floor. "Ah, Detective Mac-Laren and I are working on a case together," she said, skirting the boyfriend issue.

Not to be deterred, Sarah skewered Gabriel with implacable blue eyes. "But is he your boyfriend?" she insisted.

"Sarah, honey, you're squashing the bread," Barbara said, coming to the rescue.

"But Mommy, I want to know—"

"Do I look like her boyfriend?" Gabriel asked.

Sarah nodded.

At this point, Rae seriously considered crawling under the table. Before Sarah could answer, however, Mike appeared, setting a tray on their table with a flourish worthy of the Ritz.

"There," he said. "Barbecue."

He looked at Barbara then. She looked back, and the air between them fairly sizzled. Rae felt her jaw drop. Mike and Barbara? she thought incredulously. She glanced at Gabriel, and saw her surprise mirrored in his eyes.

Sarah held her arms out to Mike. "Ride," she said imperiously.

Chuckling, he swung the child onto his shoulders and carried her as he returned to his counter. The boys followed like pearls on a necklace. The Pied Piper of Barbecue, Rae thought. She turned to look at the other woman.

"I know what you're thinking," Barbara said.

Rae held her hands up. "It's none of my business—"

"Yes, it is," Barbara said, retrieving a chair from one of the other tables. Gabriel jumped up to help her.

When she was settled, she clasped her hands on the table in front of her. "Rae, you came to the rescue when I was completely alone and the world had caved in on me. I consider you family, and I hope you feel the same. Deal?"

Rae's throat tightened. Family. She'd wanted to be a part of one, but she'd had to be lonely for so long she'd told herself she'd gotten used to it. "Deal," she said. "So, give. What's with you and Mike?"

"I love Mike," she said. "And he loves me."

Rae opened her mouth several times, but nothing came out.

"When it happens, you know," Barbara continued. "You look into each other's eyes, and in one moment the world seems to shift into a whole new pattern."

Oh, yes, that's how it happens, Rae thought, her heart contracting in sudden, painful memory. Oh, yes.

"Why Mike?" Gabriel asked.

Barbara turned to him, her face almost seeming to glow with happiness. "Have you ever seen kinder eyes on a human being?"

Rae watched as Mike showed Sarah how to fold napkins into triangles. Infinitely patient, he held her tiny hands in his huge ones, gently guiding her movements.

"No," she said, swallowing against the lump in her throat.

"I'm just as surprised," Barbara said. "After being married to a man like Peter, well, I just assumed I'd never want to be with anyone again. But now I know I have the courage to take life by the throat. I won't allow Peter to destroy my ability to trust."

Courage to take life by the throat. Those were fighting words, brave words, reckless, happy words.

In her heart, Rae thrilled to them. She would have given her right arm to possess even a shadow of the joy she saw in Barbara's eyes.

She put her hand on the other woman's arm. "Go for it, Barbara. You deserve it."

Barbara smiled at her. Then the door opened, signaling the arrival of some more customers, and she hastily rose to her feet. But she bent to give Rae a quick, hard hug before walking away.

Tears stung Rae's eyes. Quickly, she dropped her napkin on the floor. She bent to retrieve it, hiding her face from Gabriel.

When she straightened, however, she found him staring at her with an all-too-knowing gaze. "You're crying," he said.

"I always cry at weddings," she snarled.

"You think this is all terribly romantic, don't you?" he asked.

His tone was dark with cynicism. A few weeks ago, Rae would have had the same reaction. But not now. For it had happened to her, as swiftly and powerfully as it had happened to Barbara.

There was one big difference, however: Barbara's man loved her back. And oh, things were not so good when love didn't happen to both people.

A great, roaring recklessness gripped her, urging her to try. For herself, and for Gabriel. She had to take the chance.

"Don't you see?" she asked.

Surprise flickered in his eyes. "See what?"

"Look at them." She pointed at Mike and Barbara and the kids.

He glanced at the group behind the counter. "Yeah, so?"

"They look like a family already," she said.

Gabriel leaned back in his chair and studied her with narrowed eyes. This was a Rae he'd never seen before. Her eyes were stark and defenseless, and yet demanded more from him than ever before. Alarm bells rang in his head, more so because his heart wanted to give her anything and everything.

"What are you trying to say?" he asked.

"I'm talking about faith," she said, her voice low and intense. "Those people were abandoned by Smithfield in the cruelest way possible. But they haven't lost the ability to trust again. And to love. That, Detective, is the gift of faith.''

His eyes narrowed. "What are we really talking about here?"

"About us. You and me."

His brows rose. "And faith?"

"Yes. You were the one who said we have something big and powerful, something you couldn't name. Maybe…'' She paused for a moment, struggling to contain her tumultuous emotions. "Maybe if you could learn to trust, you might learn to put a name to this."

Ah, Gabriel thought. He saw the trap now. It was a very good one, tempting simply because it was baited with Rae herself. But he'd learned already how treacherous she could be.

"What's the angle this time, Rae?'' he asked.

She blinked in astonishment. "What are you talking about?"

"Maybe this time you can actually get me kicked off the force,'' he growled.

Rae took a deep breath, stunned by the extent of her own hurt. She'd laid herself open to him in a way she'd never done before, and he didn't care.

She'd lost. Finally and forever, she'd lost. A vast, echoing emptiness bloomed in her soul, and for a moment she was afraid she couldn't hold it all. Then she took a deep, shuddering breath.

Of course she would handle this. Of course she would go on, and in time she might even be able to forget him. Of course. And the sun might freeze in place, the moon might be proven to really be made of green cheese.

"Cops have no hearts,'' she said.

"Cops can't afford to have hearts."

Tears washed through her, a tropical rainstorm of loss that she kept sternly inside. She'd shown him too much already. With a convulsive movement, she rose to her feet.

"Where are you going?'' he demanded.

"Back to the office. I've got work to do.''

"You haven't eaten."

"Maybe not," she replied. "But I've had enough."
Turning, she walked out.

Chapter 15

Rae made it all the way to the car before she started crying.

Half-blinded with tears, she retrieved Tom the Dog from the back seat and cuddled him. Sensing her distress, the puppy wriggled closer, covering her tear-streaked face with comforting dog kisses. She rubbed her cheek against his neck.

"I tried," she murmured into his soft, wavy fur.

Then she set off on foot. She didn't care where she went, as long as it was far, far away from Gabriel MacLaren. God, she'd been stupid to think she could reach him.

"Rae."

MacLaren. She shot a glance over her shoulder and saw the Taurus pacing her along the curb.

"Rae—"

"Go away," she said, managing to keep her voice steady.

"Get in the car," he ordered.

Her tears vanished in a wave of fury so hot it felt as though flames were shooting through her. It wasn't fair, damn it. He'd turned her life to chaos and broken her heart, and he couldn't even give her time enough for a much-needed cry.

"I don't have to get in the car," she snapped. "I don't

have to do anything you say. And this time, you can't even arrest me.''

Head high, she stalked away.

She got as far as the corner. Just as she stepped off the curb at the intersection, Gabriel brought the Taurus to a screeching halt in front of her. This time, he didn't waste time talking. He came barreling out of the car, scooped her *and* the puppy into his arms and stuffed them into the passenger seat.

Glaring over his shoulder at the gawking onlookers, he growled, ''Police business, folks. Move along.''

They scattered, surely more because of his brooding, bad-tempered scowl than because of his words.

Rae gave him her best withering look. ''Don't worry, Detective. I'm still going to help you with your case, if only to get you out of my hair. But I'll be giving you results by telephone or fax.''

He pulled out into traffic so fast that she didn't have a chance to even consider jumping out of the car. Besides, Tom the Dog wriggled out of her grasp and climbed into the back seat, and she wasn't about to leave him. She craned to look for him, but he'd slipped down out of sight.

What *wouldn't* go wrong? she wondered. At least she had her anger. It was her shield against the threatening tears, and her shield against the man she loved so desperately and futilely.

''I want to go home,'' she said.

Gabriel glanced at her with unreadable eyes. ''Uh-uh. We've still got work to do tonight.''

Rae's stomach did a steep nosedive toward her knees. She did *not* want to spend more time with him this evening. She couldn't.

''Look,'' she snapped, ''I've put my whole day into your case, and I'm tired.''

Gabriel ignored her. Not because he was so anxious to work.

But something had snapped in him when she'd walked out

of the delicatessen, and he'd followed her as though pulled by a string.

Very disturbing. Very unwelcome. After what she'd done to him, he shouldn't give a damn where she went.

"We're going to work," he said.

"I'm not efficient when I'm tired."

"Does that mean you're not going to do anything constructive?"

"Officer, I wouldn't dream of failing to cooperate with the police," she cooed.

He braced his hands on the steering wheel. The light from the streetlights overhead cast hard-edged shadows in his face as he scowled at her. "What's with you tonight?" he demanded.

"Nothing."

"You are the most aggravating woman I've ever met. One moment you're fine... Hell, you were even trying to convince me of the magical power of love. Then you just walked out in a huff."

Rae sighed at the futility of it all. He couldn't understand. His life was drug dealers and gamblers, thieves and cheats.

"I don't want to talk about it," she said.

"Why not?"

"Why should I?"

Gabriel blinked, surprised by her counterattack. Why, indeed? It was obvious they had no common ground between them. Heck, they didn't even trust each other. He didn't even know why he'd come after her, other than he'd had to.

"Hell if I know," he said.

Rae crossed her arms over her chest and lapsed into resentful silence. Only a faint violet stain in the western sky was left now, and lights bloomed in the buildings around them. As the darkness closed in, the city spread like a starlit sea around them.

Strange, she thought, how the night turned even this asphalt-and-concrete anthill into a fairyland. Somebody else would have thought it romantic. Under the cover of the darkness, she allowed herself a grimace. Romance. Not with Detective Gabriel MacLaren.

The moment he stopped the Taurus in front of her office building, she unhooked her seat belt and leaned over to find Tom. She found him crouched in the floorboards surrounded by shreds of white paper. A familiar smell drifted up to her. She turned to look at Gabriel, who obviously didn't know what was going on.

"Barbecue," she said. "You brought the sandwiches."

He leaned over to look, and groaned. "I was looking forward to that. Heck, Rae. What is it with you and barbecue?"

"Me?" she echoed. "Did I know the food was there? If you'd said something about it, I would have made sure the dog didn't get back there."

"You weren't talking, remember?" he countered.

Rae stared at him for a moment. Then she leaned over the seat and retrieved Tom. Tucking him under her arm, she got out of the car and headed for her office building. Gabriel caught up to her while she was still unlocking the outer door.

"I want you to go away," she said.

"And I want to see if you got any replies to your e-mail."

She gave him a hard stare. "You know, if you had a life outside of your job, you might be a nicer human being."

"According to you, cops aren't human beings at all."

"I have never said that."

"But you thought it."

Rae was not about to admit any thoughts of any kind whatsoever. She shot a glance at Gabriel over her shoulder. His eyes were heavy lidded and secretive, and his gaze held an intensity that was rather disturbing. It seemed as though he were sifting through her layer by layer. She had the feeling that he wanted to strip away everything and peer straight into her soul.

And he hadn't earned it.

Once in her office, she sat down in front of her computer. Gabriel leaned his hip against the desk beside her. Too close, much too close. He was arrogantly sure that his presence would disturb her, and damn it, he was right.

Tears stung her eyes, and she blinked rapidly to clear them. This was no good. Her emotions were running high and hard tonight, and it wouldn't take much to make her lose control. And, of course, he wasn't going to give her any space.

"You know, I can put all this on disk for you to put on your own computer at home," she said.

"Nice try," he replied, chuckling. "But you know I don't have a computer."

"How would I know?" she retorted. "My stay was limited—"

"To the kitchen table and the bed," he finished for her.

She was really sorry she'd brought up the subject. There were too many memories in his eyes and in her heart. With a hiss of exasperation, she turned back to the screen.

"Now, let's see what's in the mailbox," she said, going on-line to make that request.

A mellifluous electronic voice answered, telling her that she had twenty-three messages.

"You know efficient people," Gabriel said.

"Yes, I do," she said, calling up the first one.

That one was from her friend in Utah, a private eye who had helped her out in the past. He was merely acknowledging her request, and promised to send anything he could find. The next six messages were essentially the same.

MacLaren grunted. "This is going to take too long."

"It takes as long as it takes," she said.

"I know. And I know that it could take months if I tried to do it on my own resources, so I appreciate this. But I can't help but think that time is running out for Peter Smithfield."

Rae nodded, highlighting another message. This one was more interesting. It was from a woman in San Diego, home base of one of the companies owned by Elliston Enterprises. And she had information. Rae hit a key, and another page lit the screen.

Her awareness of her surroundings faded as she focused on the puzzle. No one source would have all the pieces; it was up to her to put them together into a viable whole.

She hardly heard the phone ring, and only vaguely registered Gabriel moving away from her. In fact, she was concentrating so deeply that she nearly jumped out of her skin when he put his hand on her shoulder.

"Take a break," he said.

Rae blinked. Her watch showed that nearly an hour had passed, and her nose told her that a new smell had entered her office.

Barbecue.

"Barbara stopped by to drop off some food and take the dog home," Gabriel explained.

Suddenly, he grinned, and Rae's heart did a hard double bounce.

"I went downstairs to meet her, so don't start thinking that she came in and you missed noticing her."

Rae held out her hand in silent demand for her sandwich. Then, sandwich in one hand and computer mouse in the other, she returned to the search. Gabriel settled down on the sofa with the stack of printouts she'd given him earlier.

For a while, she thought the night might be a bust. Then one thing fell into place, and she slapped her hand down on the desk in triumph. MacLaren was instantly at her side.

"There," she said, pointing to the screen. "That's the company that owns Elliston Enterprises. It's based in San Diego, but correspondence goes to a post-office box in Branson, Colorado. The box is in—" she slid her fingernail farther down the screen "—this guy's name. Albert Henry Dietrick, Esquire, a New Mexico–based attorney. Now, look here. He's got reciprocity to practice in Colorado. My guess is that he's the agent-of-record of this corporation. Now, if we can peg him as agent-of-record in any of the other corporations, then we've got something solid to go on."

"What city is Dietrick in?" Gabriel asked.

"Mmm, oh, here it is. Folsom." She reached for a nearby atlas and thumbed through to find the New Mexico map. "Look, it's nearly on the northern border." She did a quick measurement with her thumbnail. "It's about twenty, twenty-five miles from Branson, a convenient drive. Interesting."

She glanced at Gabriel and caught him looking at her with

mingled exasperation and awe on his face. The sight sent amusement rippling like sunlight through her, and she laughed.

"Welcome to the Information Age," she said. "These days, you can't tie your shoes without someone, somewhere, knowing about it." She clicked the mouse onto the Print icon. "I'm printing all this out for you to take home. I went through it so fast that I'm sure to have missed something."

He nodded, running his thumb along the angle of his jaw as he considered his next move. "I think I'll give the local Folsom law enforcement a call, see what they have to say about Albert Henry Dietrick, Esquire. One lawman to another, so to speak."

"You're suspended," Rae stated.

"They don't know that."

Rae couldn't help but laugh. "True."

Gabriel leaned over to see the screen better. Not the best of moves, for it put him in range of her scent. Rae didn't wear perfume. But she smelled wonderful, shampoo and soap and the indefinable female scent that was uniquely hers.

His awareness of the computer screen faded. Instead, his attention focused on Rae. She bent to look at the keyboard, and her hair slid forward, hiding her face but exposing the back of her neck. Crazy as it seemed, the flash of that hitherto unseen skin was more stirring than if she'd been naked. He had the sudden urge to press his mouth to that spot, to feel her arch in response.

And suddenly, nothing else mattered. Not the case, not her betrayal, nothing but this woman who had taken his heart by storm. His world narrowed until all he knew was her scent, her warmth, the deafening pounding of his heartbeat in his ears.

He reached out, sliding his fingers into her hair. With a gasp, she turned. Her eyes were startled but not hostile, and her mouth held a vulnerability that only made him want to touch her more. Holding his breath, he reached out again.

This time, she didn't move. He delved into the rich softness of her hair. It slid like pure silk across his hand, sending reaction pounding through him with every beat of his heart.

"Rae," he murmured, "I don't want to fight any more."

Rae drew her breath in sharply. His voice was stark with tenderness and desire, underscored by an edge of pleading that astonished her.

She turned to look at him, and her heart raced crazily. In this light, with the shadows of his lashes lying across his cheeks and emotion turning his eyes the color of a moonlit sea, he seemed the most beautiful man she'd ever seen. And oh, God, she loved him so much it hurt.

He would ask for everything she had to give, and he'd take all of it. Not as a gift, but as his right. She had no defenses against this, no way to protect herself. She loved him fiercely, wholly, without reservation, and she could deny him nothing. Even if it tore her heart out, she had no power to deny him.

"Tell me not to kiss you, and I won't," he said, his voice hoarse with arousal.

She meant to tell him no. Her mind shouted it, and she even opened her mouth to say it. But a vast, all-consuming need welled up in her, silencing any protest.

His hand eased down to the nape of her neck. Then he slid his other arm around her waist, bending close. Rae's eyelids drifted closed as he claimed her mouth with his.

Oh, it was sweet, so sweet. Her heart ached with love for him; her body ached with desire. She wrapped her arms around his neck and met his kiss almost savagely, inciting him, drawing him deeper, harder, hotter.

He made a harsh sound deep in his throat. With startling ease, he pulled her out of the chair and into his arms. Then he carried her to the sofa and laid her down. He knelt over her, his face in shadow, his hair limned with gold from the lamp behind him.

Dark angel, she thought. A being of mingled dark and light, vulnerability and danger.

She ran her hands up his sinewy arms to his shoulders, reveling in his strength. He drew his breath in sharply, and she knew she'd stirred him. That was no surprise; from the moment they'd first touched, they'd had this effect on each other.

Slowly, he eased down, fitting himself against her. A heavy feeling of inevitability settled in her heart as she accepted him. She had nothing to lose any longer. Nothing. She'd already given him everything she had to give.

He kissed her. She met him eagerly, pouring all her tumbling emotions into her embrace. Hot, wet, primitive, unrestrained, giving, taking... It was quite a kiss, and it left her shaken to her soul. She no longer cared what he might take from her as long as she could hold him like this, even for a moment.

His fingers spread out over the curve of her hip in a gesture of male possession. Then he slid his hand to her derriere, cupping her, lifting her pelvis against his.

A low groan rumbled deep in his chest, and he tore his mouth from hers. Slowly, almost as though it hurt him, he levered himself to a sitting position. Rae lay frozen in shock, not knowing what to do, what to say, what to feel.

"Oh, damn it," he muttered, raking both hands through his hair. "Why the hell do I let you do this to me?"

Rae drew her breath in sharply. "You think I planned this?"

"I don't know what goes on in your mind," he said, his voice bitter and harsh. "All I know is that I get sideswiped every time I turn my back on you."

She couldn't believe how much this hurt. She'd thought herself prepared for anything he might say or do. But this... It would have been less painful if he'd struck her. And still she wanted him, desperately, and it wouldn't take much to make her forget all about saving herself again.

That was when she broke. Tears welled up in a stinging flood that she couldn't control, and she turned her face toward the back of the sofa in an attempt to hide them. But he drew his breath in sharply, and she knew he'd seen.

"Rae," he said, laying his hand on her shoulder.

She jerked away from him. "Don't touch me."

At another time, Gabriel would have walked out. But she

sounded so lost, so hurt, that his heart contracted with pain. With a muttered exclamation, he pulled her up into his arms.

Rae might have been able to stop crying if he hadn't touched her. But now, all the heartache, all the confusion and anger and love, came pouring out in a wild torrent, and she cried like she'd never cried before.

Gabriel had never heard anyone cry like this, great, jagged sobs that sounded as though they hurt coming out. But then, Rae was not the kind of woman who cried easily. Or at all. She'd needed to be tough and hard and self-sufficient, and he knew she'd think of tears as weakness. Whatever emotion had opened these floodgates was a very powerful one. And he wondered. He wondered.

He stroked her hair, almost overwhelmed by a great surge of tenderness that swelled his heart almost to bursting. "That's all right," he murmured, burying his face in the hair at her temple. "Let it all out, sweetheart."

Rae couldn't stand it any longer. Tearing free of his arms, she fled the office. She, Rae Ann Boudreau, who had never run from anything in her life, couldn't get away fast enough.

For once, Gabriel didn't follow. Stunned by what had happened, he sat watching the door slowly swing shut.

He'd seen the real Rae. Stripped bare to her soul, scoured shiny and pure by tears, she had shown all of herself to him. And she was exactly what she'd presented herself to be. There was no subterfuge in her, nothing dishonest.

She had taken four strangers into her home, befriended them, gave them a chance for a new life. There had been no possible motive for gain. There had been no reason for her to take the Smithfield case at all, let alone pursue it with such determination and at such cost, except to help Barbara and the kids.

He'd been surrounded by cons and players so long that he'd lost sight of what was real. And cynicism was a poor ruler by which to measure truth.

Rae hadn't called his captain and cried harassment. She hadn't hounded her ex-husband off the force. This woman was a stand-up, in-your-face fighter. She'd never play it underhanded. And Gabriel had come to that belief without any evidence except that which he saw in her eyes. He needed nothing more than that.

Gabriel MacLaren had found his faith. He'd found it in a beautiful, passionate, infuriating woman named Rae Boudreau. But it wasn't enough that *he* knew this.

Somehow, he had to convince Rae, for he knew she'd accept nothing less.

Rae's doorbell rang at seven the next morning.

She sat up, tumbling the puppy off her thighs as she reached for her pistol. "Barbara?" she called. "Don't open it if you—"

"Don't know who it is," the other woman called back. "It's all right, Rae."

With a sigh, Rae snuggled down into the covers. Tom the Dog hurled himself at her, all yips and eagerness and wet, slapping tongue. "Okay, okay," she said, trying vainly to fend him off.

She got up. The moment she opened the bedroom door, Tom raced out. She could hear his claws skid madly as he hit the wood floor in the living room. With a yawn, she scrubbed at her sleep-tousled hair with both hands.

It hadn't been a good night. She should have gone back to the office, to a bar, anywhere but here, where she'd had to spend her night dreaming about Gabriel MacLaren.

"Get over it, Boudreau," she muttered.

She took her usual scalding, ten-minute shower, then pulled on a pair of jeans and an oversize cotton shirt in a scandalous shade of orange. Just buying it had been an act of defiance; wearing it was a sartorial raspberry to anyone who saw it. She wished she'd had the foresight to buy lipstick the same shade. Then, armed and armored against the world, she walked out of the bedroom.

Gabriel MacLaren sat at her kitchen table. Sarah had dragged a chair close beside his, and was chattering away while he worked on a plate of eggs and sausage. Mike and Joey worshipfully imitated his every gesture.

Gabriel glanced up at her. Their gazes locked, hers reluctant, his so intense she thought it might burn her. And her heart, treacherous thing that it was, banged against her ribs.

"Good morning," he said.

Rae would have liked to say a lot of things, none of which had anything to do with morning, good or not. But not in front of the kids. She looked at Barbara, who was busily breaking eggs into a cast-iron skillet. The blond woman shot her a glance out of the corner of her eye, and her face bore an unmistakable I-know-better-than-you expression.

No, you don't, Rae thought. "Morning," she said.

She grumped over to the table, feeling very antisocial. In fact, she was feeling a definite urge to stick a fork somewhere in Gabriel's anatomy, preferably somewhere sensitive. The thought must have showed in her face, for he gave her one of his sharp-edged cynical smiles.

"Give me a kiss, Rae," Sarah said.

With real affection, Rae bent and kissed the little girl's cheek. Then she looked at the boys. "You, too?"

Their eyes widened in alarm. "Uh-uh," Joey said. "I'm not kissing any girls."

Gabriel laughed, and the deep, smoky male sound seemed to fill the room. "I've got news for you, fellas. The day will come when you'll *beg* to kiss girls."

"No way!" Mike exclaimed.

Apparently driven from the room by sheer horror, they retreated into the living room to watch TV. Lured by the sound, Sarah slid out of her chair and went to join her brothers.

Rae pinned Gabriel with her best withering stare. "If you speak to me again, I'll become violent," she whispered, her voice no less intense for its lack of volume.

"Become as violent as you please," he replied. "Because I intend for us to have a nice, long talk."

"You—"

"Be nice, Rae," Barbara said, setting a plate before her.

Rae stared down at her food. The sunny-side-up eggs stared back at her as though mocking her helplessness to do anything about MacLaren. She could no more have eaten them than she could have cut her own throat. With a hiss of frustration, she pushed the plate away and got to her feet.

"Let's get this over with," she snapped.

Gabriel rose with lazy grace. "Fine by me."

Turning toward Barbara, Rae said, "I'm sorry about the food. I just can't eat this morning."

"I understand," the other woman said. Adding in an undertone, "I just hope you do."

Rae shot her a glare. Barbara met it blandly, and smiled. MacLaren called goodbye to the kids, then turned toward the door. There was nothing for Rae to do but grab her purse and follow him.

The ride to her office passed in frosty silence. Icily polite, Rae stepped into the elevator and waited until he joined her. When the doors closed, she turned to look at him.

"I'd rather have my teeth extracted than spend the day in close quarters with you," she said.

He didn't even frown. "Whether you want to or not, we need to talk. No quarreling this time, no competition, no games. Just talk. You and me."

"Don't you think it's a little late for talking? she asked.

"It's never too late," he replied. "As long as two people care about each other."

Startled, Rae stared at him. Then the elevator doors opened, forestalling any reply. She walked down the hall to her office, overly aware of him striding beside her like some great jungle cat. His eyes were closed and blank, showing nothing of what might be going on behind them. And still...there was an air about him, a tense sort of anticipation that sent her nerves twanging crazily.

Her hand shook just a little as she fitted the key into the lock. He laid his hand over hers, steadying it.

Then he smiled, a tender, infinitely possessive smile that completely paralyzed her brain, and pushed the door open. With an effort of will that left her shaking, Rae managed to disengage from those blue crystal eyes and turn toward her office.

And found herself looking into chaos.

Chapter 16

Rae stared openmouthed at the wreck someone had made of her office. All the papers had been dumped out of the file cabinets and lay in drifts on the floor. The drawers of her desk hung open, and the sofa cushions were disemboweled. Worst of all, her diskette storage boxes lay open and empty on the floor.

MacLaren pulled a gun from his back waistband and moved into the room ahead of her. She followed, her feet slithering on what had once been her well-organized files. Outrage shot through her with every beat of her heart. How *dare* they!

"Looks like somebody thought we were getting too close," she said.

"Yeah." Satisfied that the room was safe, Gabriel returned his pistol to its hiding place.

"I thought they made you turn in your gun," Rae said.

"They made me turn in *a* gun," he replied.

Rae went to her computer and tried to boot it up. Instead of going through the usual run-through, however, the screen brought up a "No operating system found" message. She let out a cry of sheer rage and frustration.

MacLaren drew his pistol again. "What's the matter?"

"They slicked my drive!"

"I don't know what slicking a drive is," Gabriel said. "But if I were them, I'd erase everything you had."

"Bingo, Detective. Everything we did yesterday is gone."

"We still have the printouts you made for me," he said.

"Well, okay." She slapped her palm down on the desk. "But they wiped my case files, three years of business records—"

"Are you going to let that stop you?" he asked.

Slowly, Rae turned around to look at him. His eyes held the same outrage she felt, but there was also a light of challenge that appealed to that stubborn part of her that had sustained her through greater losses than this.

"They don't have enough men, money or intimidation to stop me," she said.

Looking into Gabriel's reckless eyes, she knew he felt the same. Their gazes lingered for a long moment. Then she righted her chair and sat down in front of the computer.

Gabriel came to stand beside her. He looked tough and hard and infinitely capable, and made her pulse leap. They might fight each other bitterly, but now, when it really mattered, they'd stand side by side against a common enemy.

That knowledge sent a thrill racing through her. She didn't know what to do about it, or whether the feeling would last once the crisis was over. But it felt good to have a partner.

"Unless they defragged the drive after wiping it, I can retrieve the information," she said. "The only problem is that reinstalling DOS will mess up my files. But I can pull this drive out, put a new one in, then designate the old drive as something else." She tapped her fingertips on the arm of the chair, then glanced up at him. "There's a computer store right next to Mr. Fedderman's flower shop. Do you remember Mr. Fedderman?"

"How could I forget? He gave you that blue-eyed dog." But Gabriel remembered the florist because of that stunning portrait Rae had made with her face framed in blossoms. "Let me guess. You want me to buy a hard drive."

She took her wallet out of her purse and handed him her credit card. "I've been wanting one of those 2-gig hard drives for a while. When this is all over, I might even thank those bozos for making me take the plunge."

"I'm not sure I want to know what a gig is," he said. "But this is going to be my treat."

She raised her brows. "Most guys think a treat is taking a girl out for ice cream."

"I'm paying," he said. "This—" he waved at the trashed office "—is my fault."

"Sure, it is," she agreed, enjoying the look of shock that crossed his face in the wake of her statement. "After all, you came here and forced me to take the Smithfield case."

"Oh," he said, "I get it now. Sarcasm."

"I pay my own way, MacLaren."

"So take me to lunch sometime."

He tossed her credit card like a Frisbee, dropping it right into her lap. Before she could say anything else, he walked out, leaving her with no one to argue with.

"Men," she muttered.

She walked to the office next door. Harry Stryzinski, financial adviser. Rae had never quite understood exactly what Harry did, but she knew he did it with other people's money. A real shark, was Harry. Since she never had money to invest, she and Harry had reached a sort of nonaggression treaty, and he never failed to give her a box of chocolates at Christmas.

The secretary looked up as Rae walked in. "Morning, Rae."

"Morning, Charlene. I've got a problem."

Charlene's dark eyes widened. "I know a good doctor—"

"No!" Rae held her hands up in a warding-off gesture. "I need to borrow some software."

"Oh, is that all? Darn. I thought you might actually give me some excitement for a change. And all you came here for was something for your computer. Go figure."

"You still have Microsoft Undelete, don't you?" Rae

asked, hastily sorting through Charlene's comments for something that could be safely answered.

"Of course. You know how many times Harry pushes the wrong button," Charlene said, handing over a large diskette-storage case. "Have fun. God knows this is the least we can do after you debugged that virus for us last year."

"Thanks, Charlene. I appreciate it."

Rae went back to her office. She couldn't do anything with the computer until Gabriel got back, so she started cleaning up the mess. Computer tools being a priority just now, she first got her desk in order. Then she started on the scattered papers.

"Whoever you are, I hope I get to take this out of your hide," she muttered.

She was on her hands and knees when Gabriel came back in. Her back was to him, so he had plenty of time to admire the view. Those jeans were just a bit on the tight side, and lovingly showed off the enticing curve of her derriere.

Then she leaned forward to retrieve a paper that had slid partway under the sofa, and Gabriel nearly dropped the box he was carrying. His imagination took over, painting her absolutely, stunningly naked.

Ah, what a sight that would be.

He took a step toward her, drawn by a need too powerful to resist. Papers crackled underfoot. She jumped to her feet, turning toward him in the same startled motion.

"Hi," he said.

Rae looked him up and down. He held a large manila envelope in one hand, and in the other, an enormous bouquet of flowers. Roses. Suddenly, she remembered what Mr. Fedderman said about roses being the thing to buy if a man got himself into real trouble. Oh, no. He wanted to be forgiven.

"Forget it," she said. "There aren't enough roses in the world to buy you that."

"Of course there are," he replied. "Mr. Fedderman guaranteed this method. Although I can't figure out why he wouldn't sell me a plant for you. There was this really neat hanging basket—"

"I kill them."

He blinked. "Huh?"

"I'm the kiss of death for anything green," she said.

"These are red," he argued.

"Semantics."

He smiled. "No, roses."

Her gaze faltered and fell. Then her expression changed completely. "My drive!" she cried, pouncing.

Before he could react, she'd snatched the bag out of his hands and pulled the drive out of it.

Look at this," she crowed, cradling the drive in both hands. "Two gig. And with my other drive as storage backup, I've got so much room I won't know what to do with it."

Chuckling, Gabriel tossed the roses on the desk. Rae was something else, he thought in mingled rue and admiration. Other women got excited about flowers or diamonds or real estate, but what popped Rae's cork? Gigs.

She'd already dived into the computer's innards. "Here, hold this," she said, extracting the old disk drive and plopping it into his hands.

He watched as she installed the new drive. "Hey, they're just components. Slide them in and out, and you're done."

"Dead on, Officer," she said, glancing up. "Once this is installed, I'm going to designate it as drive C, and the old drive as D. Then I'll install my DOS operating system and reload my programs. There are several that can retrieve erased information."

"Right. But the most pressing thing now is to trace our gambling buddies."

She nodded. "Did you call Folsom?"

"Yeah. The sheriff there didn't think a lot of Dietrick. The term he used was 'shyster.' Seems Dietrick isn't a home-grown fella, moved there about five years ago. He doesn't seem to have much of a local practice."

"Aha."

"'Aha' is right."

Gabriel sat down on the sofa to start on the printouts, and Rae turned back to the computer. Within a half hour, she'd loaded the programs she needed into the new drive. Once she got her computer to recognize all its innards again, she went on-line.

"Did you get anything from that printout?" she asked.

He nodded. "As far as I can tell, Elliston Enterprises is running as an umbrella for five different corporations. But in the past four months, three other corporations passed out of Elliston's hands, either through bankruptcy or being sold."

"Names?" Rae asked.

"Twylie, Inc., E & L Corporation, Krueger Realty—" He broke off as revelation hit, and saw Rae swivel in her chair to look at him with surprise in her eyes.

"They could buy and sell their own properties," they said in unison.

"Who owned Krueger originally? Someone bought it recently—who?" Gabriel ticked points off on his fingers. "How many properties did Krueger buy? And where are they?"

Rae turned back around and started typing again. Silence fell, broken only by the tapping of her fingers on the keyboard. Still, the air fairly crackled with energy. Rae knew it for what it was: the thrill of the chase. Gabriel was a puzzle-solver, just like she was.

"Look," she said, pointing to the screen. "Three more corporations to add to the tangle."

"Hey, why not?" Gabriel countered. "Pile it all on. After all, this is already twisted beyond belief."

She glanced at him over her shoulder. "Do you have any access to banking information?"

"Why?"

"I'd like to know if a lump-sum amount of twenty thousand dollars has run through Peter Smithfield's account recently."

"Darlin', the only account Smithfield keeps is with the gambling boss—" Gabriel broke off suddenly as he realized the significance of her question. "Why do you want to know?"

"Because someone sent me a twenty-thousand-dollar bribe."

Gabriel knew his blood pressure must be life threatening just now. A bribe. "What bribe?" he inquired with what he felt was admirable calmness under the circumstances.

"Somebody dropped an envelope with twenty hundred-dollar bills in my mail slot," she said. "And a note that said, 'A prudent woman knows when to back off,' or something like that."

"It never occurred to you to mention it?"

She shot him a glance over her shoulder. "You weren't exactly forthcoming with information yourself."

"You should have told me," he growled.

"Come on, MacLaren. If I had told you about it, you'd have become all officious and bureaucratic. Then the moment passed, and I sort of got distracted."

He scowled, brooding over that. "I would not have become officious. I would have become protective."

"That's worse," she countered. "The last time you got protective, I nearly had to watch you get run over."

Gabriel's cellular rang. With a wordless growl, he flipped the phone open. "MacLaren," he snarled.

His partner's familiar voice came over the line. "I've been trying to get you for hours," Eddy complained. "Remember that gambling house we staked out on Riverwalk Drive? Well, last night our people saw Smithfield go in, but they never saw him come out again."

Gabriel stiffened. "Didn't they go in after him?"

"Not for a while. We've got to clear everything through Roth now, and he wasn't available for a couple of hours. Once we got permission, we went in. And found zip. Tables, Smithfield, nothing—the place looked like a preacher's house."

"Thanks," Gabriel growled, flipping the phone closed. He stood for a moment, just thinking. Then he went to Rae and spun her chair around so that she was facing him. "Peter Smithfield just ran out of time."

Her warm-sherry eyes narrowed. "They snatched him?"

"Last night."

"What do you want to do?" she asked.

"This is taking too long," he said, glancing at the computer. "You're going to have to get a list of all the realty transfers made in the past five years. Then integrate it with the list of corporations to see if any name comes up more than once."

"True," she agreed.

He straightened. "Honey-child, I'm checking out of the Information Age and returning to plain old police work. There's an answer in here somewhere, something so simple it'll be embarrassing once I spot it. But you're throwing me so much information that it's blinding me."

"There's no such thing as too much information," Rae countered.

He fixed her with a challenging stare. "Tell you what. I'll take what we've got right here, right now, and run it down my way. We'll see who comes up with the answer first."

"Gee, Detective, don't you want to place a bet or something?" she drawled.

"Sure," he countered, surprising her.

"And what do you want to bet?"

So swiftly that she had no time to protest, he slid one arm around her and pulled her close. Even if she weren't pressed up against his hard body, she would have had trouble breathing. His gaze burned into hers. Of their own volition, her eyelids drifted downward. Her body felt heavy and too warm, as though she'd been drugged by his presence.

"I'll bet everything," he murmured, so close that his breath brushed warm across her mouth.

Rae had lost the ability to speak. She hung unresisting in his embrace as he leaned closer, closer still. Then he claimed her mouth. Slowly. Deeply. Completely. Her body thrummed with arousal, acknowledging his claim. When he let her go, she nearly fell back into her chair.

And then he was gone.

She sat stunned, feeling as though she'd been swept up by a tornado and spun until nothing made sense any longer. Surely Gabriel MacLaren was the most confusing man ever born!

But Rae Boudreau had never backed away from a challenge yet, and she wasn't about to start now. She turned to her computer.

"Too much information, indeed!" she muttered.

It took her a couple of hours to get the list of realty transfers. She copied it into four different files and sorted each one by name, date, buyer, seller and agent. Her breath went out sharply as she finally realized the full scope of the picture. She printed what was on the screen, then sat back in her chair, feeling as though all her bones had turned to mush.

Krueger had been the agent for several of the known gambling houses. Three others had been bought within the past six months, none of which the police department had known about.

And one belonged to Peter Smithfield.

"They're not going to kill him until he signs that house over to them," Rae said aloud. Then she added, "Unless they get scared enough."

She grabbed for the phone. The time had come to forget the competition between her and Gabriel. He needed this information to save Peter Smithfield, and fast. She dialed his cellular number. The phone rang and rang, but he didn't answer.

Quickly, she jotted down the three addresses. Then she got up and got her .380 out of her purse and tucked it into her waistband.

"I've got to do it myself," she muttered.

She wasn't afraid. Not really. But for the first time in her life, she wished she had someone with her. No, she admitted, not just anyone…she wanted Gabriel.

The outer door swung open. Rae, her nerves twanging, whirled, pistol in hand.

Gabriel stood framed in the doorway, his wide shoulders almost filling the opening. Relief washed through her in a warm flood.

"Oh, it's you," she said, hiding her joy at seeing him beneath a scowl. "You shouldn't sneak up on people like that."

"Yes," he agreed, his ice blue gaze settling on her pistol. "But I wanted to see what you were doing."

She slid the little gun back into her waistband. "And?"

"And." Satisfaction curved his mouth upward. "Rauter Street. Holland Drive. St. James Street."

Those were the addresses of the three houses she'd found. "How did you get those?" she demanded.

"Sweetheart, I told you there was a simple solution," he said. "Since this case is political, and this an election year, I merely checked the lists of contributions made to all the people running for office. I found which candidate held contributions made by companies on our hit list. From there, I traced real estate holdings, and voilà!"

"Good for you," she said. "So it's a tie."

"Uh-huh. We both win." His smile broadened. "And where do you think you're going, beautiful Rae?"

"I'm coming with you."

"No, you're not."

She scowled. "Yes, I am. I've got business with Peter Smithfield."

"No."

Rae put her nose in the air and started to walk past him. His hand clamped down on her wrist, and a moment later she felt the touch of cold metal on her skin.

"Don't you dare!" she cried.

"Save it, honey-child," he replied, chuckling as he snapped the handcuff closed.

Keeping a firm grip on her, he looked around the office for a good place to stash her. She didn't want to come. But there were definite advantages to superior size and strength, and Gabriel was willing to use all of them. Tucking her under his arm like a sack of grain, he hauled her over to the desk and snapped the other end of the cuff onto the heavy metal leg.

He stepped back to survey his work. She'd have to lift the entire desk, computer and all, to get out.

"Damn you," she raged.

Gabriel crossed his arms over his chest and regarded her

levelly. Oh, she was mad! He could almost feel the crackle of her anger like lightning in the room.

"I wish I was sorry about this, Rae, but I'm not," he said. "This is going to be dangerous enough without me having to worry about you. That's it. End of story."

"You arrogant—"

"I admit it," he said. "Damn, I had a pretty speech all laid out and I've forgotten it. But here's the gist. We've got a real thing on our hands, Rae. I don't know what to call it, and I'm damned unsure what to do about it, but one thing I'm sure of is that I want to be with you."

Rae had already opened her mouth to protest, but the words died in her throat when she realized what he'd said. "What?"

"You heard me," he growled. "I want you, you want me and it's the biggest, most powerful thing I've ever felt. We can't stay away from each other, and I'm not going to try anymore."

She drew her breath in so deeply she got dizzy. Or maybe it was the look in his eyes that made her feel so strange. Then fury came flooding in on a red-hot tide, and she tugged noisily on the handcuffs.

"You let me out of these, MacLaren," she snapped. "Damn you, how *dare* you tell me something like that while I'm stuck—"

He strode to her, snatching her close with an aggressive tenderness that dried the words in her throat. Then he kissed her. Hard. Long. Completely. A shock wave of sensation rolled through her, and she was helpless to stop him. Or herself. Before she quite knew what was happening, her arms had crept around him, pulling him closer still.

When he finally broke the kiss, she hung unresisting in his arms. She felt as though her mind had gone floating off into a rose-colored fog, leaving her body stranded in a riptide of sensation.

"Rae," he murmured, "look at me."

She was almost afraid. Almost. But her spirit knew, as perhaps it had always known, that she would be safe with him. Her breath caught in her throat as she obeyed.

His heart and soul blazed in his eyes. It wasn't a gentle sort of emotion—that wasn't possible with a man like him—but a wild, tempestuous, all-consuming passion. She lost herself in his eyes, and in her own desire.

"I don't believe you got me suspended," he whispered, his voice as intense as his eyes. "I don't believe any of those things they said about you hounding your ex-husband off the force."

"I—"

"Let me talk for once," he growled. "I've got no evidence, no facts, nothing but what I see in your eyes. And that's enough. Damn it, it shouldn't be, but it is."

"Will you stop—?"

"I will not stop. You fill my dreams and my waking hours, and I want you so badly I shake every time I get near you."

"Look, MacLaren—"

"I just wanted you to know how I felt, Rae," he said, letting her go so abruptly she didn't have a chance to grab him. "Now, I've got a job to do. Wish me luck."

He strode out of the office, closing the door behind him. Rae jerked on the handcuffs so hard the metal grated.

"Don't you dare walk out now," she panted. "Come back here and finish this, you arrogant, infuriating, self-righteous... Oh, God, something might happen to you, and I never got the chance to tell you that I love you."

"MacLaren!" she shouted, pulling on the cuffs with all her strength. *"MacLaren!"*

Of course, he didn't come back. The rat. Frantically, Rae glanced around for her purse, hoping she'd dropped it somewhere close. She spotted it beside the sofa, a good five feet away.

"Mr. Know-It-All MacLaren," she muttered. "Never thought to look for a spare set of locksmith's tools, did you?"

She smiled a not very nice smile, anticipating the moment when she showed up in spite of him. Arrogant so-and-so that he was, he deserved a comeuppance. He'd put her through hell. But oh, had he ever come through when it mattered! In those few brief moments when he'd opened his soul to her, he had given her everything she'd ever wanted, things she'd never known she'd needed until he'd come into her life.

And she'd been *handcuffed*.

"You aren't going to leave me behind like this," she said, planting her feet and giving another jerk on the cuffs.

The desk budged about half a millimeter. She tugged again, and gained another fraction of an inch. That was when she got mad.

Taking a firm grip on the links with both hands, she pulled with all her strength. This time, she gained an inch.

"If my computer falls off, I'll... I'll..." She couldn't think of anything bad enough. "Damn you, MacLaren. If you think for one moment I'm going to sit here and twiddle my thumbs until you come to collect me, then you've...got... another...think...coming."

The last few words were punctuated by a jerk on the handcuffs. Panting, she took a short break. Then she started pulling again, each time gaining a precious inch. Each one upped her determination a notch, as well. Even if the stakes weren't this high, she would have *died* before giving up.

Finally, she'd moved close enough to reach the purse with her foot—maybe. She lay on the floor, extending her cuffed arm as far as possible, then easing her foot under the strap of the purse.

"There!" she gasped, pulling the purse toward her.

It only took her a couple of minutes to release herself. Police handcuffs were ridiculously easy to pick. Scrambling to her feet, she printed out another copy of those three addresses.

Gabriel was bound to take them in order, first to last, because he had no reason to do otherwise. Rae, however, was going to take the last first, because...because she had no reason to do what Gabriel did. Chuckling at her own logic, she thrust a couple of twenties into her pocket and headed for the door.

Her laughter soon faded, however, as worry came creeping through her mind on cold, clammy feet. Gabriel wouldn't call for backup until he found Peter Smithfield, knowing that someone in the department couldn't be trusted.

So Gabriel, that...that brave, magnificent idiot, was going to walk in alone, and trust that he'd have time to call for help if he needed it.

"Do I know cops, or do I know cops?" she asked.

Maybe not all cops, she amended silently. But she knew *that* one. Gabriel MacLaren—stubborn, arrogant, infuriating, incredibly sexy and man enough to strip his heart bare so that she could see how deeply he cared. Somehow, they'd been meant for each other from the beginning of time, and had flailed away at life until that night when their gazes had met and their souls had joined.

In their blindness, they had nearly thrown it all away. They had ignored their hearts and listened to logic, which only recognized facts and figures, never Fate. It had been close, so close. But somehow, they'd both come to see the truth.

Her mood turned grim as she checked her pistol, making sure the magazine was fully loaded, and shifted it out of sight in the back of her waistband.

Gabriel MacLaren was her love, her lover, the mate of her spirit, and loving him had made her whole.

She intended to keep him.

Chapter 17

Rae had the taxi stop a block away from the house. She went the rest of the way on foot, walking casually down the opposite sidewalk as though she belonged there.

This was a neighborhood in upward transition. Many of the large, 1930s-vintage brick homes had been allowed to fall into disrepair, but a few shrewd people had begun buying them and fixing them up. In a couple of years, this area would be very like Georgetown in Washington, D.C.

She bent to tie her shoe, giving herself time to take a good, long look at the place. The brick exterior had been power-washed, and the wood trim freshly painted. She could see a little of the inside from here, and it had obviously been renovated.

"Interesting," she muttered. "Verrrry interesting."

According to the printout, Krueger Realty had bought this house, number 23, and sold it a month and a half later to one Donald Culpepper. At a loss. If she guessed right, Krueger Realty had spent thirty or forty thousand renovating the place before selling it at a loss. Uh-huh. Money-laundering, maybe? If so, the Feds would like to know.

"'What a tangled web we weave...' Say, what have we here?" she muttered as a black Lexus pulled up in front.

Two men got out of the back and went inside. She couldn't see their faces. But since the driver had noticed her, she continued walking. Spotting a liquor store a half block farther on, she went inside and browsed through the stock nearest the window.

A minute or so later, the two men came out again. The Lexus passed the store and turned right at the next corner. Rae had the feeling that a decision had been made, orders given.

She had to get in that house.

The proprietor was staring at her as though she might be an ax murderer, so she bought a bottle at random from a nearby display. Obviously mollified by charging her fourteen-fifty for a five-dollar bottle of champagne, the man even smiled at her as she left.

Fortunately, there were alleys behind these old houses. She took a roundabout way to the rear of number 23. From here, she could see into the kitchen. It looked like a regular kitchen, but there was no wallpaper, no canisters on the counter, no baskets or trivets or any of the clutter that marked a lived-in house.

A man walked into the kitchen. If this was Donald Culpepper, he really went in for oversize biceps, ponytails and .45 semiautomatics. Now, Rae liked .45s as much as the next girl, but she didn't feel the need to wear one in her own kitchen.

"Who are you guarding, fella?" she murmured.

After making himself a cup of coffee, he left the kitchen again. Rae set the bottle of champagne down near the outer wall of the house, then set about finding a way in.

She started with the obvious first, the door. It was locked, but the kitchen window wasn't. All she had to do was remove the screen and put it back once she was inside.

The house smelled like stale cigarette smoke. She opened the kitchen door a crack, and heard the sound of a television playing nearby. A soap opera. She listened for a moment, and finally placed it: "All My Children." Apparently, Ponytail was a fan.

The best way to deal with a thug with a .45 was to avoid him, and hope there were no more like him around. She doubted that he'd keep his prisoner down at street level, where Peter Smithfield might find a way to signal a passerby.

She moved silently down the hall away from the sound of the television. The shades in all the front windows had been pulled down, leaving the stairs in dimness. She started up, keeping close to the banister to minimize possible squeaks. Not that the thug could hear her over the soap, but she wasn't about to take chances. Once upstairs, she moved as quickly and silently as possible as she went from room to room.

She found Peter Smithfield in one of the bedrooms. He'd been gagged with duct tape and trussed like a Christmas goose, and looked very silly and very scared. She moved farther into the room and closed the door behind her.

"You're in big trouble, Smithfield," she whispered.

He nodded frantically, and for a moment she thought he might start to cry. Rae sighed. He had to have *some* good in him, she thought, or he wouldn't have fathered such great kids. Of course, it might be a case of nurture over nature....

Smithfield made a muffled noise through the gag, and she got back to business. Her business. Taking the subpoena out of her pocket, she dropped it on his chest.

"This is official notice that you're due in court to explain why you don't pay your child support," she said softly but with great satisfaction.

Something clattered downstairs, and her heart jagged into high gear. With a smooth motion, she drew her .380 and chambered a round. Smithfield's eyes widened, and he made bleating noises through the gag.

"I'm not going to shoot you," she said. "Not that I don't think you're a waste of skin."

He obviously didn't believe her. With a hiss of exasperation, she grabbed the front of his shirt and hauled him to a sitting position. This time, he did start to cry.

"Come on," she snarled. "I'm going to get you out of here."

Preferably out the upstairs window, she thought sourly.

Jamming her fists onto her hips, she glared at him. "I'm going to take your gag off. But before I do, I want you to know that if you make any noise, those men will shoot us."

He bobbed his head up and down, indicating understanding. Mercilessly, she ripped the duct tape off his face. His mouth opened into an O of shock.

"Hey," she said, untying the bindings on his arms and legs, "it's like taking a Band-Aid off. The faster, the better. Now, tell me how many guards are in the house."

"Two." He rubbed his wrists. "They were going to kill me."

"Yeah. Right after you signed the house on Aberdeen back to them."

His eyes widened. "You know about that?"

"Did you ever hear the saying about not fooling all of the people all of the time?" she asked.

Another clatter came from downstairs, and Rae chopped the air with her hand, demanding silence.

"Time to go," she said.

He turned that smarmy smile on her, and she regained her original urge to stuff him out the window and use him for a landing pad. She gazed at him for a moment, fighting some very uncivilized urges, then turned away.

Silently, she opened the door a crack and peered out. Finding the hallway empty, she moved out, keeping her back to the wall and her gun ready. With a jerk of her hand, she motioned for Smithfield to follow her.

He oozed out after her, making sure she was between him and the stairs. She grimaced. And here she'd been angry at Gabriel for being protective.

She realized now that he hadn't been trying to take the least bit of her independence away from her, nor had he thought her incapable of handling the situation. It had merely been the instinctive reaction of a courageous man to danger.

After seeing the contrast between him and Smithfield, she found she greatly preferred Gabriel's brand of manhood.

Not, she amended, that she intended to forego discussing it with him. At length.

She and Smithfield eased their way down the stairs. "All My Children" was still on. She paused, assessing the situation. Then she started down again, motioning for Smithfield to stay close.

"Hold it right there." The voice was male and full of threat.

Unfortunately, it came from below and a little behind her, and she knew there was nowhere to run. Up or down, she'd be a dead-on target. Or rather, dead. Slowly, she raised her hands.

She glanced down, and saw that Ponytail had a partner. This one had blond hair cut so short she could see the sheen of his scalp below. Her gaze drifted down to his gun. Amazing how big a 9 mm barrel seemed when one was looking down into it.

"Toss the gun and come down," Blondie said.

No choice. She dropped the .380 into his hand and went the rest of the way down the stairs. Peter Smithfield followed, keeping slightly behind her, of course. Blondie patted her down for other weapons, then stepped back.

"Into the den," he ordered.

Rae, guessing, followed the sound of the television. She pushed the door open and went in. Smithfield crowded her so closely he nearly tread on her heels. A good thing, it turned out, because the first thing she saw was Ponytail lying unconscious on the rug.

And he was handcuffed.

She reacted instantly, instinctively. Even as she sprang to one side, dragging Smithfield with her, she saw Gabriel come hurtling toward Blondie. Hitting the other man broadside, he knocked him down so hard they both bounced. Gabriel landed on top. Jamming his forearm against the blond man's throat, he squeezed the other man's gun hand until Blondie cried out and dropped the weapon.

Gabriel slung the other man over onto his stomach, swiftly handcuffing his wrists. "You're under arrest," he growled as he straightened.

His chest heaved, and the light of battle turned his eyes to ice blue slits. Rae's own breath came fast and shallow, but it wasn't from exertion.

Gabriel MacLaren was much man. More man than she'd ever thought to find. And oh, Lord, he was looking at her as if…as if… Suddenly, she lost the ability to breathe at all.

He reached her in one long stride. Sweeping her against him with one hard arm, he kissed her. It was like being caught up in a hurricane, that kiss, and rational thought went spinning off in a firestorm of reaction. She clung to him, wanting more, more.

Just when her knees started to give, he tore his mouth from hers. "Seeing you here, a gun held on you…" His voice was low and intense, harsh with barely restrained emotion. "I've been stupid, Rae. Stupid and blind and stubborn."

"So what's new about that?" she asked, although her own voice betrayed the wild tumult of her feelings.

He didn't smile. "I should have seen it before. Now that I do, I'm not going to let another moment go by without telling you." Framing her face between his hands, he gazed into her eyes. "I love you, Rae. I love you hard and crazy and wild, and I will love you for as long as I draw breath."

Rae looped her arm around his neck. He claimed her mouth again in a searing, torrid kiss, and this time her knees really did buckle. Finally, he let her up for air.

"I was so mad when you left me today," she gasped against his mouth. "And I was so afraid that something would happen to you before I had a chance to tell you how much I love you."

"Ah, damn it," he groaned. "Think of the time we wasted."

"I wasn't fair to you," she said. "Because of what my ex-husband did, I asked more of you than was reasonable. I demanded faith without having the courage to give it in return."

His grasp tightened. "There are so many things I want to say to you, so many things I want to share—"

Someone chuckled. Gabriel broke off, swinging around to look in the direction from which the sound had come. Ponytail was sitting up, his eye just beginning to turn a rich shade of purple.

"Mind your own business," Gabriel growled.

"You gotta be kidding," Ponytail said. "This is better than 'All My Children.'"

Rae couldn't help but laugh. "This isn't television, boys. It's the real thing."

Ponytail laughed with her, then looked at Gabriel. "While you were romancing the lady, my associate and I discussed the possibility of working with the police."

"The police are always agreeable to working with people who cooperate," Gabriel said, adding, "and who have something of value to tell us."

"Would you be interested if we told you that we were hired by a member of the city government?"

"I think I would," Gabriel said.

Ponytail smiled. "What do they say in Hollywood? Oh, yeah. Have your people call my people."

Rae took Gabriel aside. "You can't make the arrest stick," she whispered. "You're under suspension."

"Hah," he whispered back. "On the way over here, I called my captain in the hospital. He was still woozy, but awake enough to call the commissioner and get me reinstated on the proviso that I come up with results. I'd call this results."

"I'm so glad," she said.

The sound of far-off sirens drifted in. With a shock, Rae realized that the door was open, and Peter Smithfield was nowhere to be seen. She met Gabriel's cynical gaze.

"He's run away again," she said.

"Did you serve him?"

She smiled. "Do you doubt it?"

Gabriel laughed. Then he suddenly became serious, and the

look in his blue crystal eyes made her tremble. "I will never doubt you again."

"And I will always believe in you," she murmured. "Always."

The sirens grew louder. Rae moved into the circle of his arm, feeling as though the world had taken on a whole new shine.

Ah, love was a good thing. A very good thing.

Rae stood in the shower in Gabriel's town house, letting the hot water rinse away the day's happenings. She'd come here to wait for Gabriel to accompany his prisoners to the station to see that they were properly booked, printed and installed in a holding cell.

All in all, a job well done.

Peter Smithfield would probably never show up in court. Coward that he was, he'd simply disappear without a thought as to what might happen to his children. But Barbara would be all right, and Mike would make it even better.

And Rae had an idea. It would take some time, but she thought she might be able to work things the way she wanted.

For some reason, the tune of "Moon River" popped into her mind and took hold. She started humming along, and before she knew it, she'd started to sing. A slight noise told her she was no longer alone, but she only smiled and kept singing. Of all the places in the world, she was safe here. With Gabriel.

His hands came down on her shoulders, and she moved back a pace, bringing herself against his body. She rubbed herself playfully against him.

"Oh, darlin'," he groaned. "'Moon River'?"

"I couldn't help myself. It just popped into my head and wouldn't go away." Goodness, she thought, he was *very* happy to see her. "How did everything go?"

"They implicated the vice-mayor," he said.

"Anton Taggett?"

"The one and only. And get this—Roth, the guy who suspended me, has been riding Taggett's coattails toward the commissioner's office. Talk about having friends in high places."

"Well, I expect he's not going to be on the department's golden-boy list much longer."

"And I'm off the hook. Roth fabricated that complaint to get me bumped off the case. But now, Taggett is finished. Thanks to you..." Gabriel paused, having a great deal of trouble keeping his mind on business. "Damn it, Rae, I don't want to talk right now."

"Talk," she said, merciless.

He took a deep breath. "Thanks to you, the Feds have come in on the money-laundering angle, and they were quite interested in that network of companies. They're also sending someone out to talk to that Dietrick fellow."

"Then we've won."

"Darlin'," Gabriel said, "we won the moment we touched."

He soaped his hands and began to wash her. Rae gasped, aroused almost unbearably by the sensation of his soap-slick palms upon her skin. Reaching behind her, she grabbed a double handful of his hair, giving him unrestricted access to her body. He made the most of it, stroking and rubbing, exploring, teasing, caressing until she was shaking with need.

"Now that I've got your attention," he murmured.

"Yes?"

"I want to talk about handcuffs—" his fingers stroked her swollen, aching nipples "—and your sudden appearance in that house."

"I always keep a spare set of locksmith's tools," she breathed, closing her eyes against the exquisite sensation.

"I didn't want you in danger."

She nodded. "And I didn't want *you* in danger."

Gabriel considered her words and the meaning behind them. This was a new beginning for them, and he wanted it to be right. "Okay," he agreed, "I can understand your feelings on that."

"And I can understand your feelings in wanting to protect me. But—"

"But," he finished for her, "we're both in occupations that involve risk, and we both have to accept that."

"Can you?"

He was silent for a moment, and her entire soul hung suspended, waiting for his answer.

"Yeah," he said, "I can. Provided, however, that I'm allowed to back you up."

"Wh-what are you saying?" she stammered.

"I'm impressed with what you do and how you do it. More than that, I envy the freedom you have. I want that for myself. And you have to admit that we make a formidable team, you and I."

"I don't understand what you're driving at."

He turned her around to face him. The intensity of his gaze all but burned her. She stood transfixed, her awareness of her surroundings fading as she became lost in his eyes. Mist rose around them, further enclosing them in a world created by love.

"I want us to be partners."

"Boudreau and MacLaren?" she asked, half teasing.

"I don't want you to change the name of your firm," he said.

"You built it, and it should bear the name you gave it. But on a more personal level, I was hoping for something along the lines of MacLaren and MacLaren."

Stunned, she could only stare. He smiled at her, a smile so full of tenderness that her heart felt as though it might twist itself into knots. With hands that trembled just a bit, he tilted her face up.

"I'm offering myself," he said in a tone that made her pulse race. "Here's my heart. It's yours. Keep it or throw it away, but it belongs to you. It will always belong to you."

It took her a moment to find her voice. When she did, it sounded strangely subdued. "You want...you want—"

Sliding his arm around her waist, he pulled her against him with an aggressive male possessiveness that sent a thrill racing through her.

"Marry me, Rae."

How arrogant, she thought, shifting position so that they fit together just a little more fully. Arrogant and not quite civilized, insufferable at times...and brave enough to love, truly and without reservation, holding nothing back. To be loved like *that*... Holy cow, she must have done something right in her life.

They would be partners. He wouldn't try to limit her, or to hold her back. Rather, he'd stand beside her, giving her support with his mind, his will and yes, his strong right arm. And at night, when the world narrowed to one woman, one man, he would sweep her straight up to heaven. Guardian angel, bad boy, lover.

Marry him?

"Oh, yes," she said.

Epilogue

"What do you think about a nice, elegant church wedding?" Barbara asked.

Rae glanced at Gabriel. He lay on the sofa like a great cat, with Tom the Dog and the three kids climbing all over him. He grinned at her, but didn't offer to help.

With a sigh, Rae turned back to her friend. "I'd rather have my toenails pulled out with rusty pliers."

"Oh, come on, Rae," Barbara said. "I survived the wedding experience."

"Barely."

"Smart aleck," Barbara retorted. "You've set a date less than two months from now. You have to let me make some plans."

"We could elope," Rae said with another hopeful glance toward her intended. "Gabriel?"

Gabriel carefully hid his amusement. *He* wasn't about to get sucked into this conversation, a surefire lose-lose situation for the guy in the middle.

"I want what you want, lover mine," he said. "If you insist on eloping, then elope we shall."

"You will not," Barbara said. "My children would never forgive you. You know Sarah wants to be your flower girl. And Little Mike wants to give you away—"

"Yeah, as long as I promise not to do any of that disgusting kissing stuff," Gabriel said, his voice muffled by Joey's knee. He lifted the child straight up, which instantly resulted in a chorus of demands for a ride. "Have mercy, Barbara. How about a nice service performed by the police chaplain, and then a wild party afterward? Most of the guys I know prefer beer and hot wings to pâté and asparagus."

"Did I say anything about pâté?" Barbara inquired.

Rae laughed. Barbara and Mike had been married a month now, and only wanted Rae and Gabriel to experience the same happiness.

But Rae was already so happy she thought she might die of it sometimes. She simply didn't care about the how, when or where of their wedding, as long as she got to keep him forever.

"Barbara, honey, I give you permission to do the wedding any way you see fit, as long as I don't have to wear anything confining, say anything stupid or invite anyone I don't like."

Barbara threw her hands up in a gesture of defeat. "You've just taken away everything that makes up a normal wedding, so I guess we'll have to do the chaplain-and-wild-party thing."

"As long as Big Mike agrees to do the food," Gabriel said. "If he won't, tell him I'm going to make the dog best man."

"Barbecue and beer?" Barbara asked, making a face.

Tom the Dog fixed those mesmerizing blue eyes on her and barked.

"I know," Barbara groaned. "I should have spelled it."

"Oh, he recognizes the spelling now," Gabriel said.

Barbara rolled her eyes. "Mike says that dog is smarter than most people he knows." Then she pinned them each in turn with a suspiciously bland look. "Oh, by the way. Do either of you know anything about a twenty-thousand-dollar deposit made mysteriously in my account?''

Rae whistled. ''Twenty thousand! Hey, if you've got a mystery, you're rich enough now to hire us to solve it.'' She whipped out one of her new business cards, which read, MacLaren & MacLaren, Private Investigators.

''You both passed the P.I. test!'' Barbara cried. ''I'm so proud of you.''

''Of course, the MacLaren & MacLaren won't be official until we get married,'' Rae said. ''But I couldn't resist the cards.''

Barbara smoothed her blond hair and got to her feet. ''Now that you think you've distracted me about that twenty thousand, we'd better get back to the store. It's almost lunchtime, and since Mike expanded, we're busier than ever.'' She raised her voice. ''Let's go, kids!''

The boys were too cool to actually hug anyone, so Rae just waved and said, ''See you later, dudes.''

But Sarah gave Gabriel a hug, then ran to Rae and kissed her cheek. ''I love you, Rae,'' she said.

''And I love you, sweetie,'' Rae murmured, touched by the girl's gesture. ''Be good.''

After the others were gone, Rae walked over to the sofa.

Gabriel sat up, snatched her into his arms and settled back onto the cushions with her in his lap.

''I love you, too, beautiful Rae,'' he murmured, rubbing his cheek against her hair. ''I adore you. I worship you. I want you to scratch my back—''

''Watch it, buster.''

He laughed, his voice a low, smoky rumble against her temple. ''You're a genius, getting rid of that bribe money that way.''

''It came to me because of Peter Smithfield, so it ought to be hers. It's the only legacy those kids will ever have from their father.''

''They never had a father, except in the physical sense,'' Gabriel said, his voice turning harsh for a moment. ''Now they've got Mike, and he'll do right by them all. Oh, by the way, Anton Taggett was arrested today. And there will be more arrests as the cases against his accomplices are prepared.''

''It's about time.''

''The whole case is built on the research we did, and Captain Petrosky has convinced the powers-that-be to hire us to teach a course to the detectives on information-gathering via computer.''

She blinked. ''Petrosky did that?''

''Hey, he might seem like a grouchy old dinosaur, but he's got vision. And he doesn't see a reason to ignore any tool that might help solve cases.''

''Well, what do you know,'' she said. ''I might even find another cop I can like. It's a miracle.''

Gabriel looked up at her, and his heart gave a now-familiar lurch. He loved her so much, so very much. And to think he'd almost been stupid enough to throw her love away. She'd since told him what had really happened between her and her ex.

''I saw Brett Wilson today,'' he said.

Rae tensed. ''You didn't hit him this time, did you?''

''Uh-uh. But he's not off the hook yet. I—''

''Let it go,'' she said.

His mouth thinned. ''Why?''

''Because since Eddy told everyone what he found out about Danny, Brett Wilson's name is dirt.'' She framed his face with both hands, letting her thumbs drift along the hard, arrogant line of his jaw. ''None of that matters. It's the past, gone, forgotten. And you and I have everything. For the rest of our lives.''

His gaze bored into hers, sending a message of acceptance and passion that made her quiver inside. Oh, yes, they had everything. Slowly, she lowered her head. Slowly, he lifted his.

Their lips met. Their spirits melded, entwined.

And the world went away.

* * * * *

IN CELEBRATION OF MOTHER'S DAY, JOIN
SILHOUETTE THIS MAY AS WE BRING YOU

a funny thing
HAPPENED ON THE WAY TO THE
Delivery Room

THESE THREE STORIES, CELEBRATING THE
LIGHTER SIDE OF MOTHERHOOD, ARE
WRITTEN BY YOUR FAVORITE AUTHORS:

KASEY MICHAELS
KATHLEEN EAGLE
EMILIE RICHARDS

When three couples make the trip to the delivery
room, they get more than their own bundles of
joy…they get the promise of love!

Available this May,
wherever Silhouette books are sold.

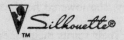

Silhouette®
TM

Look us up on-line at: http://www.romance.net

MD

Take 4 bestselling love stories FREE

Plus get a FREE surprise gift!

Special Limited-time Offer

Mail to Silhouette Reader Service™

**3010 Walden Avenue
P.O. Box 1867
Buffalo, N.Y. 14240-1867**

YES! Please send me 4 free Silhouette Intimate Moments® novels and my free surprise gift. Then send me 6 brand-new novels every month, which I will receive months before they appear in bookstores. Bill me at the low price of $3.34 each plus 25¢ delivery and applicable sales tax, if any.* That's the complete price and a savings of over 10% off the cover prices—quite a bargain! I understand that accepting the books and gift places me under no obligation ever to buy any books. I can always return a shipment and cancel at any time. Even if I never buy another book from Silhouette, the 4 free books and the surprise gift are mine to keep forever.

245 BPA A3UW

Name	(PLEASE PRINT)	
Address		Apt. No.
City	State	Zip

This offer is limited to one order per household and not valid to present Silhouette Intimate Moments® subscribers. *Terms and prices are subject to change without notice. Sales tax applicable in N.Y.

UMOM-696   ©1990 Harlequin Enterprises Limited

As seen on TV!
Free Gift Offer

With a Free Gift proof-of-purchase from any Silhouette® book,
you can receive a beautiful cubic zirconia pendant.

This gorgeous marquise-shaped stone is a genuine cubic
zirconia—accented by an 18" gold tone necklace.

(Approximate retail value $19.95)

Send for yours today…

compliments of ▼ *Silhouette*®
TM

To receive your free gift, a cubic zirconia pendant, send us one original proof-of-purchase, photocopies not accepted, from the back of any Silhouette Romance™, Silhouette Desire®, Silhouette Special Edition®, Silhouette Intimate Moments® or Silhouette Yours Truly™ title available in February, March and April at your favorite retail outlet, together with the Free Gift Certificate, plus a check or money order for $1.65 U.S./$2.15 CAN. (do not send cash) to cover postage and handling, payable to Silhouette Free Gift Offer. We will send you the specified gift. Allow 6 to 8 weeks for delivery. Offer good until April 30, 1997 or while quantities last. Offer valid in the U.S. and Canada only.

Free Gift Certificate

Name: _____

Address: _____

City: _____ State/Province: _____ Zip/Postal Code: _____

Mail this certificate, one proof-of-purchase and a check or money order for postage and handling to: SILHOUETTE FREE GIFT OFFER 1997. In the U.S.: 3010 Walden Avenue, P.O. Box 9077, Buffalo NY 14269-9077. In Canada: P.O. Box 613, Fort Erie, Ontario L2Z 5X3.

FREE GIFT OFFER   084-KFD
ONE PROOF-OF-PURCHASE
To collect your fabulous FREE GIFT, a cubic zirconia pendant, you must include this
original proof-of-purchase for each gift with the properly completed Free Gift Certificate.

084-KFD

This summer, the legend
continues in Jacobsville

A LONG, TALL
TEXAN SUMMER

Three **BRAND-NEW** short stories

This summer, Silhouette brings readers a special
collection for Diana Palmer's LONG, TALL TEXANS
fans. Diana has rounded up three **BRAND-NEW**
stories of love Texas-style, all set in Jacobsville,
Texas. Featuring the men you've grown to love from
this wonderful town, this collection is a must-have
for all fans!

*They grow 'em tall in the saddle in Texas—and
they've got love and marriage on their minds!*

Don't miss this collection of original Long, Tall Texans
stories…available in June at your favorite retail outlet.

Question: Who was born, bred—and bound to be wed—in Texas?

Answer: You'll have to read

award-winning author **Maggie Shayne's** irresistible new miniseries for Intimate Moments:

June 1996: If **THE LITTLEST COWBOY** on his doorstep makes Garrett Brand a daddy... *who's the mother?* (#716)

June 1997: She's young, she's innocent, but Jessi Brand will be **THE BADDEST VIRGIN IN TEXAS** to get the man she wants.... (#788)

September 1997: Will **BADLANDS BAD BOY** Wes Brand be able to convince a sexy, by-the-book beauty to give him a fighting chance? (#809)

And don't miss The Texas Brand as the series continues into 1998, only in—

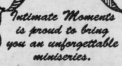

*Intimate Moments
is proud to bring
you an unforgettable
miniseries.*

BEVERLY BIRD

*Wrapped in the warmth of family tradition,
three couples say "I do!"*

LOVING MARIAH
(Intimate Moments #790, June 1997)
Adam Wallace searches for his kidnapped
son...which leads him to the Amish heartland
and lovely schoolteacher Mariah Fisher.

MARRYING JAKE
(Intimate Moments #802, August 1997)
Commitment-shy Jake Wallace unravels the
ongoing mystery of stolen babies and helps
Katya Essler learn to believe in love again.

SAVING SUSANNAH
(Intimate Moments #814, October1997)
Kimberly Wallace needs a bone marrow donor
to save her daughter's life. Will the temporary
nanny position to Joe Lapp's children be the
answer to her prayers?

▼INTIMATE MOMENTS®
▼ Silhouette®

From the bestselling author of
Iron Lace and *Rising Tides*

**When had the love and promises they'd shared turned
into conversations they couldn't face, feelings they
couldn't accept?**

Samantha doesn't know how to fight the demons that
have come between her and her husband, Joe. But she
does know how to fight for something she wants: a child.

But the trouble is Joe. Can he accept that he'll never be the
man he's expected to be—and can he seize this one chance
at happiness that may never come again?

"A great read and a winner in every sense of the word!"
—Janet Dailey

**Available in June 1997
at your favorite retail outlet.**

MIRA The brightest star in women's fiction